"You called me Hunter. Do you know me? Is that my name?"

Of course Leah knew him. How could she not know her own husband? Mixed feelings surged through her; then, suddenly, his face and the porch began to spin.

"You look like you're about to pass out. Are you sick?" He reached out and wrapped his arm around her shoulder to steady her. His touch was a jolt to her senses, and memories of all the other times he'd touched her assailed her.

For four, long, hellish months of agony she'd been sick with guilt and remorse. If it hadn't been for her, he wouldn't have gone out that night, wouldn't have had the accident in the first place.... He wouldn't have died.

But he hadn't died.

How could he have died when he was standing next to her, talking to her, touching her?

Dear Reader,

The holidays are here, so why not give yourself the gift of time and books—especially this month's Intimate Moments? Top seller Linda Turner returns with the next of her TURNING POINTS miniseries. In *Beneath The Surface* she takes a boss/employee romance, adds a twist of suspense and comes up with another irresistible read.

Linda Winstead Jones introduces you to the first of her LAST CHANCE HEROES, in *Running Scared*. Trust me, you'll want to be kidnapped right alongside heroine Olivia Larkin when bodyguard Quinn Calhoun carries her off—for her own good, of course. Award-winning Maggie Price's LINE OF DUTY miniseries has quickly won a following, so jump on the bandwagon as danger forces an estranged couple to reunite and mend their *Shattered Vows*. Then start planning your trip Down Under, because in *Deadly Intent*, Valerie Parv introduces you to another couple who live—and love—according to the CODE OF THE OUTBACK. There are *Whispers in the Night* at heroine Kayla Thorne's house, whispers that have her seeking the arms of ex-cop—and ex-*con*—Paul Fitzgerald for safety. Finally, welcome multipublished author Barbara Colley to the Intimate Moments lineup. Pregnant heroine Leah Davis has some *Dangerous Memories,* and her only chance at safety—and romance—lies with her husband, a husband she'd been told was dead!

Enjoy every single one, and come back next month (next year!) for more of the best and most exciting romance reading around—only in Silhouette Intimate Moments.

Yours,

Leslie J. Wainger
Executive Editor

Please address questions and book requests to:
Silhouette Reader Service
U.S.: 3010 Walden Ave., P.O. Box 1325, Buffalo, NY 14269
Canadian: P.O. Box 609, Fort Erie, Ont. L2A 5X3

Dangerous Memories

BARBARA COLLEY

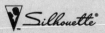

INTIMATE MOMENTS™

Published by Silhouette Books

America's Publisher of Contemporary Romance

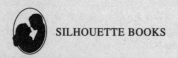 SILHOUETTE BOOKS

ISBN 0-373-27408-4

DANGEROUS MEMORIES

Copyright © 2004 by Barbara Colley

Visit Silhouette Books at www.eHarlequin.com

Printed in U.S.A.

BARBARA COLLEY

is a native of Louisiana, a mother and a grandmother. She and her husband live in a small suburb of steamy New Orleans. Besides playing with her grandchildren, writing and sharing her stories, one of Barbara's favorite pastimes is strolling through the New Orleans historic French Quarter and Garden District, both of which often inspire ideas and the settings for her books.

Barbara has always loved mystery, suspense and romance and, according to her mother, has always had a vivid imagination. Also writing under the name Anne Logan, Barbara has had books published in over sixteen foreign languages and has appeared on several bestseller lists. She has also been nominated for a *Romantic Times* magazine Reviewers Choice Award and is the recipient of the Oklahoma RWA National Readers' Choice Award, the RWA Artemis Award and the Distinguished Artist Award, in honor of outstanding contributions to the literary arts in Louisiana. In addition to writing romantic suspense, Barbara is the author of an ongoing mystery series.

Barbara loves to hear from readers. You can write to her at: P.O. Box 290; Boutte, LA 70039 or visit her Web site: www.eclectics.com/barbaracolley-annelogan.

To my dear friends, Jessica Ferguson
and Rexanne Becnel.

Chapter 1

The sight of the sleeping man on Leah Davis's front porch gave her a start. He was slumped in a heap of humanity near the steps. His back was to her, his face hidden in the crook of his arm. And just beyond where he lay, on the top step of the porch, was the newspaper, the reason she'd ventured out in the first place.

"That's just great," she grumbled, shoving a stray strand of auburn hair behind her ear. "Just what I need." Between the August heat and humidity and the double shifts she'd been pulling at the hospital, not to mention the occasional bouts of nausea, she'd just about gone her limit. And now this.

Shading her eyes against the bright glare of morning sunlight that not even the deep porch of the old Victorian home could block, she stared hard at him.

At least this one appeared to be still breathing, she thought as she noted the slight rise and fall of his back. The last one she'd found on the porch had been dead, cancer and malnutrition according to the coroner's report.

Still staring at the man, she slowly shook her head. The fact that they kept showing up amazed her. It was almost as if every bum in New Orleans had some kind of built-in radar that directed them to her front porch.

"Thanks a lot, Grandm'ere," she muttered as she tightened the belt of her thin cotton robe more securely then stepped out onto the porch to get a closer look.

Almost a year had passed since her generous, softhearted grandmother had died, and still they came. Leah had inherited her grandmother's house, but she had no intention of taking over her grandmother's charity work as well. Even so, no matter how many times she called the police to come and haul away one of the unwelcome, indigent visitors, more kept showing up to take their place.

Most of them were harmless and simply there for a handout, but Leah had learned not to be as trusting as her grandmother had been.

"Enough's enough," she grumbled as she crossed her arms protectively around her slightly rounded abdomen and tapped her bare foot against the wooden floor of the porch. Unlike her grandmother, who had felt that it was her calling in life to help every hungry, homeless man who showed up on her doorstep, Leah didn't feel that she could take such chances, especially now that she had her unborn baby to protect.

With her eyes still on the man and with every intention of returning inside to call the police, Leah took a step backward toward the door. Instead of going inside though, she hesitated.

Tilting her head and narrowing her eyes, she frowned. There was something different about this one, different from the normal run-of-the-mill bums who had showed up in the past.

For one thing, even though he could use a haircut, his thick, dark hair looked fairly clean and well kept instead of long, greasy and dirty. And instead of the usual sweat and dirt-crusted pants and shirt, this man was wearing what appeared to be hospital scrubs.

Hospital scrubs?

Leah's frown deepened. Strange. Very strange indeed.

Even so, the hair and clothes had nothing to do with why he seemed different. Though it was probably a silly notion, she could swear there was something familiar about him. That she'd seen him before…somewhere.

Growing more puzzled with each passing moment, she continued staring at him. Was it possible that he was a former patient, someone she'd treated at Charity Hospital? Leah frowned. Now she was really getting paranoid. There was no way a former patient would know where she lived.

So why the nagging feeling of familiarity? Leah had no answer. Maybe if she saw his face, maybe then she'd know.

Just forget it. Go call the police and have his butt hauled off.

Leah glared at the man as indecision warred within her. "Oh, for Pete's sake," she muttered. There was only one way to find out for sure, and though she was curious, she wasn't careless. Her experiences working as a nurse at Charity Hospital had taught her to be cautious.

She reached just inside the doorway and grabbed the baseball bat that she kept propped there. Unlike her grandmother who, in Leah's opinion, had always been far too trusting, Leah kept the bat handy, just in case of trouble.

Taking a deep breath for courage, she gripped the bat with both hands and eased over to within a couple of feet of the sleeping man. Using the tip of the bat, she poked him just below the shoulder blades.

"Hey, you!" she called out. "Wake up!"

The man groaned, but he didn't budge.

Gripping the bat tighter, she poked him again, pushing harder than she had the first time. "You're trespassing, mister. If you don't leave I'm calling the police." She poked at him once more for good measure. "Now, get up!"

Suddenly, like a coiled spring, the man jumped to his feet.

With a yelp of surprise, Leah immediately jerked the bat into a swinging position as she stumbled backward. "Please leave," she shouted, her legs trembling. "Go on, get out of here."

Then, the man turned to face her, and she froze. Her breath caught in her lungs, and all she could do was stare at him, her eyes wide with disbelief, her heart pounding like a bass drum against her rib cage.

"Hunter?" she whispered. The baseball bat slid through her nerveless fingers and fell to the porch with a clatter. "No," she moaned as she slowly shook her head from side to side, trying to deny what was before her eyes. Had she finally lost it, gone over the edge? "Not possible," she protested. Hunter was dead.

Yet, even while logic dictated that there was no way this man could be Hunter, her insides quivered with the ache of recognition. The same ruggedly handsome face, made even more rugged by the shadow of his dark beard…the same deep-set, steely blue eyes…

Though myriad questions rushed through her head, for the moment, she didn't care. For the moment, more than anything, she longed to throw herself at him, to once again feel his arms around her, just to assure herself that the man really *was* Hunter.

Then, their gazes collided, and when she saw the clouded, confused look in his eyes, her mind reeled with her own confusion. Something was wrong…terribly wrong.

He held up his hands defensively. "I don't mean you any harm," he said in that rich whiskey voice that had always sent goose bumps chasing up her arms. "You called me Hunter. Do you know me? Is that my name?"

He didn't know her.

Leah fought to gain control over her runaway emotions.

"Lady, do you recognize me?"

Lady? Even more disconcerted, Leah could do little more than nod. Of course she knew him. How could she not know her own husband? But why did he even have to ask such a question?

Mixed feelings surged through her, then suddenly, without warning, his face and the porch began to spin. Her vision grew hazy then dark around the edges even as she felt her knees buckle.

"Whoa—hey, lady—" He reached out and wrapped an arm around her shoulder to steady her. He was a tall man, six foot two to her mere five foot five, and her shoulders fit just beneath his armpit. His touch was a jolt to her senses, and memories of all the other times he'd touched her assailed her.

"Take it easy. You look like you're about to pass out. Are you sick?"

"No, not—not sick," she whispered, shaking her head as she gave voice to the half lie.

She had been sick though. For four, long, hellish months, she'd been sick with guilt and remorse. How could she not? After all, it had been her fault. If it hadn't been for her, he wouldn't have gone out that night, he wouldn't have had the accident…he wouldn't have died. Despite the heat, a chill ran through her. But how could he have died when he was standing next to her, talking to her, touching her? She began to shiver.

"Hey—" His arm around her shoulder tightened. "You'd better sit down before you fall down."

Hunter. But was Hunter his first name or his last name? the man wondered as he silently repeated it. He nudged the woman toward the porch swing. She looked exactly as he'd pictured her in the brief flashes of memory he'd had over the past month…well, almost exactly. Same warm brown eyes shot with flecks of jade, same alabaster skin sprinkled with a faint dusting of freckles across a pert, ski-jump nose, all framed by thick shoulder-length auburn hair. The only difference was her body. In his memory she'd appeared to be a lot slimmer. Not that she was fat, far from it; but then again, it was highly possible that his memory couldn't be totally trusted.

Now that he'd seen her, there was no doubt that she was the one he'd traveled hundreds of miles to find. And even better, just as he'd hoped and prayed, she knew him. But how did she know him…?

Unable to do much else, Leah allowed Hunter to help her to the porch swing. After she was seated, he knelt in front of her.

Leah searched his face. If she'd had any doubts that the man was Hunter, they disappeared. This close there was no denying who he was, right down to the tiny scar on the right side of his forehead where a bullet had grazed him.

"You know me, don't you?" he asked again. "Is Hunter my name?"

Leah nodded, still trying to make heads or tails of what was happening.

"First name or last name?" he asked.

"Your—your n-name is Hunter Davis," she blurted out. "And you're—" Whether it was instinct or her overcautious nature, for reasons Leah didn't understand, she couldn't complete the sentence, couldn't tell him that he was her husband…not just yet.

"Hunter Davis," he repeated softly, almost in awe, as if savoring each syllable.

"Don't you remember?" But even as she asked the question she knew he didn't. If he did he wouldn't be asking in the first place. Even so, she'd had to ask, if only to hear him say it, to hear him admit it.

His head slumped forward until his chin almost touched his collarbone. "That's just the problem," he said. "I don't remember." He slowly raised his head until he could look her in the eye. "They tell me I have amnesia."

It was just as she'd suspected. But who on earth were "they"?

"I was told that I was in an accident and almost died," he continued. "They said that the car I was driving went out of control and hit an eighteen-wheeler hauling gasoline, then burned. The only reason I survived at all was because I was thrown free." He cleared his throat. "When I finally woke up, it was a month later—so I was told. I was in a hospital in Orlando, Florida, and didn't remember any of it, not even my own name. They told me I'd been in a coma."

Leah frowned. As shocked as she was to see him, she could still think enough to realize he should have been identified right away. So why wasn't he?

"But what about your billfold? And fingerprints? Didn't they run a check on your fingerprints?"

He gave a one-shouldered shrug. "My ID must have burned with the car, and when the police ran a fingerprint check, they didn't find a match."

"But that's imposs—" Leah broke off the sentence and clamped her mouth shut.

"What?" he asked. When Leah refused to answer and shook her head, he narrowed his eyes. "You were about to say something. What was it?"

"Nothing." She forced a smile, hoping it would take the wary edge off her tone. And suddenly, she was wary, big-time wary, and growing more so with each passing minute. Too much of what he'd told her simply didn't make sense. After all, the police were the ones who had told her he was dead in the first place.

Leah shuddered. They had said he'd been burned beyond recognition, burned to the bones, and she'd buried those bones in the same tomb that held her grandmother's remains. Then, there were the fingerprints. Hunter was a cop from New York City who had been on leave for medical reasons. His fingerprints would definitely be on file somewhere.

Why would the police have lied to her…and to him? What reason could they possibly have for such a deception?

And whose bones had they given her to bury?

Chapter 2

Leah's mind raced as she tried to find answers. Her stomach grew queasy just thinking about the hell she'd gone through the night Hunter disappeared. It had been her twenty-eighth birthday. They'd just returned to the hotel room after having dinner, and she'd sent him to the drugstore. She'd waited for Hunter to return…one hour…two hours, then three, until she couldn't stand to wait a minute longer.

Now, she realized she should have thought it strange that when she finally called the police, they showed up almost immediately. But by the time they had knocked on the hotel-room door, she'd been in such a state she hadn't been thinking straight. And afterward, after they told her what she'd dreaded the most, she'd been too distraught to think of anything but her loss and her guilt. And she'd spent four months grieving and blaming herself for his so-called death.

But grieving wasn't all she'd done in that time. She'd spent a lot of it thinking, mostly about their hasty courtship and marriage.

Under normal circumstances, there was no way she would have married a man, any man, after only knowing him for a few weeks.

Leah swallowed hard against the tight ache in her throat. But that particular time had been anything but normal, and Hunter wasn't just any man. She'd been in mourning when she'd met him, mourning for her beloved grandm'ere, the woman who had raised her since she was five. With her parents' deaths, her grandmother had become everything to her. When her grandmother had died, the world as Leah had known it, along with the love and security she'd always felt, had disappeared.

Hunter had been on an extended medical leave from the New York City Police Department for psychiatric reasons. He'd been involved in a bad shoot-out, and had accidentally shot and killed an innocent bystander, a ten-year-old girl. As a result, he'd been unable to fire a gun ever since.

For Leah, it had been a time of adjustment and mourning, of coming to grips with being all alone in the world. For Hunter, it had been a time to heal.

They had both been vulnerable and needy and had taken solace with each other and within each other's arms.

Leah suddenly went still as yet another strange discrepancy occurred to her. "There's something I don't quite understand," she told Hunter. "You say you have amnesia. But if you have amnesia, and you didn't even know your name, why are you here on my doorstep? What made you think that I might know you? In fact, how did you even know where I lived?"

He shrugged. "I guess that does seem kind of strange, even a contradiction of sorts. But I do have an explanation," he hastened to add. "I was told that there was a good chance I would regain my memory."

A momentary look of embarrassment crossed his face and

he got to his feet. "This might sound weird," he said as he rubbed the back of his neck and paced the width of the porch in front of her. "But about a month ago I began having flash-backs—memory flashes. Most of them didn't make sense to me. But in one particular flashback I kept seeing a woman's face, and an address kept running through my mind."

He stopped in front of her and motioned toward her. "Your face," he said. "The same auburn hair, the same brown eyes, the same face."

Hunter felt heat climb up his neck as he stared at her. He'd seen more than just her face in his recurring flashback, much more. In his mind he'd seen her completely naked. He'd seen himself hovering over her, stroking her, felt her smooth, silky skin, felt her writhing beneath him in the heat of passion, her hands urging him to…

He squeezed his eyes shut. There was no way he could tell her the rest, not until he knew if it what he'd seen in the flash-back was true or simply wishful dreaming on his part. With a shake of his head, he opened his eyes then gestured broadly. "And this address. I'm not sure why—" He raked his fingers through his hair. "But, like I said, this address kept flashing through my head. It took me days of hitchhiking to get here from Orlando, but I felt I had to do it or I might not ever find out who I am."

He dropped down beside her then turned to face her, his left arm across the back of the swing. "I was right, wasn't I?" Tilting his head to one side he held her gaze. When she nod-ded, he said, "I need to know what else you can tell me about myself. Please," he added.

Leah's mind raced as she considered just how much she should tell him, and after a moment, she decided that di-vulging some of the facts couldn't hurt.

"You're thirty-two years old, and you're a police officer with the New York City Police Department," she said. "We met when you took an extended vacation to New Orleans after you were placed on medical leave. You said that you had always wanted to see Mardi Gras but had never had the time off."

A frown creased his forehead as he mulled over what she'd said, and Leah laced her fingers together tightly in her lap to keep from reaching up to smooth the frown away.

"Medical leave for what?" he finally asked.

As Leah explained about the shoot-out and the ten-year-old girl, a multitude of emotions played over his face. But when she told him the part about him being unable to fire a gun, he stared at her as if she'd just grown horns.

"So it wasn't just a simple medical leave? I wasn't physically injured?"

Leah shrugged. "I—I don't know all the details," she hedged.

"Who does?"

Leah shook her head. "I don't know. Maybe your captain or your doctor."

"You mean my shrink, don't you?"

"I told you, I don't know," she repeated slowly, emphasizing each word.

"Then, how do you know me?" he retorted. "And just what was our relationship?"

The answers to his questions stuck in Leah's throat. She'd known he would eventually ask, and she'd dreaded it, especially since she wasn't sure how to answer him.

With all of her heart, she wanted to tell Hunter that he was her husband, and she wanted to share with him the wonderful news that he was going to be a father. But even as her hands strayed protectively to her abdomen, a little voice inside warned against revealing everything, warned that she should proceed with caution until she knew more about Hunter's circumstances. What she'd realized in the months since Hunter's death was that she didn't really know him very well at all.

For long moments, a battle raged within her. *Tell him... No, don't tell him. But he's your husband...but what if there was more to his medical-leave story than he'd admitted? After all, you only know what he told you, and he could have lied, could have lied about everything. Can you afford to take the chance? You've got your unborn baby to protect.*

Leah finally decided that what she needed was time. Time to digest what he'd told her, and time to further assess his mental state.

"We're friends," she finally said. "We're just really good friends."

Again, he seemed to mull over what she'd told him, and Leah tensed. She'd never been a good liar, and there was nothing in his expression to indicate whether he did or didn't believe her. If he didn't, then what?

After a moment, he finally said, "So, *friend*, do you have a name?"

Leah's stomach knotted. He didn't believe her. Somehow he knew they had been more than just friends, knew that she wasn't telling the whole truth. "My name is Leah. Leah...Johnson."

"Leah Johnson," he repeated slowly, thoughtfully. But to her acute disappointment, his eyes remained blank, without even a spark of recognition. After a moment, he squeezed them tightly shut and whispered, "Damn."

When Hunter opened his eyes, the brief look of confusion and disappointment that Leah saw in them almost broke her heart. It was evident that he'd hoped that hearing her name would awaken some of his lost memory. But it hadn't.

"What about family?" he asked. "Do I have any family? Mother, father, brothers or sisters?"

Leah shook her head. Only me, she wanted to say, but she whispered, "No. Your parents both died in an accident when you were a young teenager. After their deaths you lived with an aunt, your mother's only sister. But she died of cancer not long after you graduated from the police academy."

Again that same brief, miserable look of confusion and disappointment flashed in his eyes. "Then there's no one," he mumbled, pushing out of the swing.

No one but me, Leah added silently as she watched him pace the length of the porch. That they had both been alone in the world had been just one more thing that sealed the bond of need between them despite the short time they'd known each other.

I'll be your family and you'll be mine, then neither of us will have to be alone. The words he'd whispered to her when he proposed echoed in her mind, and knife-stabbing guilt pricked at her conscience.

Hunter stopped his pacing near the porch steps and sudden panic seized her. What if he left? After all, as far as he knew, there was nothing to keep him here.

"Why don't you come inside?" she blurted out before she had time to change her mind. There was no way she could let him leave…not just yet…not until she got some answers that made sense.

"The least I can do is fix you a bite of breakfast." Half-afraid he would say no, Leah pushed out of the swing. With an eye on Hunter, she stepped over, picked up the bat, then walked purposely toward the front door, leaving him little choice but to follow.

"You don't have to do this," he protested, his gaze sliding warily to the bat. But even as he protested, he took a step toward her.

"Don't be silly." She motioned for him to follow her.

The look of relief on his face pricked her conscience again, but she ignored it. Once inside, she leaned the bat against the wall, then led him through the parlor and down a short hallway.

"As long as you're here," she told him when they entered the kitchen, "maybe you'd like to take a hot shower—clean up a bit—while I cook breakfast?" She turned to see him inspecting the large kitchen and breakfast area.

"I could definitely use a shower," he muttered, his gaze settling on her face. "But I really couldn't impose on you like that."

"We *are* friends," she emphasized. "And it's not imposing if I invite you. I might even be able to rustle up a clean change of clothes for you as well. Last time my uncle came for a visit, he left a few of his things in the closet."

While it was true that she had an uncle—a great-uncle— the jeans and shirts had actually belonged to Hunter. When she returned from Orlando, she'd packed them away in a box with intentions of giving them to Goodwill. Only problem was, she never seemed able to remember to put the box in her car.

Leah turned away quickly for fear he would somehow be able to see that she'd lied yet again, and she walked over to the phone sitting on the kitchen counter. "Right now, I need to make a phone call and let the hospital know that I won't be coming in today."

"You work at a hospital?"

Leah punched out the numbers of the floor she worked on. "I'm a nurse."

Her call was answered on the third ring, and in a matter-of-fact tone she explained that she needed to take a sick day.

"You didn't have to do that," Hunter said when she hung up the receiver. "Not on my account."

If only you knew, she thought, and taking a deep breath for courage, she turned and faced him. "It's no problem. Really it's not. It seems like forever that I've seen you and I could use a day off." She motioned toward the breakfast table. "Why don't you have a seat and wait right here while I get you those clothes. Feel free to pour yourself a cup of coffee. It's decaf." She turned and headed toward the door leading to the bedrooms. "Coffee mugs are on the counter," she called out over her shoulder.

When Leah reached her bedroom, she glanced over her shoulder again, just to make sure he hadn't followed, then she headed straight for the dresser. Sitting on top was an eight-by-ten framed photograph of the two of them taken on their wedding day. She hadn't hired a professional photographer, and the picture was only an enlarged snapshot taken by a friend, but she'd worn a short veil to go along with the white-lace dress she'd bought, and Hunter had rented a tuxedo for the occasion. One look at that picture, and he'd know that they had been more than just friends.

Leah glanced over her shoulder again, just to make sure that she was alone, then she removed the framed picture and placed it in the bottom drawer of the dresser beneath a stack of out-of-season sweaters. After a quick inspection of the room to make sure there was nothing else incriminating, she headed for the closet. In the bottom of the closet near the back was the small cardboard box that contained the remainder of Hunter's clothes.

After a brief stop in the guest bathroom, Leah returned to the kitchen. Hunter was seated at the breakfast table, staring out the bay window. His hands were wrapped around a steaming coffee mug.

Just beyond the bay window in the tiny backyard, her grandmother had created a lovely garden oasis surrounded by a wall of camellias, azaleas and a host of other evergreens that thrived in the Uptown neighborhood. In the midst of it all was a small goldfish pond, complete with lily pads, and edged by palmetto palms. A water fountain shaped like a fish rose in the center of the pond, and a water spray flowed continuously from the mouth of the fish.

A heavy feeling that had nothing to do with pregnancy settled in Leah's stomach. Hunter had loved that particular view, and seeing him sitting there, staring out the window was déjà vu. He'd once told her that all that lush greenery had a soothing, calming effect and was a stark contrast to the depressing shades of gray he was used to seeing. He'd said that the only green to be found in New York City was in Central Park.

When Hunter pulled his gaze from the window and stared up at her, the uneasy, jittery feeling she'd had when she'd first seen him on the porch returned with a vengeance. She quickly placed a pair of jeans and a folded knit shirt on the table. "These should fit you," she said as she backed away. "Sorry there's no underwear, but even if there was—I mean, even if my uncle had left some, I figured you wouldn't want to wear someone else's."

She was babbling, she realized, babbling because being in such proximity to him, along with the lies she'd already told, was making her nervous. But who wouldn't be nervous, given the circumstances?

Taking a deep breath, Leah motioned toward the doorway that led to the guest bathroom. "Just down that hallway to the right is a bathroom you can use when you're ready. I laid out a couple of clean towels and a washcloth. I also left a new razor and toothbrush on the countertop next to the sink."

Hunter narrowed his eyes and stared at her. "Why are you doing this? There's no way I can repay you."

Leah felt her cheeks burn with guilt. Unable to face him, she quickly turned away. "What are friends for?" she murmured, almost choking on the words as she busied herself with preparations for breakfast. "Friends" didn't begin to describe their relationship, but until she knew more about what had happened to him and why, being friends was a lot safer.

* * *

Hunter Davis.

As Hunter entered the bathroom, he mulled over his name. Not wanting any unwelcome surprises, he locked the door behind him, and then glanced around the small room. The name felt right, felt as if it fit and was a hell of a lot better than just plain John Doe. But he didn't remember it. Even knowing his name hadn't produced the breakthrough that he'd hoped for. His mind was still a blank.

He eyed the jeans and shirt that the woman named Leah had given him and wondered if, like his name, they would fit. Anything had to be better than the hospital scrubs he'd worn for the past three days. Like him, the scrubs were beginning to smell a little too ripe.

Hunter closed his eyes and breathed deeply and slowly. Leah…Leah Johnson…Leah Johnson… He silently repeated the woman's name.

Nothing. No revelation, no sudden memories. Nothing.

With a frustrated sigh, he picked up the toothbrush and tore off the packaging. When he'd finished brushing his teeth, he used a bar of soap to lather his face and shaved.

His insides quivered with frustration as he rinsed then dried his face. Throwing the towel on the countertop, he stepped over to the shower, jerked back the shower curtain, and turned on the water. Then he took off his watch and slipped off the shoes. After he stripped off the hospital scrubs, he kicked them into the corner.

There was no doubt that Leah Johnson was the woman in his flashbacks. She was even more beautiful face-to-face, and the extra pounds made her look even more womanly, more sexy.

Friends…

She'd said they were just "really good friends." So if they were only friends, why would *her* face be the one he remembered? Even more puzzling, why the ache in his gut when he'd first seen her in the flesh, and why the overwhelming urge to crush her into his arms and taste her lips.

With a shake of his head, Hunter stepped into the shower. "Depends on her definition of 'friends,'" he muttered. Just how good of friends were they? According to the visions he kept having, "friend" was far too tame to describe the relationship between them. Besides, he couldn't imagine why he would be "just friends" with a woman as beautiful as she was…unless he was married.

Married. "Damn," he grunted. It had never even occurred to him to ask her if he was married. Surely she would have said so if he was, wouldn't she? And she hadn't said so. Besides, if he was married, it stood to reason that he would have had flashes of his wife's face, instead of just his friend's face. And if he was married, why would he have come to New Orleans alone, instead of staying in New York? She'd said he'd come for an extended vacation, but that brought up yet another question. If he lived in New York and had just come for a vacation, why was it this address he remembered?

Too many questions and not enough answers, he decided as he turned his face into the spray. The water was steamy hot, and Hunter savored the feel of it against his skin.

It had been three days since he'd had a real shower. With almost no money, he'd been unable to afford even the shabbiest of motel rooms, neither for sleeping nor for cleaning up. Instead, he'd had to make do with washing up in public rest rooms along the way.

What he really needed was a hot whirlpool to soothe his aching right leg. It had been broken in two places when he'd been thrown from his car. According to the doctor who had treated him, it had healed nicely, but it still ached when he walked a lot. And he'd walked a lot during the past three days.

In addition to his leg aching like hell, the two nights he'd spent with hardly any sleep had exhausted him. By the time he'd found the address that kept flashing in and out of his head, it had been past midnight, far too late to be knocking on anyone's door, especially someone he wasn't sure he even knew.

He hadn't meant to fall asleep on the porch. He'd only meant to sit there and wait until morning, until a decent hour to knock on the door. He'd chosen the spot near the steps to wait because he'd needed cover from the prying eyes of neighbors and any patrol cars that might pass by. After everything he'd been through, the last thing he'd wanted was to be picked up by the police, and the huge bush near the steps was wide enough and tall enough to provide just the right amount of cover.

Hunter wrinkled his nose and sniffed. The bathroom door was closed and the shower was running full blast, but he could swear he smelled bacon frying.

She'd said she would fix him breakfast, and Hunter's mouth watered at just the thought of food.

Not only had it been three days since he'd showered, but the last meal he could remember eating was the egg sandwich he'd had yesterday morning. Unfortunately, it had been the last of his money as well.

At the thought of the money, Hunter swallowed hard and lathered his upper body. Then, using the washcloth, he scrubbed with a vengeance, as if doing so would scrub away the thoughts of how he'd gotten the money.

Stolen money.

Jumping the hospital guard outside his room and knocking him unconscious had been bad enough, but stealing the man's wallet, his watch and his shoes was even worse. Hunter heaved a sigh. Desperate measures called for desperate actions, and he had been desperate…desperate to escape. Besides, it hadn't been much money, just barely enough to eat on during the three days he'd been hitchhiking. The shoes weren't that great, either. They were too tight for one thing. But wearing tight shoes beat the hell out of going barefoot. As for the watch, it wasn't as if it was gold or anything. It probably didn't cost more than twenty dollars at most.

Even with all his excuses for doing what he'd done, he felt badly about it. Even before Leah had told him he was a cop, stealing from the guard had bothered him enough to realize that, whatever he was, he was no thief. And somehow, some way, he fully intended to repay every penny he'd taken, including enough to buy the man a new pair of shoes and a new watch. But first he needed to figure out why there had been a guard posted outside his hospital room…and why the hospital had been holding him prisoner.

Hunter turned off the shower, grabbed the towel Leah had left for him and vigorously dried himself. He'd been lucky. When he'd gone in search of something to wear other than the skimpy hospital gown, he'd come upon an unattended cart of sheets, towels and blankets not far from his hospital room. On the cart, secured in a clear plastic bag, were clean scrubs. He'd snatched the bag, and just as he ducked into an empty room to change, he heard the footsteps of the attendant returning to distribute the contents of the cart. Wearing the scrubs and the security guard's shoes, he'd been able to walk right out without a hassle.

Once outside, he'd only had to walk a couple of blocks before he spotted an all-night café. Judging by all the eighteen-wheelers in the parking lot, the café was also a popular truck stop. Thanks to the generosity of one wizened old trucker, he'd been able to hitch a ride all the way to Alabama.

Hunter pulled on the jeans and shirt. He'd had a lot of time to think on the road, and it didn't take a rocket scientist to realize that there was more to his situation than just the accident, more than just having amnesia. And despite Leah's statement about them being "just friends," Hunter's gut feeling told him that there was a good possibility that she knew more than she was telling. With every fiber of his being, he was certain that she was the key that could unlock his memory, the key to the whole puzzle.

But could he trust her? Should he trust her? After what he'd been through, he wasn't sure he could trust anyone.

No fingerprints on record.

"Impossible," Leah muttered as she cracked an egg and dropped the yoke and egg white into the skillet of heated oil. The oil popped and crackled as the egg cooked, and Leah tilted her head to one side when she heard the water pipes in the old house groaning, an indication that Hunter had cut off the shower.

She returned her attention to the egg, and in one smooth motion, flipped it over.

No fingerprints.

Definitely impossible…unless…unless he'd lied about the police not being able to find a match. But what reason would he have to lie?

Leah shook her head. *No reason.* To be fair, there could be another explanation. The police could have lied to him, just as they had lied to her.

Again though, why? What she needed were answers. But she didn't have a clue as to how to get them or even where to begin. For all she knew, Hunter could have lied about everything from the very beginning. About being a cop. About his medical leave.

"No!" she muttered with a determined shake of her head, denying the possibility of such a thing. There had to be something else, some other reason for all that had happened.

Suddenly, Leah grew stone still, the spatula in her hand

poised just above the skillet. She couldn't explain it, but without looking, she knew the exact moment Hunter entered the kitchen.

She cleared her throat, mostly to swallow the lump that had formed in it. "You timed that just about right," she said, scooping the egg from the skillet and sliding it onto a plate next to the first one she'd cooked.

Only then did she glance over her shoulder. Sure enough, he was standing just inside the doorway.

He'd shaved, she noted. The clothes she'd given him didn't fit quite as well as they had the last time she'd seen him wear them. He'd lost weight, just enough so that the jeans no longer hugged him like a second skin, and the knit shirt was loose instead of molded to his body.

Leah frowned. Though he'd combed his hair, it was still damp from the shower. She should have thought to tell him where she kept the hair dryer.

The sight of Hunter standing there with wet hair reminded her of the first time she'd seen him, and like an old-time movie reel, a kaleidoscope of images played through her mind.

It had been the end of February, the week before Mardi Gras Day, and she'd worked a night shift at the hospital. Though it wasn't something she normally did, after she left the hospital, she'd let her friend, Christine, persuade her to meet a couple of their co-workers at Café Du Monde in the Quarter for coffee and beignets. Surprisingly the outdoor coffeehouse hadn't been overly crowded from the influx of tourists in town for Mardi Gras festivities. Leah had decided that most of the visitors were probably still in their hotel rooms sleeping off their previous night of debauchery and carousing.

The sky had been overcast with dark clouds, the damp air of the Mississippi River chilly and breezy. She'd just seated herself with her friends, when it suddenly began to rain. She'd

glanced up, and that's when she'd seen him. He'd been running across the street to take shelter beneath the deep over-
hang around the outdoor coffeehouse. In his path was a
bedraggled bag lady struggling with her shopping cart full of
junk that she'd collected.

Then, something amazing had happened, something rarely
seen in the Quarter. Though it meant getting soaked, he had
stopped long enough to help the old woman push her cart up
out of the street onto the sidewalk that ran in front of the coffeehouse. Then he'd pushed it beneath the shelter of the over-
hang. By the time he'd sat down at a nearby table, he'd been
soaking wet.

"Is something wrong?"

Hunter's question jerked her back to the present. "No—
nothing's wrong," she told him. She motioned toward the
plate of food on the cabinet. "I hope you like your eggs fried."
She already knew he did, but did *he* remember that he did?

Hunter shrugged. "Beggars can't be choosers." He stepped
farther into the room.

With the spatula, she motioned toward the refrigerator.
"There's orange juice and apple juice in the fridge. Pour yourself a glass of whichever you want and be seated." She
grabbed a mitt and opened the oven door. "Yep, perfect timing," she reiterated. "Even the biscuits are ready." A couple
of minutes later, she placed the plate of food on the table in
front of him. On the plate were the two fried eggs, grits,
bacon and a couple of the hot biscuits that she'd buttered as
soon as she'd removed them from the oven.

"This looks great," he told her.

"I'm afraid that the only kind of jelly I have is fig pre-
serves," she said. "Is that okay?"

Before she realized his intentions, he grabbed her wrist.
"You tell me."

Chapter 3

Leah swallowed hard. Hunter's manacle grip was anything but gentle, but it was the hard, cold look in his eyes that sent a shiver of fear racing up her spine. "Tell you?" she cried. "Tell you what?" She tugged on her wrist, but his grip tightened.

"If, as you claim, we're such good *friends*," he sneered, "then you would damn well know my likes and dislikes, wouldn't you?"

Leah tensed and desperation clawed at her insides. She'd been a fool, a lovesick fool. Only a complete idiot would let herself get caught alone with a man with no memory of a past that was questionable.

Stay calm and think. Use your brain. If it came down to a physical confrontation, she'd lose, hands down. Even though Hunter had lost weight, he still outweighed her by nearly a hundred pounds. The only thing to do was try to bluff her way out of the situation.

"I don't know what you think you're doing—" She looked

pointedly at his hand around her wrist. "Whatever it is, stop it," she demanded. "And let go of my arm. Now, please."

For long seconds he simply stared at her as an array of expressions crossed his face. First confusion, then, when he glanced down at his hand wrapped around her wrist, he paled and confusion changed to shock.

"Oh, God," he whispered, immediately releasing her. Propping both elbows on the table, he dropped his head forward, and supporting his head with the heels of his hands, he squeezed his eyes closed. "Sorry." He slowly shook his head from side to side. "I didn't mean to—it's just that—" He dropped his hands and looked up at her, his eyes reflecting his genuine remorse. "Everything's so damn confusing. I don't know what to think, who to trust, how to act."

Leah was still wary, but her heart ached for him as she watched him struggle for composure. "It's okay," she told him gently. "I guess I'm a bit jumpy, too. It's not every day that a long-lost friend shows up on my doorstep. In hospital scrubs, knowing my name." Though she was serious about being jumpy, the last was said in an effort to relieve the tension, an effort that fell flat if his expression was any gauge.

He shook his head. "No—you don't understand. I need some answers."

"Well, of course you do," she said.

At her placating tone, warning bells went off in Hunter's head, and he threw her a wary look.

"Considering your condition it's only natural that you want answers," she continued.

Her tone and expression were full of what seemed like genuine concern, but beneath it all, he sensed fear as well. Was she simply telling him what she thought he wanted to hear? Was the concern reflected in her eyes real or fake?

"Yeah, I want answers," he finally agreed. "But there's more to it than just the amnesia." The not knowing about his past was driving him crazy, and while it was true that he needed answers, even worse than not knowing about himself was the issue of not knowing who to trust. Once again he had to ask himself if he could trust her.

Hunter stared deep into her eyes as if doing so would tell him whether she was trustworthy. He wanted to trust her, and the last thing he wanted was for her to be afraid of him.

At some point, you have to trust someone. Either that or end up running for the rest of your life.

There was no way he could keep running and, to give her credit, so far she'd done nothing suspicious, nothing but try to help…the food, the clothes…

Hunter swallowed hard. "You know that hospital I told you about?"

Leah nodded.

"They didn't just release me. I was being held there against my will, and I had to escape."

Leah backed away from him. First the amnesia, and now he was delusional as well, unless… It had been her experience that the only people they locked up in hospitals were mental patients.

Stay calm. Don't panic. She forced a sympathetic smile. "I'm sure it *seemed* like that to you, but—"

His eyes suddenly blazed with fury. "Not just seemed, dammit!" He slammed his fist against the top of the table so hard the dishes rattled. "I'm telling you that I was being kept a prisoner."

Leah threw up her hands in a placating gesture. "Okay, okay." She forced calmness in her voice that she didn't feel. "Just take it easy."

Hunter sighed heavily. "Sorry." His face was bleak with regret. "I did it again, didn't I?"

Leah's tensed muscles relaxed somewhat and she felt her professional instincts kick in. In an even, soothing voice, she said, "Maybe if you talk about it, I might understand better. Why don't you tell me about it—about your stay at the hospital—and the reasons you think you were being held prisoner."

After a moment, he finally nodded.

Keeping an eagle eye on Hunter, Leah sidestepped over to the cabinet. "Just let me get something to drink." Without waiting for a response, she poured a glass of apple juice, then seated herself across the table from him. She motioned toward his plate. "Your food's getting cold. Eat first. Then talk."

When something that resembled a grin tugged at the corners of his lips, Leah relaxed even more.

"Yes, ma'am," he drawled and gave her a two-fingered salute. "Aren't you eating, too?"

Leah shook her head. "I ate earlier," she lied. Truth was, she was far too nervous and her emotions in too much chaos to eat, even if she wanted to.

Before Leah had finished even half her juice, Hunter had polished off every bite of food on his plate.

"That was the best meal I've had in a long time," he told her. "From the bottom of my heart and my stomach, thank you."

"You're welcome," she responded with a smile. "When was the last time you ate?"

"That obvious, huh?" But instead of answering her question, Hunter shoved the plate aside and wrapped his hands around his coffee cup. "Please understand that I'm just trying to figure things out, trying to understand what happened to me and why."

Leah nodded and in spite of her earlier apprehension, sympathy welled up inside her. "Why don't you tell me about it?"

For several seconds he stared at her, then, as if he'd come to some kind of decision, he began. "When I came out of the coma, I was placed in rehab. My right leg had been badly broken in the accident, and it was almost six weeks before I could walk again without assistance."

He took a deep breath and let it out in a sigh. "Once I could walk," he continued, "I was placed in a private room. I was still pretty weak, and at first, I didn't think about it too much. I mean a John Doe, a charity case, being placed in a private room," he clarified. "I was just grateful that I didn't have to share the room with anyone else." He frowned. "Later, I realized that I was never allowed to go anywhere outside of my room without an orderly accompanying me.

"Anyway—" He gave a one-shouldered shrug. "As I felt stronger, I began to feel antsy. I was ready to get out of there so I could find out who I was—find out about my life. But each time I asked the doctor about being discharged, he always came up with an excuse as to why I wasn't ready. Well, I got enough of that real fast and decided to simply leave.

"Since all I had to wear was a hospital gown, I talked an orderly into getting me some scrubs, and—" Hunter shook his head. "A lot of good that did me. I only got as far as the hospital exit door before they caught me. Before I knew what hit me, one of the nurses popped me with a shot and the lights went out. When I woke up, I was back in my bed with restraints on my wrists and ankles. The scrubs were gone, and I was in a hospital gown again."

Unbidden outrage and anger at the treatment that he'd received welled within Leah. "Didn't anyone bother trying to explain?"

Hunter shook his head. "No matter how many times I asked, no one would tell me what was going on, and each time I raised hell, they drugged me. It didn't take me long to figure out that if I ever hoped to leave that place, I was going to have to play along. I'd have to pretend that I was cooperating. After about a week, they finally removed the restraints and began giving me the sedatives by mouth."

Restraints…sedatives… Leah frowned, not liking what she was hearing. Until she knew more though, she figured that humoring him would be the best thing to do for now. "So, just how did you escape?" she asked.

"The last couple of nights I was there, I pretended to swallow my pill, and as soon as the nurse left, I spit it out. As long as they thought I was drugged they didn't watch me as close."

Hunter paused. He'd seen the fear in her eyes earlier, and since the last thing he wanted was to scare her again, he decided against telling her about the guard outside his door. He'd caught the man half-asleep, and before the guard had realized what hit him, he'd knocked the man unconscious and dragged him into the bathroom out of sight. He'd debated on whether to take the guard's uniform, but one look at the short skinny man and he'd known that there was no way he could squeeze into the clothes.

"I found some clean scrubs on an unattended utility cart down the hall from my room," he continued. "With the scrubs on—" He shrugged. "No one paid me any attention. The only door that wasn't locked was at the emergency-room entrance. Once I found that, I walked right out."

When Leah shifted in her chair, he could tell she was unsure of how to react to what he'd told her, and he wondered if she would catch his discrepancy about the clothes, specifically the shoes, the one thing he'd glossed over.

As Leah stared into her glass of juice, she tried to digest everything that Hunter had just told her. Everything he'd said, the restraints, the sedatives, all of it only served to confirm her suspicions about him being held in the hospital mental ward. There were also huge discrepancies in his story about escaping. Mental wards had locked doors, and patients didn't just wander around at will. He wasn't telling her everything, and every instinct within cried foul. Something just didn't add up.

"You're right about one thing," she finally said, looking up at him. "We do need to find out more about what happened to you and why." *And I need a little time to do some checking around,* she added silently. If she could determine exactly which hospital in Orlando had treated him, then maybe she could get some answers. But first she had to figure out how to do so without Hunter knowing that she was checking up on his story.

When Hunter reached up to cover a yawn, Leah figured she'd been handed the perfect opportunity.

"For right now though," she told him as she stood, "in my professional opinion, I think what you need even more is rest." She picked up his plate and juice glass. "If you'd like, you can take a nap on that bed in the first bedroom down the hall. Then, when you've rested some, we can figure out where to go from here."

Hunter yawned again. She was right about him needing rest, and the fact that she'd said "we" was certainly encouraging. Did he dare hope that she believed him?

"I am tired," he admitted. Tired didn't begin to explain how drained and exhausted he felt, and since he had no money, nowhere else to go and no one else he could trust for the time being... "Maybe just a short nap—if you're sure that's okay?"

Leah nodded. "That's more than okay with me." She walked over to the cabinet, where she paused. "Tell you what though," she said. "Why don't you nap in the bedroom at the end of the hall, instead of the front bedroom? It's a lot quieter back there. Less street noise."

There would also be less chance of him overhearing any phone conversations she had. She placed the dirty dishes in the sink, then motioned toward the hall door. "We'll talk more after you've rested."

Once Hunter had disappeared around the hall doorway, at the last minute, Leah remembered that she hadn't yet made up her bed that morning. Too bad, she finally decided. As he'd said, "Beggars can't be choosers."

Leah frowned as she wiped off the table. But Hunter wasn't a beggar, not by a long shot. She transferred the dishes in the sink to the dishwasher. He was her husband, and from the looks of him, he wouldn't care if there were clean sheets on the bed.

Glancing around the kitchen, Leah began what she'd always called busywork. Wiping the stovetop, the counter, and cleaning the glass front of the oven and microwave. She wanted to give him plenty of time to get to sleep before she began making phone calls.

When Hunter entered the bedroom at the end of the hallway, he immediately realized that it belonged to Leah. For one thing, the bed was unmade.

As he stood, staring at the sheets, just the thought of climbing into the bed that she'd slept in did funny things to his libido. Surely he wouldn't be feeling this way unless there was a good reason, which, in turn, made him more certain than ever that she hadn't been exactly truthful about their so-called friendship.

Then, another thought occurred to him. If she'd been untruthful about their relationship, she could be lying about other things as well. What if she was using the same trick he'd used at the hospital? What if she was just lulling him into a false sense of safety so that once he was asleep, she could call the police to come get him?

Get a grip, man. If she'd meant to call the cops on him, she could have easily done so while he was in the shower. Hunter shook his head. Too many days of plotting and planning his escape from the hospital had taken its toll, and he was seeing a conspiracy in everything. Again he reminded himself that at some point, he had to trust someone, and right now, Leah was the only game in town.

Hunter stared at the doorknob. Too bad there wasn't a lock on the door, but the doorknob, like the house, was old, the kind that required a key.

Near the bed, Hunter pulled off the knit shirt, unsnapped and unzipped the jeans and shucked them as well, then climbed into bed. As he lay his head on the pillow, a musky flowery scent filled his nostrils. The scent felt familiar and safe. Was he imagining things, or was it a memory?

Hunter closed his eyes and breathed deeply. Whether imagined or a true memory, he was too dog-tired to worry about it.

Leah eyed the doorway leading to the hallway. She needed to put some clothes on instead of walking around in her pajamas and housecoat. And she needed a shower. And since she'd sent Hunter off to her bedroom, there was no way she could get into her closet without disturbing him, and disturbing him was the last thing she wanted at the moment.

Leah stood in the middle of the kitchen, debating what to do next, when suddenly the solution to her clothing problem came to her. Maybe, just maybe, there was something in the laundry room that she could wear. If she remembered right, she'd neglected to put away the last load of clothes she'd dried.

In the laundry room, she rummaged through the dryer. Sure enough, she found a pair of jeans and a T-shirt. Both were faded and wrinkled, but too bad, she thought as she headed for the bathroom. Wearing faded wrinkled clothes was the least of her problems at the moment.

When Leah entered the bathroom, she paused, her hand on the doorknob as she debated whether to leave the door ajar or lock it. But just thinking about being locked up in the small room was enough to make her break out in a cold sweat. For as long as she could remember, being in a small, closed-up space was a surefire guarantee that she would have a panic attack.

Leah pushed the door almost closed, leaving about a six-inch gap. Besides, she comforted herself, if Hunter had meant to harm her, he could have already done so.

She glanced around the bathroom. Hunter had left the room the way he'd found it except for the wet shower curtain and the damp towels and washcloth. Leah's gaze landed on the small trash basket in the corner. And except for the scrubs he'd been wearing. He'd shoved those into the trash.

She walked over to the basket, pulled out the scrubs, and carefully examined them. "Yes," she whispered when she finally found what she'd been looking for. Most hospitals stamped their names on the scrubs that they provided to their surgery doctors and nurses. Just as she'd suspected and hoped for, inside the neck of the shirt, stamped with permanent ink, was the name of the hospital, Orlando Memorial. Knowing the name of the hospital would save her a lot of time and trouble, not to mention the cost of making a bunch of long-distance calls.

"Now, that's strange," she murmured, noticing, for the first time, the square lump in the pocket of the pants. The lump turned out to be a black billfold, made of plastic that was supposed to resemble leather.

But Hunter's billfold had been burned in the wreck, so where had this one come from? And why would Hunter have thrown it away? she wondered as she searched through the different compartments.

Leah frowned. Empty. The billfold was empty. *Well, duh, what did you expect? Why else would he have thrown it away?*

Still perplexed and more wary than ever, she stuffed the scrubs and the billfold back into the trash basket. The answer had to be that he'd stolen it. He'd needed money, and with no available resources, he'd resorted to taking what he needed.

But from whom? And what had happened to the person he'd stolen the billfold from? A shiver ran up her spine. Just one more reason to proceed with caution, she decided.

From experience, Leah knew that it usually took about thirty to forty minutes for her to brush her teeth, shower, wash and dry her hair, and dress. By the time she'd dried her hair and was pulling on clean underwear and the jeans, she figured that she'd given Hunter plenty of time to fall asleep. There was just one problem, she thought as she glared down at the front of the jeans. She couldn't snap the jeans and still breathe.

With an oh-well shrug, she zipped up the jeans as far as they would go and left the snap undone. Once she pulled on the T-shirt, she gave a soft sigh. The T-shirt was midhip length, just long enough to cover the unsnapped, half-zipped jeans.

She glanced at her profile in the full-length mirror attached to the back of the bathroom door, and sighed again. Due to her body build and in spite of her slightly swollen abdomen, with loose clothes on, she didn't look pregnant yet. Even so, her clothes were getting a bit too snug for comfort, and it wouldn't be long before she would have to buy maternity wear.

The only way that Hunter would know that she was pregnant was if he saw her naked. Even then, he might think she was simply out of shape or a little overweight.

Just the thought of Hunter seeing her naked sent a wave of both apprehension and desire rushing through her. Lying to him about their relationship was bad enough, but how would he react once he realized she was pregnant?

Leah turned away from the mirror. Best not to think about it for now. There was no point. Until she knew more about what had happened to him, she didn't intend to get that close. No matter how much her body wanted him.

Once Leah had straightened the bathroom, she stepped into the hallway and stared at the door leading to her bedroom. Hunter had closed the door, but was he asleep yet? Only one way to make sure.

For the most part, her bare feet were noiseless on the wooden floor, but the house was old, and there were places where the floor creaked. Though she tried to avoid those spots, completely avoiding them was impossible. Each time the floor creaked, she froze, her ears straining for the slightest sound coming from the bedroom. When she finally reached the bedroom door, she held her breath, slowly turned the doorknob then eased the door open just far enough to see inside.

Only when she saw that Hunter was indeed asleep did she dare breathe again. He was on his back with his arms thrown out to the side, his chest bare, and he was breathing deeply and evenly. As her gaze settled on his bare chest then moved lower to where the sheet just barely covered his hips, a quiver surged through her veins and her mind burned with the memory of the last time they had made love. Knowing that he was naked in her bed sent another familiar ache of desire surging through her.

Momentarily paralyzed by the depth of her feeling, Leah eased the door shut again. But even with the door shut, the old adage "out of sight, out of mind" didn't work, and it was several moments before she could finally force her limbs to do her bidding.

Back in the kitchen, she went straight to the telephone, called directory assistance and asked for the phone number of the Orlando Memorial Hospital. The sooner she found out what she needed to know, the sooner she would know for sure exactly what had happened to Hunter.

Once she'd scribbled down the number and disconnected the call, she hesitated long enough to come up with a plan of action. As a nurse, she knew that getting any information about a patient without that patient's privately assigned patient number was out of the question, a long shot at best, because of HIPA, the Hospital Informational Privacy Act.

Long shot or not, she had to try. Taking a deep breath, she punched out the number. "Admissions, please," she told the woman who finally answered her call. After several moments she was finally connected.

"Admissions," a woman's voice answered. "Virginia Cole speaking. How may I help you?"

At least Ms. Cole sounded friendly enough, which would make her inquiry easier than it might have been.

"Yes—hello, Ms. Cole. Any help you could give me would certainly be appreciated. My name is Leah Johnson, and I'm with Charity Hospital in New Orleans, Louisiana. We've just admitted an amnesia patient who claims that he was recently a patient at your hospital. We'd like to start procedures to have a copy of his medical records transferred."

"What's the patient's name and his patient number?"

"He says his name is Hunter Davis," Leah told the woman. "But he doesn't remember his patient number, and of course there's no way we would know it. He said he had been at your hospital a number of months. He was a victim of an automobile accident and he also says that he was in a coma for a couple of weeks."

"I'm sure you realize that I really can't give out patient information without the number or proper authorization."

Leah drummed her fingertips against the kitchen countertop. "Yes, I do realize that, but these are special circumstances. The man has amnesia."

"Well, I suppose I could check with my supervisor. Can you hold a minute?"

"Yes, I'll hold."

While Leah waited, she kept her ears tuned to any noise that would indicate that Hunter had awakened.

Finally, after what seemed like forever, the phone clicked in her ear. "Ah—Ms. Johnson? You still there?"

"Yes," Leah answered.

"I'm sorry, Ms. Johnson," the woman said. "But we can't help you."

Leah's fingers stilled. Though it was just a gut feeling, there was something in the carefully controlled tone of Virginia Cole's voice that set off warning bells, a guarded reticence that hadn't been present when Leah had first asked about Hunter.

"Are you sure about that?"

"Absolutely sure," was the woman's emphatic answer. "Sorry."

But Leah wasn't the type to give up easily, especially with so much at stake. "Well, can you at least tell me if any John Doe's were admitted about that time?" she asked.

"No, I can't," the woman retorted in a flat tone that brooked no argument. Then, without further explanation or even so much as a goodbye, the woman promptly disconnected the call.

"Well, thanks for nothing," Leah muttered to the dead line. But as she slowly hung up the receiver, her mind raced.

In spite of the woman's refusal to cooperate, she had proof that he'd been there. How else could he have gotten the scrubs?

Leah turned away from the phone. There was an answer, but it wasn't one she liked or wanted to dwell on. The only other way he could have gotten the scrubs was by stealing them. But even that answer only conjured up more questions. Why would he have bothered to steal someone's scrubs in the first place unless he'd been in a position where he'd needed clothes? And the only reason he would have needed clothes was if he'd been a patient in a hospital.

Hunter didn't want to wake up, but no matter how hard he tried to ignore the building pressure in his bladder, further sleep was impossible.

With his eyes still closed, he groaned and pushed himself to a sitting position. He reached up, rubbed his eyes, and finally opened them. Then, he went stone still.

"What the hell?" With a fierce scowl, he glanced around the unfamiliar, spacious bedroom that was decorated with lace and ruffles. Definitely a woman's bedroom. But what woman?

His eyes narrowed suspiciously, and as he glanced around the room, searching for something, anything, that might give him a clue, his gaze found and rested on a framed photo on the bedside table.

In the photo were two women. One was an attractive older, woman who was probably in her seventies, but it was the other one, the younger woman, that snapped his memory into focus. And along with recognition of the woman, all the doubts and confusion he'd experienced over the past weeks surged through him with a vengeance.

Leah Johnson...the woman he'd seen in his flash-backs...his so-called *friend*.

Beside the photo was a clock radio, and the digital dial showed that it was 4:00 p.m.

Hunter shook his head in amazement. He'd slept like a dead man for over eight hours, a record for him. No wonder his bladder was about ready to burst.

He dragged himself to the edge of the bed, but when he stood, he did so cautiously. His leg was stiff. From experience, he knew that once he began moving around, it would loosen up.

On the floor beside the bed, exactly where he'd left them, were the jeans and shirt that Leah Johnson had provided. Hunter stepped into the jeans, snapped and zipped them, then pulled the knit shirt on over his head. As he approached the bedroom door, too many days of looking over his shoulder and expecting that any minute he'd get caught made him wary. He tilted his head and listened, but all he heard was the hum of the central air conditioner.

With a shake of his head and a sigh, he eased the door open. The most opportune time for someone to grab him would have been while he was sleeping. Since no one had, it stood to reason that no one was waiting for him to wake up so they could pounce on him.

The hallway was empty, and as he made his way to the bathroom, he listened for any sound that would tell him where Leah was in the house, or even if she was still there.

As he entered the bathroom, he heard the distinct rattle of dishes and caught a whiff of food. Realizing that she was in the kitchen made him aware of just how hungry he was. How long? he wondered. Just how long would she be willing to extend her hospitality? And if she didn't, then what?

He could always try to contact the New York City Police Department, and he would…eventually. But without money or transportation, his options were limited. Besides, his gut feeling told him that the woman named Leah had all the answers he needed.

The toilet flushing was the first warning Leah had that Hunter was awake, and she tensed as she stirred the pot of soup on the stove top.

Though he hadn't made a sound, when she ventured a glance over her shoulder, he was standing just inside the kitchen doorway. Deep lines of concentration creased his forehead.

He motioned toward the stove. "Whatever that is you're cooking smells out of this world," he said, stepping farther into the room.

In spite of her feelings of trepidation, a tiny smile pulled at the corner of her lips. "I call it ham-bone vegetable soup. If you're hungry, you're welcome to have a bowl."

An hour and two bowls of soup and a thick ham sandwich later, Hunter groaned, then shoved back from the table and stood. "My memory might be out of whack, but there's nothing wrong with my appetite. That was good. But you should have stopped me after the first bowl."

"I'm glad you enjoyed—"

The sharp rap coming from the front door interrupted Leah midsentence.

"Are you expecting anyone?" Hunter demanded.

Leah shook her head. "No, not really." Trying to ignore the tense wild look in Hunter's eyes, she tried placating him. "I'll get rid of whoever it is." She turned and headed toward the hallway. Before she'd taken two steps, Hunter grabbed her arm, then stepped in front of her, blocking her path to the door.

"I don't know how, but they might have tracked me down," he said, his voice low. "Don't let on that you've seen me or that I'm here... Please," he added. "I'm trusting you. I can't be locked up again, not without first finding out why."

For several moments Leah stared at him. The wild look in Hunter's eyes, along with his paranoia, was a stark reminder of just how little she knew about him. It also reminded her that there was a good chance that Hunter had been locked up because he was a mental patient.

Leah covered his hand with hers. "You're safe here," she told him. "You can trust me." But even as she uttered the lie, guilt for the other lies she'd told him reared its ugly head.

Another sharp rap echoed throughout the house, and after a moment, Hunter finally nodded and released his hold on her.

From behind the heavy curtain that draped the front window in the parlor, Leah peered out at the two men who stood on the porch. Both had short, military-style haircuts, and both were dressed in suits and ties. Other than the fact that one was just a bit taller, and one had dark hair and the other one was sandy-haired, they could have been cookie-cutter look-alikes.

Whoever they were, Leah had an uneasy feeling that they weren't there for a social call. Glancing over her shoulder to make sure that Hunter was out of sight, she walked to the front door. Once she was at the door, she called out, "Who is it?"

"FBI, ma'am," one of the men answered. "Open up. We've got a search warrant."

Stay calm...don't panic. "Just a second, please." Leah slipped the slide bolt of the chain lock into the doorplate, then opened the door as wide as the chain allowed.

"I'd like to see some ID," she said. "And the warrant," she added.

The taller, dark-haired agent flipped open a badge and held it up to the narrow opening of the door.

The badge looked authentic enough, but of course she'd never had reason to see an FBI badge, so there was no way for her to know if it was real or fake. Then he slipped a paper through the opening.

Leah glanced over the paper, and once she saw that it was a warrant to search the premises and she recognized the name of the local judge who had signed it, she decided that the warrant and the agents had to be authentic.

"Ma'am, I'm Agent Lance Martin, and this is Agent Ray Harris." He motioned toward the sandy-haired man. "Open the door. We need to talk to you."

"About what? And why do you need to search my home?"

"This is about Hunter Davis," he said.

The uneasy feeling she'd had a few minutes earlier grew. Leah took a steadying breath as she fought to keep her panic felt from showing on her face.

For several moments she simply stared at the man, trying to buy time. Where was Hunter? she wondered, fighting the temptation to look over her shoulder. Even more important, was he within earshot? If the FBI was there looking for him, he'd be caught for sure. Then another thought suddenly occurred to her. The FBI would also know that she was married to him. What if they said her full name?

"Why are you looking for Hunter?" she demanded.

"I'm not at liberty to discuss that with you."

"Then just go away," she told him. "Hunter is dead."

"Afraid we can't do that, ma'am. We have good reason to believe that he's alive, and that you know he's alive. We also have reason to believe that he's here in this house. One way or—"

"How do you know that?" she retorted. "Just what makes you think he's here?"

"We have our sources, ma'am. Now open up. We don't have a lot of time, and one way or another, we're coming in. It's up to you whether we do it peaceably or by force. If you don't let us in, we can and *will* break down the door."

Leah's heart pumped double time beneath her breasts. She was between a rock and a hard place and had no choice. As she unlatched the chain, she silently cursed her trembling fingers. Glaring at first one man, then the other one, she opened the door.

"This won't take long, ma'am," the agent named Ray Harris told her as he and the other agent pushed past her. When both men whipped out guns from the holsters beneath their jackets, a hard fist of terror lodged in Leah's stomach.

Ray turned and headed for the hallway. "I'll check back here," he told the other agent, "while you check through there." With his head, he motioned toward the door on the opposite side of the room.

Leah stood frozen, her heart racing, as the dark-haired agent disappeared through the doorway and the sandy-haired agent crept toward the hall. Suddenly, she couldn't breathe. Where was Hunter? Surely he'd overheard what the agents had said, and surely he'd had sense enough to escape through the back door.

The second Ray Harris turned the corner into the hallway, Hunter jumped him, and Leah screamed.

Chapter 4

As Leah's scream echoed in the house, Hunter grabbed the agent around the neck in a chokehold and latched on to the gun.

Across the room, the dark-haired agent came charging back into the room just as his partner elbowed Hunter in the gut. Hunter grunted from the blow but held on to the gun and tightened his grip around the other man's neck.

Before the dark-haired agent got halfway across the room, quick as lightning, Hunter twisted the gun, pried it loose from the agent's hand and rammed it against the man's temple.

Hunter's captive stiffened then went still, and the dark-haired agent skidded to a halt. Using his captive as a shield, Hunter forced him into the parlor.

"Easy now," Hunter told the dark-haired agent, his voice deceptively soft but edged with steel. "Just take it easy and no one will get hurt. Put your gun down and kick it over here. And no funny business."

Leah's heart pounded. Would the agent give up his gun?

"We're not here to hurt you," the agent told Hunter. Then he knelt down and placed the gun on the floor. "We're here to protect you." He straightened, then kicked the gun toward Hunter.

The sound of metal skidding against wood grated loudly in Leah's ears as the gun slid across the floor then stopped just to the right of Hunter's feet. Using the heel of his foot, Hunter kicked the gun back behind him into the hallway.

All Leah could do was stand frozen and watch. Was Hunter running a bluff on the agents or had he lied to her about being a cop, about being unable to fire a weapon? Surely if he was a cop the FBI would know about his medical leave and the reasons behind it. But then, maybe they didn't. Maybe such things came under patient-doctor confidentiality. After all, the agent did give up his weapon.

"Down on your knees," Hunter ordered. "Hands behind your head." When the dark-haired agent dropped to his knees and raised his hands, Hunter loosened his hold on the captive agent and shoved him in the direction of the one on his knees. "You, too," he snarled. "Down. Hands behind your head."

The agent stumbled but caught himself, and with a backward glare at Hunter, he joined his partner on the floor.

The minute the agent was down, Hunter yelled, "Answers! I want some damn answers. And I want them now! You! Martin!" He waved the gun at the dark-haired man. "Start talking."

"Easy does it, Hunter," the agent said. "Like I said, we're not here to hurt you. We're only here to take you into protective custody. All I can tell you is that you're a material witness to a murder committed in Orlando."

"Yeah, right!" Hunter snarled. "And I've got some ocean-front property in Arizona for sale."

"It's true," the sandy-haired agent told him.

"Well, the joke's on you," Hunter sneered. "The only thing I remember about Orlando is being held prisoner in that damn hospital. I didn't even know my own name until this morning. Seems I have this little problem called amnesia."

"We know that," the dark-haired agent said evenly. "It's because of the amnesia that we can't tell you anything else. You have to remember it on your own, without any prompting or help or else your testimony won't hold water."

Breathing hard, Hunter glared first at one man and then the other. Though he didn't trust either agent as far as he could throw them, their body language told him they were telling the truth.

Body language? Now, where in the hell had that come from? *More memory returning or instincts and training? Cop instincts and training?* Leah had said he was a cop. No time to think about it now.

"Okay," Hunter drawled. His steely gaze slid to the sandy-haired agent, then back to the dark-haired agent. "Just for argument's sake, say I believe you. What then?"

"For your own protection, we've been instructed to take you and your wife into custody and take you both to a safe house."

His wife? Hunter felt as if he'd just been sucker punched. His eyes cut to Leah. *You're safe here... You can trust me.* As her words swirled in his head, a cold feeling settled in the pit of his stomach. She'd lied. And if she'd lied about something like that, what else had she lied about? Was she the reason the feds had showed up? Had she called them after all?

Leah felt her insides shrivel. Hunter's expression was tight with strain and anger as he glared at her, but the stony look of betrayal in his eyes cut her to the quick. "Hunter," she entreated. "Please, let me explain."

Icy contempt blazed in his eyes, but before she could utter another word, he shifted his gaze back to the agents. "Then what?" Hunter demanded, glaring at the men.

Leah swallowed against the ache in her throat. She should have trusted him.

"We'll keep you in the safe house until a transfer back to Orlando can be arranged," Lance Martin answered. "There's a doctor in Orlando that we think can use hypnosis to break through your amnesia without compromising your testimony."

Safe house? Raw rage boiled up within Leah, rage with herself for not trusting Hunter, but mostly rage against the police and the two agents, the very people who were supposed to uphold the law and protect the innocent.

Her eyes narrowed and she glowered at Martin. She'd been lied to from the get-go, purposely deceived. She'd spent months in anguish, thinking that Hunter was dead and wondering how she was going to raise a child on her own. And while she'd been grieving, these people had kept Hunter locked away, had kept him a prisoner without telling him why. And now they expected to waltz right in and have her and Hunter go along with them like meek little lambs. Well, no more. Enough was enough.

Leah slammed her hand down on a nearby table. "Hey!" she shouted. All three men jerked their heads her way. "My turn to ask questions! Just who the hell do you people think you are, messing in other people's lives? I'm not stepping foot out that door, not until I get some answers. And if you think otherwise, you've got another think coming."

"Now, now, Mrs. Davis, just calm down," Martin told her.

"Don't you dare tell me to calm down," she snapped at him. "And don't you dare patronize me." Leah knew she was losing control, but for once in her life, she didn't care. "I want some answers," she screamed at him. "And I want them now!"

"All in good time, ma'am," he told her.

"All in good time?" she cried. "That's all you've got to say? Well, we'll just see about that!" Leah shifted her glare to Hunter. "Shoot him, Hunter. Just shoot the bastard."

Though Hunter kept his eyes and the gun trained on the agents, his shoulders tensed and the look on his face bordered on desperation and confusion. It was only then that Leah realized what she had said. How desperate she sounded. She didn't really want the man dead, she just wanted some answers.

Leah's face burned with regret.

Out of the corner of her eye, she spotted the baseball bat propped next to the door where she'd left it. Time for a different approach, she decided. Before anyone realized her intentions, she reached over, snatched the bat and jerked it up into a swinging position. Tightening her grip and careful to keep a safe distance, she edged closer to the agent called Martin.

"Back off, Leah," Hunter demanded.

Leah ignored him, her eyes on Martin. "I said I want answers," she stormed. "And one way or another, I intend to get them. Either you tell me what I want to know or I'm going to use this bat to hit a home run with your head." To emphasize her point she squared off and raised the bat a notch higher. "First question," she snapped. "Why was I told that Hunter was dead? Why not just take us both into protective custody to begin with?"

The agent hesitated only a moment. "It was for your own protection," he told her. "And for Hunter's," he added. "In the beginning we didn't know if Hunter would live or die, so it was decided that it would be safer all the way around if the perpetrators believed that Hunter had died in the accident. And to make it real, to make them believe that he was dead, you had to believe he was dead, too. If we had told you the truth and taken you into protective custody, they would have known that he was still alive."

Leah's anger died a slow death as logic took over. The agent's answer made sense, and without realizing she'd done so, she eased her grip and lowered the bat.

The moment she lowered the bat, the agent nodded his approval, then turned his gaze to Hunter. "Be reasonable, Hunter. Don't you see that by refusing protective custody, you're putting your life as well as your wife's in grave danger? All it would take would be for the wrong person to spot you—and it could happen. These people we're talking about have connections everywhere."

She had been told he was dead? Endless thoughts raced through Hunter's head, but he kept seeing Leah, brandishing the bat and demanding answers. He could not even imagine how shocked she must have been when she found him on her porch. Though she certainly hadn't shown it, until now. If she was so ready to defend him, her husband, why had she lied in the first place?

"You know I'm right," Martin said, interrupting Hunter's thoughts. "Think about it, man. We can protect you."

Protect you...protect you...to serve and protect... The agent's words echoed in Hunter's head, and without warning, scenes flashed through his mind. With a heart-stopping jolt, he suddenly recognized the scenes for what they were— memories, unbidden memories of another time and another place.

Leah had told him the basics about the incident, and though it could be argued that he was simply being influenced by those words, Hunter knew deep in his gut that the flashes in his head were too detailed and graphic to be anything but real.

It had been New Year's Eve. Even now he could feel the sting of the bitterly cold night. The 911 call had come from a hysterical child. Her mother's ex-boyfriend was drunk, threatening to kill her and her mother. Hunter and his partner, Jack O'Brian, had been sent out to investigate the call.

Even before they reached the third floor of the apartment building, they heard the woman's screams. Together, they kicked in the door. The man had the woman pinned against the wall near a door. From the look of her bloody face, he'd used the gun to beat the hell out of her. It all happened so fast that Hunter had reacted out of pure instinct. Hunter went in low and Jack entered high. Just as they cleared the door, the man, gun in hand, whirled to face them. The man fired and missed, then he dropped to the floor. But in that split second before he dropped and just as Hunter squeezed the trigger of his own gun, the door behind the man flew open. The little girl had died on impact.

Hunter's insides shriveled as the memory faded. He'd taken an oath to protect the innocent and on that night he'd broken the oath and lost his soul in the process. Putting himself in danger was one thing, but he couldn't risk another innocent. Not again. Leah had said he couldn't fire a gun, and he was damn sure she was right, so there was no way he could protect her even if he wanted to.

Taking a deep breath and praying that he was doing the right thing, Hunter slowly lowered the gun, then he turned it butt forward and held it out to Lance Martin.

"You made the right decision," the agent told him, scrambling to his feet as he reached for the weapon. He handed it to his partner. Addressing both Leah and Hunter, he said, "We don't have much time. You've got about five minutes to pack."

Ray Harris followed Leah and Hunter back to the bedroom while Lance Martin stayed in the living room to keep watch out front. Once in the bedroom, the agent positioned himself near the window that overlooked the backyard. Hunter was

standing at the foot of the bed, and as Leah crammed underwear, a nightgown, T-shirts, a pair of loose-fitting jeans and
a couple of pairs of knit pants into a backpack, she could feel
Hunter watching her every move.

"I take it these belong to me and not some fictitious uncle."
Hunter plucked at the knit shirt he was wearing. "Are there
more where this came from?"

Nodding, Leah reached down and took the cardboard box
from the bottom of her closet. "Not many," she said as she
handed the box to Hunter. "You packed most of your stuff for
the trip to Orlando. I just left it there." Unable to maintain eye
contact, Leah turned away, then began searching through the
closet until she found the spare backpack she was looking for.
She threw it to Hunter, and while she made a trip to the bathroom for toiletries, and to change into a better-fitting pair of
jeans, he began stuffing the backpack with the clothes from
the box.

"Time's up," Ray Harris announced when Leah returned.
"We've got to get out of here."

With Harris bringing up the rear, Leah and Hunter headed
down the hall. When they entered the living room, Lance
Martin glanced their way. "Ready?" he asked.

Leah shook her head. "What about my job? I can't just disappear without telling them something."

"You'll have to call and say that you're resigning."

Leah glared at Martin. "I can't just up and quit."

"Yes, you can," the agent told her. "And after this is all
over, the hospital will be apprised of the circumstances. Now,
are you ready?"

Leah shook her head. "I don't care what you say, I'm not
quitting my job. And one more thing—I've got to make sure
my house is secure," she insisted. "Make sure all the windows
are locked, stop the delivery of the newspaper, have my mail
stopped."

Martin rolled his eyes, then, with a sigh, he said, "Ray and I will check the house now—and later, we'll take care of the newspaper and your mail. You and Hunter wait there." He motioned toward the hall where Hunter had jumped Ray Harris.

Within minutes, both agents returned. "All the windows are locked and the back door is secure," Martin told her. With him in the lead and Harris bringing up the rear, they hustled Leah and Hunter to the car.

Harris drove and Martin rode shotgun. Leah sat as close to the door as she could while Hunter sprawled out behind Martin on the passenger side.

"So where is this so-called safe house?" Hunter asked once they were on their way, bumping along the narrow, uneven street that Leah lived on.

Martin shifted sideways in the seat. "It's just outside the city, near Kenner," he said over his shoulder.

"How long before we're transferred to Orlando?"

"Probably a day or two at the most."

Leah, still avoiding eye contact with Hunter for fear of seeing only condemnation, listened to his questions and the agent's answers as they drove beneath the overhanging branches of the towering oaks that shaded the narrow street. As she gazed out the side window at the century-old homes they passed, her mind's eye kept seeing the betrayal on Hunter's face when he'd learned that she lied about their relationship.

She should have told him the truth. Shoulda, woulda, coulda, she thought with sarcasm. And hindsight was a wonderful thing.

Across from her, Hunter shifted in the seat. "Another question," he said, directing his attention to Martin again and interrupting Leah's self-flagellant thoughts. "How did you know where to find me?"

Leah tensed as her gaze flew from the window to the agent.

"We weren't sure where to look at first," the agent said. "The minute you disappeared from the hospital, we put a tap on your wife's phone, and we also instructed the staff at the hospital to immediately report any inquiries made about you. Then, this morning, we hit pay dirt. Your wife's phone call to the hospital was what tipped us off."

"Her phone call?"

Hunter whipped his head around to glare at Leah. At the expression on his face, a cold knot formed in her stomach.

"And just what kind of phone call did she make?" Hunter retorted, sarcasm oozing with each word as his eyes burned a hole in her that went all the way to her soul.

Leah swallowed hard. Caught again. Yet another lie, another betrayal found out.

"She was trying to confirm that you had been a patient there," Martin answered. "For all the good it did her," he added. "But it was just the red flag we'd been waiting for. We were dispatched immediately to bring you in."

"We've got trouble!" Harris interrupted in a tense, clipped voice. "We picked up a tail. The black SUV."

When Martin shifted his gaze to the vehicle's side-view mirror, Leah heard a pinging sound. The rear windshield splintered and Leah screamed.

Chapter 5

Hunter grabbed Leah. "Get down!" he shouted. He shoved her down onto the seat, then covered her with his own body. Leah's scream was muffled by the car seat. Panic and fear for the safety of her unborn baby streaked through her as she struggled to breathe beneath Hunter's weight.

"Damn Bureau leak," she heard Harris mutter as she felt the car careen first to one side then to the other.

Suddenly shots exploded from the passenger side of the car as Martin returned fire.

More shots rang out from behind. Martin groaned then yelled, "Dammit to hell! I'm hit!"

"How bad?" his partner demanded.

"My arm! Can't return fire!"

"Hunter—the gun!" Harris floored the accelerator and zigzagged between the vehicles in his path. "Get his gun!" Harris shouted as horns blared and tires squealed.

"Stay down," Hunter told Leah. When he sprang up,

reached over the seat and grabbed for Martin's gun, Leah gulped in air and splayed her hands protectively over her abdomen. Just as Hunter latched on to the gun, another spray of bullets pelted the rear end of the car, and he ducked. Again Harris floored the accelerator. More horns blared.

"Coming up to Valence Street," Harris shouted. "They're at least three cars behind. When I make the turn, I'll slow enough for you both to bail out. Just pray that they keep following me!"

"Take this." Martin pitched Hunter his cell phone. "And keep the gun."

Only seconds passed before Harris yelled, "Get ready! Here it comes."

"Keep low," Hunter ordered, his mouth inches from her ear.

Fear within Leah increased tenfold as tires skidded and she felt the car lurch to the right as Hunter grabbed her arm with the grip of a vise. What if she fell? What if she lost the baby? *Don't think about it. Just concentrate on staying alive.*

As she tensed in readiness, out of the corner of her eye, she spied her purse on the floor. With her free hand she latched on to to it just as Hunter shoved open the door. He yanked on her arm, and the force of it propelled Leah sideways. Hunter jumped, pulling Leah with him. When they hit the pavement, Hunter's firm grip was all that kept her from falling flat on her face. The second Hunter slammed the door shut, Harris gunned the engine.

"Run!" Hunter yelled.

Leah had barely regained her balance when Hunter jerked her sideways again. Half pulling, half dragging her, he jumped the curb, and Leah had no choice but to follow.

"Take cover behind the tree!" Hunter yanked her behind the trunk of a huge oak off to the side of the walkway, then pinned her to it with his body. The rough bark bit into her chest, and she could feel every gasping breath that Hunter took against her back. Within seconds, they both watched as the black SUV streaked past, following the agent's car.

Before the agent's vehicle had gone half a block, more shots were fired from the SUV. Leah cried out when the agent's car careened out of control and crashed into a line of vehicles parked on the side of the street. The SUV skidded to a stop just beyond the tangle of wrecked cars.

"Dammit to hell," Hunter growled as he eased just to the side of her. "Here!" He shoved a cell phone into Leah's hand. "Keep out of sight and call 911."

Leah was thankful to have the tree to lean against since she could barely stand. She looped her purse strap over her shoulder, then punched out 911 with trembling fingers.

Three men spilled out of the black vehicle, and Hunter yanked the gun out of the waistband of his jeans.

"Need help," Leah yelled into the phone. "Shots fired near the corner of Prytania and Valence!"

Using both hands, Hunter took aim and tried to squeeze the trigger, but his trigger finger froze. With a growl of frustration, he tried again. But it was no use. Again his finger froze and failed to do his bidding. Hunter cursed, shoved the gun back into the waistband of his jeans. "We've got to get out of here," he said, keeping a wary eye on the shooters. "In about five seconds, they're going to realize we bailed."

It never once entered Leah's head to argue or question Hunter's judgment. One glance at the smashed agents' car and the three men from the SUV advancing on it was enough to convince her. Leah motioned with her head toward a tree-shaded driveway several yards away. "This way," she said, and when Hunter nodded, she took the lead.

Leah had lived in the Uptown area for most of her life and was familiar with the neighborhood. As she and Hunter jogged through a maze of driveways, jumped a low hurricane fence and sprinted through backyards, all she could think about was putting distance between the shooters and themselves.

When Leah slowed near a line of thick shrubs to search for a break to the other side, Hunter asked, "Where are we headed?"

In the distance, police sirens screamed, and Leah prayed that help for the agents hadn't arrived too late. Finally spotting a break and trying to catch her breath, she said, "We're headed for Magazine Street—more commercial, more people. Easier to blend with a crowd." She scrambled through the opening and Hunter followed. "There's a coffeehouse where I figure we can duck inside and wait," she told him once they were through the hedge.

But wait for what? she wondered as they trotted down yet another narrow driveway. When Hunter didn't argue, she figured that they could decide what to do next once they got to the coffeehouse.

The portion of Magazine Street that Leah led Hunter to was lined with a variety of small specialty shops. Just as Leah had predicted, there were a considerable number of people milling around. Judging from the way they were dressed and the cameras hanging around their necks, most were tourists out taking in the sights and window-shopping.

The small coffeehouse they entered was crowded near the front, and the aroma of brewing coffee and the low buzz of conversation filled the air. Hunter glanced around then leaned closer. Keeping his voice low, he said, "Head for one of those tables in the back." He motioned toward a group of three empty tables. "They're close to the side exit, and I should still be able to keep an eye on the entrance. Just in case we get some uninvited company," he added.

Self-consciously aware of how disheveled they must look,

Leah stared straight ahead and ignored the stares as they made their way through the tables.

Once seated, Leah stared down at the red-and-white checkered vinyl tablecloth. Several moments passed before her legs stopped shaking and her heart slowed. They were safe, but for how long? And how long before Hunter began demanding answers from her?

"Hunter, I'm sorry," she whispered. She ventured a glance at his face, but Hunter was staring past her, his eyes on the entrance to the coffeehouse, and his only response was the muscles tensing in his jaw. That he didn't look at her or ask what she was sorry for was telling. "You have to understand though. I—"

Hunter cast a warning look her way. "Don't!" He ground the word out between his teeth. "Now is not the time or the place to discuss our relationship or your lies. We've got more pressing things to worry about at the moment." With a cold dismissing look, he turned his gaze back to the front entrance.

Leah swallowed hard against the ache in the back of her throat and squeezed her eyes shut against threatening tears. There would be a time of reckoning. Of that she had no doubt. But Hunter was right. Now was not the time or the place. "Do—do you think those agents are dead?"

"One way or another," he answered.

Leah shivered. "What are we going to do?" she asked.

He leveled a no-nonsense look at her. "We're going to stay alive," he said. "Stay alive and survive until I can figure this whole mess out." After a pregnant pause he sighed. Folding his arms and resting them on the tabletop, he said, "At the moment though, I'd give my right arm for a cup of coffee." He eyed her purse then quickly returned his gaze to the entrance.

They'd only dated a few weeks before they'd married, but one of the things she'd learned about Hunter in that short time was that he was a proud man, the type of man who liked to pay his own way. She could only imagine how it galled him to be in the position he was in.

"I have some money." She unsnapped her purse and dug out her wallet. From out of the wallet she took a ten-dollar bill, placed it on the table, then, with her forefinger, she shoved it across the table to Hunter. "Get us both a cup," she said. "A decaf *café au lait* for me."

Hunter simply stared at the money.

"Oh, for pity's sake," she told him. "It's just a cup of coffee."

After a moment, he unfolded his arms, picked up the ten, and with a sardonic twist of his lips he said, "I'll be back in a minute."

Leah watched Hunter as he walked toward the counter to place their order. The way he moved in between the tables reminded her of one of the sleek panthers she'd seen at the Audubon Zoo. Like the panther, his fluid, effortless movements were deceptive and masked the power and strength of the beast.

Would he ever forgive her? she wondered as she watched him place their order at the counter then turn to keep an eye on the front entrance.

Leah chewed on her bottom lip. She'd had her reasons for what she'd done—logical, valid reasons—but would he understand? Was he the type of man who could forgive easily or was he the type to hold a grudge?

Leah narrowed her eyes. Truth was, she didn't know, and once again she was reminded of just how little she'd really known about him before she married him.

The woman behind the counter said something to Hunter, and when he turned to face her again, the woman slid two cups of coffee toward him. When Hunter handed her the ten-dollar bill, it was a sharp reminder for Leah that they were in deep trouble.

Leah glanced down at her wallet, then fingered through the

bill compartment, counting her money. Two tens, a five and some change. "Not nearly enough," she murmured as she snapped the wallet closed and shoved it back inside her purse.

Her eyes sought out Hunter again, and as she watched him carry the cups to the condiment island, her mind raced. They had no money to speak of, not even enough for a cheap motel room. There was also the problem of transportation. With no money, no credit cards that she could use, no place to hide and no transportation, their options were slim to none. Surely the best thing they could do, the only logical thing, would be to contact the police. Once they had explained everything, the authorities would be obligated to help them, to protect them, wouldn't they?

But what if, for some reason, they wouldn't help? Then what?

Leah had no answer, and it was hard to even think straight with everything that had happened. First, the shock and joy of learning that Hunter was alive, then the suspicions and confusion, then the agents showing up, the car chase, bullets flying…Leah shuddered. Maybe, like Dorothy in *The Wizard of Oz,* if she just clicked her heels together, she'd find out it was all a nightmare.

Still watching Hunter, Leah was momentarily distracted when an older couple seated themselves at the empty table next to theirs.

When Leah returned her gaze to Hunter, his eyes were on the couple as well. Then he glanced her way and mouthed, "Sugar?" Leah nodded and held up two fingers to indicate that she wanted two packets.

A minute later, Hunter approached the table and set one of the cups and the sugar packets in front of Leah. Once he was seated and had taken a sip of the coffee, he leaned closer from across the table and said in a low voice, "We're going to need money and transportation, not to mention somewhere to hole up for a while."

Leah shook her head. "What we need to do is call the police." The words came out louder than she'd intended, and the two people at the next table glanced their way.

Hunter ignored them, but he pinned Leah with a glare. Though he said nothing until the couple looked away, his expression spoke volumes.

Leah felt her cheeks grow warm. The last thing they needed was to attract attention. "Sorry," she murmured, casting a quick glance at the pair.

"Just keep your voice down," he told her in a quiet but lethal voice. "And no police, local or otherwise—too risky." He cut his eyes back to their neighbors, then, seemingly satisfied that they were no longer paying attention to him and Leah, he said, "The police would be obligated to bring in the Feebs—"

"Feebs?"

"The feds—the FBI. And after what just happened, I have to believe Ray Harris was right. There must have been a Bureau leak, which means that whoever was after me knows that I'm not dead."

"You don't know that for sure—about the police calling in the feds—Feebs—whatever."

"It's standard procedure."

Leah stared at Hunter. He'd answered automatically, without a moment's hesitation, which could mean only one thing. "How did you know that?" she asked. "How did you know it's standard procedure?"

"I—" Hunter opened his mouth then clamped it shut.

"It's coming back, isn't it?" she said, unable to stem the excitement building inside. "That doctor in Orlando was right. Your memory's returning."

Hunter shrugged then shifted uneasily in his chair. "Some—but just bits and pieces, and not enough."

"But don't you see? The important thing is that the doctor was right. It's just going to take time."

"Time is a luxury I don't have," he said bluntly. "A luxury *we* don't have," he amended.

For a moment, Leah was at a loss for words. Given their situation, she couldn't argue the point. He was right. Time was of the essence, and after what had just happened, time could mean the difference in life or death.

"I still think we should contact the police," she argued in a low voice. "Couldn't we just tell them what's happened, tell them not to call the feds?"

Again Hunter shook his head. "It doesn't work like that."

Leah took in a deep breath, then exhaled. From the stubborn set of his jaw, she figured there was no use arguing the point. "Okay. You win. No police. So what now?"

Hunter shoved agitated fingers through his hair. "I wish to hell I knew." For long moments he stared at the entrance and drummed his fingers against the tabletop.

Leah dropped her gaze to her half-empty coffee cup and racked her brain for a solution. She had friends who would help, good friends who would be more than willing to give them sanctuary for a few days. But on the heels of her thoughts was the mental image of the agents and the smashed car. Leah shuddered. There was no way she could put any of her friends in that kind of danger.

So where could they go? Then, without realizing that she was thinking out loud, she whispered, "There is a place, a place no one would think to look."

"What did you say?"

At the sound of Hunter's voice, Leah jumped. "What?"

"You muttered something about there being a place we could go."

"It's just a thought," she said. "There's this place, a camp actually, located on Lake Pontchartrain. It sits out over the water. My grandm'ere and I used to go there every summer around the Fourth of July. The place belongs to a distant cousin of hers, and he would invite us out for a couple of days. No one would ever think of looking for us there."

Hunter narrowed his eyes. "This cousin—he lives out over the water?"

Leah shook her head. "No, he doesn't live there. He lives in the French Quarter. And unless I'm mistaken, the only time he ever really uses the camp is the week before and after the Fourth, and sometimes around Thanksgiving. There used to be a lot of people in the city who did that sort of thing, kind of a home away from home, to get away from the heat in the summer, since it's a lot cooler on the water. After the last hurricane though, not many of the camps are left."

"So—let me get this straight. On the off chance that this camp is still standing and that no one is occupying it right now, you're suggesting we could hole up there?"

Leah nodded.

"And just how do you propose we get to it? Walk?"

Hunter's sarcasm chafed. "No," she retorted. "We can take a city bus. But before we go anywhere, I have to go back home."

"Uh-uh." Hunter shook his head emphatically. "No way! That's the first place anyone, the feds or the shooters, will look."

Leah found herself growing short of patience. "Read my lips, Hunter. We need money and clothes. Without money, we don't eat, and our bags are still in that smashed car. I'd use my bankcard, but there's no money in my bank account to cover it, and my credit card is maxed out at the moment." In spite of the overtime she'd been working, keeping up with her electric bill over the summer had taken almost every penny she had in the bank. After the last rainstorm, the roof on the old house had sprung a leak. She'd decided to use her credit card to have a new roof put on the house instead of the cash she had saved.

"I have some money stashed away" she continued. "It's my emergency stash. And if this isn't an emergency, then I don't know what is. But the money's inside the house. As for getting in and out without being seen, no one knows the ins and outs of that house like I do."

As a teenager, Leah had gone through what her grandm'ere had always referred to as her "wild years." She had dearly loved her grandm'ere, but the old lady had been overly strict when it came to Leah's social life. More times than Leah cared to remember, she'd sneaked in and out of the house without her grandmother ever being the wiser.

For long moments Hunter simply stared at her as if weighing the pros and cons of what she'd proposed. Then, finally, he shook his head. "I don't like it. It's too risky."

Frustration welled within. "Well, that's just too bad," Leah retorted. "Whether you like it or not, I'm going." To emphasize her point, she stood. "I don't know about you, but I like to eat."

Again, the couple at the next table looked their way. Pasting a fake smile on his lips, Hunter glanced at them, rolled his eyes and said, "Lord save me from a stubborn woman." The older couple smiled knowingly and looked away.

"Okay, you win." Hunter motioned for Leah to be seated. Then he leaned forward and lowered his voice. "But we're going to wait until it's good and dark."

Leah glanced at her watch. Her eyes darting from Hunter to the older couple then back again, she whispered, "That won't be for another two hours or so. Just what do you propose we do until then?"

"Have you still got that cell phone?"

Leah nodded.

"Well, hand it over."

With a frown, Leah dug the phone out of her purse and handed it to Hunter. "Who are you going to call?"

"My partner, Jack O'Brian."

"Your partner? Another memory flash?"

"Yeah, you might say that. Enough of one to remember Jack's name, a phone number, and just how I came to be put on medical leave."

"Oh…"

"Yes, 'oh.'"

"I'm sorry. That must have been painful for you."

Hunter tried to ignore Leah's sympathetic tone. Painful didn't begin to describe the horror of what he'd remembered. Of all the things he could have recalled, that particular memory would have been on the bottom of his list, if he'd had a choice. And it sure as hell wasn't something Hunter wanted to discuss. Not with Leah, and not with anyone.

Hunter stared at the phone as he fought to get his emotions under control. "Only problem," he finally said, avoiding a response to her statement, "I'm not sure the phone number belongs to Jack." With a shrug, he turned on the phone. "Guess there's only one way to find out." He tapped out the number.

Four rings later he grimaced when he heard, "This is Jack. Leave a message."

Jack's voice sounded familiar. He could even picture a stocky, dark-haired man, but to Hunter's acute disappointment there were no memories attached to the mental image. His mind was still a blank.

Hunter hesitated, torn between leaving a message and simply hanging up. Even if he left a message, what would he say? Finally, with a sigh, he disconnected the call and slipped the phone into his pants pocket.

"Was it your partner's number?"

Hunter stared at Leah. "Yeah."

Leah frowned. "Why didn't you say something?"

"Voice mail."

"You could have left a message."

"And say what? Say something like, 'Hey, partner, this is Hunter. And by the way, I'm back from the dead but I don't even remember you…'" His voice trailed away.

When Leah's face softened with sympathy, Hunter narrowed his eyes. He might not want her sympathy and he might not completely trust her, but right now she was all he had. She was still privy to information that he didn't have, information that he needed about himself. So why not pump her for the information he needed?

Hunter shifted in his chair. "I need answers, and it looks like you're the only one who can give them to me. Did I happen to tell you where I worked in New York? Which precinct?"

Leah shook her head.

"What about where I lived there?"

"All you ever said was that you lived in Manhattan."

Hunter narrowed his eyes. This was getting him nowhere fast.

"Given the fact that we're married, you don't seem to know much about me. Just how long did we know each other before we got married?"

For long seconds Leah just stared at him, and when she finally did speak, there was no way he could misinterpret her sarcasm. "I thought you didn't want to discuss our relationship."

"I don't, not really," he retorted. "But I'm beginning to wonder if we even had a relationship. You don't know where I worked or where I lived, so just what the hell do you know about me? Other than my name," he added with a bit of stinging sarcasm of his own.

Leah flinched at the vehemence in Hunter's tone. She tried to tell herself that it was just his frustration talking. After all, he didn't remember her or anything about their brief time together or the whirlwind love they'd shared. All he knew was that he'd trusted her and she lied to him. But even so, his sarcasm and anger was like a sharp knife slicing her heart into tiny pieces.

Ever aware of the nosy couple at the next table, she kept her voice soft and even. "You can't have it both ways, Hunter," she finally told him. "Either we discuss it or we don't. Either you let me explain why I did what I did or you—" Leah bit off the rest of what she'd intended to tell him, and to her horror, unexpected tears filled her eyes. "I—I—" She blinked furiously and panic set in. The last thing she wanted at the moment was for Hunter to see her cry. "Excuse me," she mumbled. "Have to go to the ladies' room."

Before Hunter could stop her, she fled to the bathroom. Once inside, she locked the door. But when she glanced around the tiny closet-size room, she immediately realized her mistake. She squeezed her eyes closed against the tears and tried to take deep, slow even breaths, tried telling herself that the walls weren't closing in on her. Then, when she didn't think she could stand being closed up in the tiny room one more minute, she yanked enough tissue off the toilet roll to blow her nose. Once she'd dropped the paper into the trash, she turned on the faucet at the sink, splashed water on her face, and blotted it with a paper towel. The moment she opened the door, the panicky feeling disappeared.

Hunter stood when she approached the table, then he latched on to her wrist.

"Don't look, but there's a pair of cops just outside the door. Just take it nice and easy. We don't want to attract attention."

At that moment the couple at the next table abruptly stood, and with one last glare at Hunter, they headed straight for the front counter.

"Aw, that's just peachy," Hunter muttered as he watched them conferring with the woman behind the front counter.

"Just what we need." To Leah he said, "We've got to go and go *now*. What we're going to do is walk slowly to the side exit."

Leah swallowed hard. "I don't think we should leave," she said evenly.

Hunter shot her a look of disbelief.

"Think about it, Hunter. We've got no money, no transportation, and nowhere to go. At some point we've got to trust someone."

"Like I trusted you!" he snapped.

The accusation stung. "I told you I could explain that, but—"

Hunter's grip on her wrist tightened. "I don't want to burst your bubble, sweetheart, but those cops you're so willing to trust aren't alone. A black SUV just pulled up and one of the cops is talking to the driver."

Chapter 6

Leah's eyes darted toward the side exit, and when Hunter stepped away from the table, she followed his lead. Only when they were through the exit did she think to breathe again.

The exit spilled out into a narrow street that ran alongside the coffeehouse. Their only choice was to go right since going left led back to Magazine where the SUV was parked.

Hunter finally let go of her wrist only to sling his arm around her shoulders. His arm was heavy and warm, and Leah immediately stiffened.

"Looks less suspicious," he told her. "Just a couple out for a casual stroll, exploring the city."

There was nothing casual about the feel of Hunter's arm draped around her shoulders. *He* might not remember how it had been between them, but she did, all too vividly. From the very beginning the mere touch of his hand could set off a shiver of uncontrollable desire racing through her veins. In spite of all that had happened, even after all of the soul-searching she'd done about their whirlwind courtship in the aftermath of his accident, to her dismay, she still felt the same way.

Realizing that Leah knew her way around the neighborhood, once again, Hunter allowed her to take the lead. Though to any onlookers, they appeared to be just what he'd intended, a couple out for a casual stroll, there was nothing casual about what he was feeling at the moment.

What had seemed like a good idea had backfired, big-time. The minute he'd put his arm around her, he'd known that he'd done the same thing before and had experienced the same knee-jerk feeling of desire. It was the same feeling he'd experienced when he climbed into her bed earlier that morning, the same feeling he'd had in the erotic memory flashes he'd been having for the past month. Whether déjà vu, or simply wishful thinking—and he leaned strongly toward the déjà vu—for the moment he didn't care. As illogical as it seemed, considering that she'd betrayed him, they were connected. And for the first time since he'd awakened in the Orlando hospital, he didn't feel so alone and lost.

Out of necessity, when they reached the next block and crossed the street, he had to break off the contact. Once they had safely negotiated the intersection, he shoved his hands into his jeans pockets to keep from reaching out for her again. Touching her was too distracting, and he needed to be on his toes if they hoped to get through this ordeal alive.

"We've still got an hour or so before dark. Any suggestions?" he asked.

"I've been thinking about that," Leah answered. "How do you feel about riding the streetcar?"

"Riding it where?"

"Just riding it. That way we'll be constantly on the move,

and if we're on the move, it won't be so easy for that black SUV or the cops to find us. And it's cheap. Besides, I don't know about you, but I don't think I can keep walking. My feet are killing me."

"Yeah, my leg's not feeling none too great, either," Hunter complained. Then, after a moment, he nodded. "Sounds like it just might work." He motioned with his hand. "Which way?"

By the time they reached St. Charles Avenue, Leah was more than ready to get off her feet. It didn't happen often, but occasionally she'd had problems with her feet swelling since she'd been pregnant.

"How far does the trolley go?" Hunter asked as they crossed St. Charles to the neutral ground where the tracks were located.

"Not trolley," Leah corrected. "San Francisco has trolleys. New Orleans has streetcars. But to answer your question it runs all the way from Canal Street over to where Carrolton crosses South Claiborne."

Hunter rolled his eyes. "Sorry, but I have no idea what that means."

"Oh, well, suffice it to say, it's a nice long ride," Leah told him as they approached the nearest streetcar stop. "And we can keep riding as long as we need to," she added.

Hunter nodded. "Good."

Besides Leah and Hunter, there were only three other people waiting at the stop, and within minutes they heard the rattling hum of a streetcar approach.

Brakes squealed, the car stopped, and the doors swung open. Leah and Hunter waited their turn, then climbed the steps and entered the car. Once Leah had deposited the fare for their ride, they made their way down the narrow aisle until they found two empty seats together near the back.

Leah slid in next to the open window and groaned with relief when she finally sat down. Her feet had swollen to the point that the loafers she wore were beginning to pinch. She was sorely tempted to slip off the tight shoes but was afraid that once off, she might never get them back on.

Within minutes, the streetcar lurched into motion with a loud clatter that sounded as if the whole car could fall apart at any moment.

Accompanied by the *clickety-clack* of the metal wheels against the track, the swaying car hummed along beneath the live oaks, some so huge that the limbs reached out to form a soothing canopy of green over the avenue. At each intersection, the conductor rang a bell as a warning for crossing vehicles.

As Leah stared out the window, enormous, beautiful old homes, most over a century old, flashed by, and she couldn't help remembering another time when she and Hunter had done the same thing. But would Hunter remember?

They had been married for only a couple of days, and the weather had been unseasonably cold for March, the kind of damp cold that chilled to the bone. They'd had to delay taking a honeymoon because of her work schedule. With little else to occupy his time, he'd been like a little kid in a candy store, one who was eager to explore and taste everything the city had to offer. In spite of the cold weather, Hunter had insisted that they ride the streetcar, but it was afterward that she remembered the most, when they'd returned home.

She made hot chocolate while Hunter built a fire in the fireplace. Once the fire was burning, he spread a couple of her grandmother's Afghans on the floor and had piled pillows off the sofa on top. By the time they got around to actually drinking the cups of cocoa, the cocoa had long grown cold.

Though they had made love many times before that particular evening and many times afterward, Leah would always believe that it was on that chilly afternoon in front of a crackling fire that she had conceived their baby. And a month later, Hunter was gone.

"Okay," Hunter said, interrupting her thoughts. "Time to talk. If I'm going to figure this thing out, I have to know more than just my name or the fact that I'm a cop. Start from the beginning. When and how did we meet?"

Leah swallowed hard. "But what about what the agent said—you know, about you needing to remember on your own?"

"Did you see the murder?" he retorted.

Leah shook her head.

A feral smile pulled at Hunter's lips. "No, I didn't think so. Otherwise, they would have taken you into protective custody as well. And since you didn't see anything, there's no way that what you tell me could possibly compromise any testimony I might give. What I'm hoping is that if I know enough about what led up to that point in time, it will jog my memory."

A suffocating sensation tightened Leah's throat. She was living on borrowed time. Part of her longed for Hunter's memory to return, longed for him to remember the love they'd shared and the plans they'd made, while part of her dreaded it. Once Hunter remembered, once he realized why he'd gone out that night, she might lose him...again.

Tell him. Tell him about the baby now.

She couldn't do it. That was one thing he had to remember on his own. Without knowing that he'd loved her and she loved him, he would only see that once again she was deceiving him.

"Okay," Leah finally said. "We met at Café Du Monde—that's an outdoor coffeehouse down in the French Quarter. I was there with some friends after a night shift at the hospital. You sat down at a table near ours and overheard us making plans to go to the Bacchus parade that night."

Hunter looked confused. "So what's a Bacchus?"

Leah smiled. "When we first met, you asked me that same question. Bacchus is the name of the Krewe, and a Krewe is an organization formed by the group of people who sponsor a parade."

Leah shrugged. "Anyway, you began asking questions about the parade route, we struck up a conversation, and one thing led to another—anyway, we ended up inviting you to go with us."

Leah paused as heat climbed up her neck. For her their meeting had been love at first sight. In retrospect, after months of thinking about it, she suspected that his feelings had been more like lust at first sight, and she'd simply been ripe for the picking. After all, he'd come to New Orleans to lose himself in Mardi Gras, to have a good time and try to forget.

"I guess we were drawn together because of mutual pain," she continued. "I was still grieving. I had buried my grandmother last fall," she explained. "And you—well, you were trying to come to grips with the shooting incident. Other than what I've already told you, there's not much else. The trip to Orlando was to have been a delayed honeymoon. Delayed because of my work schedule."

When Leah didn't offer more, Hunter narrowed his eyes. "So, just how long did we know each other before we got married?"

Leah swallowed hard and lowered her gaze. "Three weeks," she whispered.

"You married me after only knowing me three weeks?" His tone was incredulous, and all Leah could do was nod.

Hunter shook his head in disbelief. "O-kay. Say I believe you for now. So how did the cops know that I saw a murder in the first place? And if I saw it, why didn't you see it, too?"

Hunter's attitude stung, but Leah swallowed her hurt and answered as best she could. "I don't know how they knew you saw the murder because I wasn't with you. The evening we arrived in Orlando, I had just come off a night shift and hadn't had much sleep. I had an upset stomach, and once we checked into the motel, you went out to the drugstore a few blocks over to get me something for my nausea."

At least that much was true. From the very beginning, she'd been queasy.

"When you didn't return within the hour I began to get worried. Then, three hours later, I began to panic. I called around to several hospitals first, with no luck. Not knowing what else to do, I called the police. The next thing I know, two detectives show up at the hotel and tell me that you've been involved in a terrible, fatal accident. They said that you lost control and hit a gasoline truck, that you were terribly burned. That there was almost nothing left…" Leah shuddered remembering the horror of it all.

"Did you never question how they identified me if I was supposedly burned beyond recognition?"

Leah nodded. "Of course I did. They said they were able to determine that the car was a rental and they traced it that way. Since I knew you had gone out and not come back, it made sense."

When Leah said nothing more, Hunter simply stared at her for long seconds. Then, with a sardonic twist of his mouth, he closed his eyes and shook his head. "Nothing, dammit," he whispered. "Nothing."

Knowing he was referring to his memory, Leah's heart ached for him. "It will come," she told him. "You just need more time."

It was almost nine before the city grew dark. With only the soft glow of the streetlights to guide them, Leah and Hunter made their way through the shadowy streets. But the closer they came to the street where she lived, the slower Leah walked.

She'd convinced Hunter that she could get in and out of the

old house without being detected, and at the time, she'd believed it herself. But she'd had hours to think about it, hours to imagine everything that could go wrong. It was true that she'd fooled her grandmother many times, but fooling an old lady was a far cry from fooling the people who were after them.

When they were four houses away, Leah slowed her footsteps even more. "We're almost there," she told him. Suddenly unsure of how to proceed, she stopped and faced Hunter, "I guess you should wait here."

Hunter shook his head. "Uh-uh. You wait here. I'm going to scout out things first and see what we're up against. Stay out of the light. Stand over there." He motioned toward a large oleander bush. "And don't go anywhere until I get back."

Before Leah had time to object, Hunter turned and headed down the street. Within seconds, he melted into the shadows and disappeared into the night.

Securing the strap of her purse over her arm, Leah shivered in spite of the heat as she moved closer to the oleander bush. Still straining to catch a glimpse of Hunter, her mind raced. What if he didn't come back? What if he got caught or worse... She didn't want to think about worse. If the worst happened, then it would be all her fault...again.

She drew in a deep breath. "No," she whispered as she released her breath slowly. Now was not the time to think negative thoughts. She had to think positive, had to believe that he knew what he was doing, had to believe that this time he would come back.

Seconds dragged by and turned into minutes. She could hear traffic on the next street over, and somewhere down the street a dog barked. Then, from a distance, Leah heard the sound of an approaching car and she quickly ducked behind the bush until the vehicle passed. Once the car had passed, she peered out from her hiding place and watched as the vehicle continued down the street.

Leah was so intent on watching the fading taillights of the car that when Hunter suddenly appeared out of the shadows within just a few feet of her, she jumped and clamped her hand over her mouth to smother the shriek that filled her throat. She removed her hand.

"You scared the daylights out of me," she told him, her voice low but edged with fury. And for a moment, she was tempted to haul off and belt him. But since she was equally tempted to grab him and hug him in relief, she did neither.

Ignoring her reproach, he said, "Look down the street. See that car parked across from your neighbor's house?"

Leah craned her head. "The neighbor on this side or the other side?"

"This side. See it?"

She nodded.

"There are two men in that car watching the house. Only there's no way of knowing if they're FBI or the shooters. There's also no way of knowing if there's someone posted around back." He shook his head. "Too risky. I think it's about time for us to rethink this little venture and get the hell out of here."

Part of Leah wanted to agree, wanted to leave right then and there, but the other part, the practical side, argued that they needed money if they were going to survive. "I'm not leaving without that money," she vowed, and though she was quivering with fear on the inside, she stood her ground.

For long seconds Hunter stared at her, and even in the dim light, she could see the conflicting emotions chasing across his face as he weighed the pros and cons of the situation.

"Hunter, we need money," she insisted.

Finally, he let out a sigh of frustration and slowly nodded. "Okay, but if you're determined to do this thing, then let's do it right. I'll keep an eye on our *friends* while you get the money. And if something goes wrong—if you get into trouble, scream bloody murder."

"And if you get into trouble, are you going to scream bloody murder, too?"

Even under the dim glow of the street lamp there was no misinterpreting Hunter's sardonic expression. "Okay, okay," she retorted. "Just forget I said that." Leah motioned to her right. "I have to go this way."

Hunter nodded. "Which side of the house are you going in on?"

"This side—my bedroom window. There's a row of bushes next to the house that will hide me from the street."

"Okay." He nodded then glanced at his watch. "It's almost nine-thirty. I'll meet you back here in, say, twenty minutes."

When Leah turned to leave, he took hold of her arm to stop her. "What?" she said, staring up at him.

For a moment he looked confused. Then, with a shake of his head, he released her arm, "Just be careful. Be damn careful."

Leah was still wondering about the look on Hunter's face when they parted ways two houses down from her house. Was his concern for her? And if it was then there was hope after all, hope that he might remember how much they had loved each other. Then again, his concern could have been purely self-serving, especially considering that she was going after money that would help keep them alive until he could figure out what had really happened in Orlando.

Leaving Hunter lurking in the shadows, she headed down the narrow driveway next to the house. Even if he forgave her for not being truthful about their relationship, once he found out that she had also neglected to tell him about their baby… A heavy feeling settled in the pit of her stomach and cold sweat trickled down her back and between her breasts as she made her way along the familiar route down the driveway. Best not to think about that now, she decided. She'd do better to concentrate on simply trying to stay alive.

At the end of the driveway, she cut over to the backyard of the house next door to hers. Once she reached the thick hedge that separated her neighbor's property from her own, she followed the hedge until she came to the break she was looking for. She ducked into the break, then stopped. As she stood crouched between the thick shrubs and scanned the short stretch of lawn between her and the bush near her bedroom window, fear and doubt again assailed her. This particular stretch was the only open space clearly visible from the street.

Leah glanced down at her clothes. Not exactly the type of clothes to go sneaking around in the dark. The jeans wouldn't be that visible but the white T-shirt would stand out like a sore thumb.

The night was still and the only sounds she heard were her own harsh breathing and the distant, muted noise of traffic as she tried to figure out how she was going to get to the bushes near her window without being seen. She peered up into the dark sky and made a face at the bright full moon.

The only way, she finally decided, was to crawl. If she stayed close to the ground and moved very slowly, there was a good chance that she wouldn't be noticed.

Leah's hand strayed to the ever-so-slight protrusion of her abdomen, and she sighed. Crawling on her stomach might not be the best idea after all. Lately, she couldn't even sleep flat on her stomach and had to be content with sleeping in a halfway position, half on her stomach and half on her side with one leg drawn upward for balance.

There had to be another way, but what?

She'd just about made up her mind that the crawl would

just have to work, when, the sound of an approaching vehicle reached her ears.

Sending up a prayer of thanks, she tensed in readiness. She would only get one shot, and the timing would have to be just right. When the oncoming vehicle was almost even with the car that Hunter had pointed out, Leah made her move. With one hand holding her purse and careful to keep a low profile, she sprinted toward the window.

It was close, but Leah reached the window and the cover of the bushes just as the vehicle passed the parked car. For long moments she stayed crouched behind the bushes, her heart pounding like a bass drum, her legs quivering, and her ears attuned to any noise that would tell her whether she'd been spotted. Finally her heartbeat slowed and, secure in the knowledge that she hadn't been seen, she stood up.

The ground around the old house was uneven, almost two feet higher in elevation toward the back than the front. Though the house had been built up off the ground, Leah could easily reach the side window of her bedroom.

Over the years, the wooden frame of the window had shrunk. She'd always meant to get it fixed but there never seemed to be any extra money for the repair. Taking a firm grip on the sash bar, she wiggled the window back and forth, then from side to side until the lock jiggled loose. As she pushed up and the window slid open, she once again reminded herself that one day soon she needed to have the window fixed…assuming, of course that she lived that long.

With a shiver, she slipped the strap of her purse off her shoulder, and lowered the purse through the opening. Turning her back to the window, she planted the heels of her hands on the windowsill behind her, gave a little jump, and with arms straining to the max, she hoisted herself up. The perch was precarious at best. She had to grab the frame to keep her balance, then she swung her legs up and around. Once her legs were inside, she scrunched down sideways and wiggled through the opening.

Ever aware of the passing time, she retrieved her purse then felt her way through the dark familiar room to the cedar chest at the foot of her bed. From inside the chest, she removed a small metal box, opened it, gathered up the money and stuffed it inside her purse.

If she remembered right, at last count, she'd laid up a hoard of almost six hundred dollars. It wasn't a fortune by any stretch of the imagination, but at least they could eat for a while.

When Leah turned and eyed the open window, sudden, momentary panic seized her. She'd gotten in without being detected, but she still had to get back across the lawn. And this time, she didn't dare hope to be so lucky that another car would happen along. This time, she'd have to crawl.

Looping the strap of her purse over her shoulder, she felt her way to the window. Once at the window though, she hesitated. The clothes she'd stuffed into the duffel bag were lost, and for a moment, she thought about at least grabbing another T-shirt and pair of pants, maybe a nightgown.

Leah shook her head. Crawling across the yard was going to be hard enough without having to worry about a bundle of clothes. Besides, she had no idea how much time had passed, and no matter how much she squinted, she couldn't see her watch in the dark.

With a resigned sigh, she turned her back to the windowsill, sat on the edge, and with her ears tuned to any unexpected noise, she grabbed hold of the frame. Just as she swung her legs through the opening, the sound of a man's voice cut the silence.

"Hey, you, freeze!"

Chapter 7

A sudden blinding light hit Leah square in the face, and icy fear streaked through her veins.

"Don't move a muscle," a deep male voice demanded. "I have a gun."

Leah was perched sideways in the window, her heels resting on the ledge. Her grip on the window frame tightened and as she fought to keep her balance, all she could think about was her baby. If she moved, he would shoot, and if he shot her, there was a good chance he could kill her baby.

"Please don't shoot." She cut her eyes sideways toward the direction of the voice, but with the light shining on her face, she couldn't see anything. "Please," she cried.

For an answer, she heard a thud, and a groan. Then, the light was gone. It took a moment for her eyes to adjust and it was then that she saw the dark form of another man.

"Leah, it's me. It's okay."

By the time it registered that the voice belonged to Hunter, she was trembling so hard that she was afraid to let go of the window frame. Then he was there, and she felt his strong steady arm wrap around her waist.

With a cry of relief, Leah twisted and grabbed him around the neck.

"You didn't scream," he accused softly as he lifted her out through the window. Even when her feet touched the ground, she still clung to him.

"He—he said he had a g-gun," she stammered.

Hunter didn't ever want to relive the terror he experienced when he saw the man leave the car and head for the side of the house. Nor the horrifying moment when he'd seen the man pointing his gun at Leah. For now though, with Leah's trembling body pressed intimately against his own, he was torn between his desire to savor and prolong the moment and his fear that the other man could show up at any second.

Were the lustful feelings stirring in his groin simply a physical need for release, or was his body remembering how it had felt to be so close to her? And how could he feel this way knowing that she'd not only lied to him about their relationship, but she'd also betrayed him when she made the phone call that had alerted the feds.

With Herculean effort, Hunter forced himself to reach up, untangle her arms from around his neck and step back. "We haven't got much time," he explained.

Though Leah heard what Hunter said, she was too caught up in the way her body had begun to react for his words to immediately register. Only when the bond between them was severed did the words finally sink in.

When Hunter stepped away and knelt beside the dark form of the unconscious man on the ground, she swallowed hard. "Is—is he dead?" she whispered.

Hunter picked up the flashlight. "No, he's just uncon-scious." He handed the flashlight to Leah. "Shine this on him."

The man was slumped on his side. Hunter patted him down then rolled him over and searched his back pockets. All he found was a billfold. He pulled it out and flipped it open. Shining the flashlight, he removed a driver's license from one of the credit-card slots.

"His name's Tony Lorio," Hunter murmured. "Address, Orlando, Florida." He shoved the license back inside the slot and searched the rest of the contents of the billfold. "That's the only ID—no badge—so he has to be one of the shooters." When he thumbed through the money in the bill compart-ment, he let out a soft whistle then glanced up at Leah. "There's well over a thousand dollars in here," he muttered.

"Take it," Leah told him without a qualm.

"I'm no thief," Hunter retorted.

"Well, neither am I," Leah snapped, stung by his inference. "But those people are trying to kill us, and I think it's only fair that they have to pay."

Hunter stared at her for several moments, and in those moments, she realized that he was actually trying to make up his mind whether to take the money or leave it.

"If you don't take it—"

In the distance, a car door slammed. Both Hunter and Leah glanced toward the direction of the noise. "You're right," he muttered as he pulled out the money and shoved it into his back pocket. "Turn off the light," he told her as he stuffed the billfold back into the man's pocket then jumped to his feet. With one hand he took the flashlight from her, and with his other hand, he grabbed her by the wrist. "Let's get out of here."

When he tugged on her wrist and took off across the lawn, Leah gladly followed.

* * *

Hunter set a steady pace, and only when they were halfway down the block did he finally slow down to a fast walk. "I think it's safe enough now," he said. "So how do we get to this camp you told me about?"

Leah was still trying to catch her breath, and instead of answering, she asked a question of her own. "How—how did you know? About that man?" she explained.

"I saw him leave the car and figured he was leaving to patrol the perimeter. When I saw him head to the side of the house, I followed."

"Glad you did. To answer your question, we ride the streetcar to Canal then catch a city bus." She drew in a deep breath. "In case you're wondering, I got my money. With what I have and with that other money—" Leah laughed. "I'd love to see the look on that man's face when he discovers that all his money is gone."

Hunter's only answer was a chuckle and a shake of his head.

When Leah and Hunter finally reached St. Charles Avenue and caught the streetcar, Leah was more than ready to sit for the length of time it took the car to get to Canal. At Canal they had to wait a good thirty minutes for the Elysian Fields bus. After numerous stops, they got off at Leon C. Simon near the University of New Orleans. There, they waited about twenty minutes for the bus going to Hayne Boulevard.

By the time Leah and Hunter stepped off the bus near the area of the camp, almost two hours had passed since they'd left her house and Leah was almost stumbling with fatigue. All she could think about was taking off her shoes and finding a pillow to lay her weary head on.

"This way," she told Hunter when the bus pulled off. With Hunter following, she crossed Hayne and walked along the bottom of the levee until they came to a small sign that read, Summer Bliss. Leah pointed at the sign. "That's the name of one of the camps. Each of the camps are given names," she explained as she kept walking. "If I remember right, the next one is the one we're looking for."

A few minutes later, she stopped and pointed at a sign that read, Old Codger. "This is it," she said.

Hunter chuckled. "Well, is he?"

"He?"

"This distant relative of yours. Is he an old codger?"

Leah laughed. "No, the old codger was his father who originally built the camp. That camp—the original one—was pretty much destroyed during a storm back in the fifties. This is the rebuilt camp and one of the few that survived the last hurricane."

"Now you've really got me curious." Hunter handed her the flashlight then motioned with his hand. "Lead on."

Sending up a prayer that the camp was unoccupied, Leah nodded, switched on the flashlight and began the climb up the levee. When they reached the top, she paused to catch her breath. A cool gentle breeze was blowing, and the dark, cloudless sky was lit by a full moon and what seemed like a million stars, all reflecting off the enormous lake.

"The camp is there at the end of the run." She directed the flashlight beam toward a long narrow wooden ramp leading out into the water. At the end of the walkway, like a small island, was the dark shape of a building.

For long seconds, Hunter simply stared out over the lake.

"It's beautiful, isn't it?" Leah murmured.

"One thing's for sure. There's no way anyone will track us here." He turned to Leah. "So, what now?"

"This way," she told him, shining the flashlight in front of her as she picked her way down a small incline and crossed a set of railroad tracks that ran along the lake side of the levee.

"It's a good thing you brought the flashlight," she said, picking her way across the rails of the track.

Leah followed the tracks for several yards then veered off toward the ramp. The wooden walkway was about the width of a sidewalk and on either side were rails. After they had walked a few more feet, they came to a wrought-iron archway and gate that blocked access to the other side of the ramp.

Leah directed the light to the heavy chain and padlock and groaned. "I forgot about the gate." She lifted her chin and peered up at the top of the archway, shook her head, then motioned below the ramp on the other side of the gate. "We're going to have to climb down and around."

She swept the beam of the flashlight across the large boulders and chunks of broken concrete that had been placed along the shore of the lake to reinforce the levee. Water from the lake lapped around and over the boulders and chunks of concrete.

Hunter shook his head. "I don't know about you, but I don't think I fancy a swim right now."

"You wouldn't have to swim," Leah told him. "The water down there and around the camp isn't much more than knee deep—hip deep at most."

"Yeah, well, it might not be deep, but I'll lay you odds that those boulders are slippery as hell. And one thing we don't need right now is a broken arm or ankle." Hunter picked up the padlock, and after he'd studied it a moment, he dropped it. "Give me the flashlight and wait here," he told her.

When Leah handed him the flashlight, he turned and retraced their steps to the railroad tracks. Within minutes, she saw him bend down and pick up something. Seemingly satisfied with what he'd found, he walked a few more feet, then bent down and picked up something else. Again, he seemed satisfied. Then he turned and headed back.

"These should do it," he told her. He handed her the flashlight and one of the two large rocks he'd picked up. "Hold these a minute." Then he turned to the gate, picked up the padlock and placed the rock he'd kept between the padlock and the gatepost.

"Hand me that other rock now," he said.

Leah frowned and shook her head. "You're never going to break that lock with just a couple of rocks."

Hunter held out his hand. "The rock, please."

With a shrug, Leah handed it to him.

Hunter laughed. "You're right, of course." He turned toward the lock. "Shine the flashlight here."

When Leah did as he asked, he lifted his arm and smashed the rock against the padlock.

Leah flinched as the clacking sound echoed out over the lake.

"By the way," he said. "I have no intention of breaking the padlock." With a grunt, Hunter struck the padlock again. "I just want to break the chain," he added as he smashed the rock against the padlock yet again. "Just-a-few-more-times," he said, emphasizing each word by pounding the lock. Then the pounding stopped. "That should do it," he muttered. He dropped the rocks, grabbed the chain and the padlock, then twisted and pulled. The chain came loose, and with a clatter, it fell to the ground.

"What did you call this thing?" Hunter asked as they made their way along the wooden pathway.

"It's called a walk or a run," Leah told him.

"Walk, run, whatever—it's still a hell of a long way to have to lug groceries."

Leah laughed. "This one's over three hundred feet," she said. "Some are shorter, some longer. Most of the camps were built before air-conditioning, and it's a lot cooler out over the water. The whole point was to get as far out as possible without having to take a boat."

At the end of the run was a small porch area that covered the front entrance of the camp. Leah held out her hand. "Give me the flashlight." When Hunter handed it to her, she directed the beam to a small ugly gargoyle, one of two that guarded each side of the door. "I hope it's still in the same place," Leah murmured as she ran her fingers over the gargoyle.

"You hope what's in the same place?"

"The key to the front door," she answered. "He always kept a spare key—yep, here it is." She pulled a key from the small opening of the gargoyle's mouth.

"So what's with the gargoyles?"

A tired smiled pulled at Leah's lips. "You ain't seen nothing yet." She inserted the key, twisted it and opened the door. When she flipped the light switch, Hunter's mouth dropped open, and all he could do was stare. Inside, mounted on both walls of the long, wide hallway, were other gargoyles spaced about two feet apart but at different heights. Instead of an overhead light, it was the eerie glow coming from each of the gargoyles' eyes that provided the light for the hallway.

"Weird," Hunter murmured, staring at the gargoyles. "This is totally weird."

Leah closed the front door and locked it. Leaving the key on a small table near the entry, she headed down the hallway. "If you think that's weird, wait until you see the rest of the place."

Leah tried to cover a yawn and stopped at the first doorway in the hall. "The grand tour's going to have to wait until tomorrow though. I don't know about you, but I'm really really tired, and I'm going to bed."

As she opened the door, she motioned across the hall. "There's a bathroom in there, and the next door down is another bedroom." When she reached inside the door she'd opened and switched on a light, Hunter couldn't help staring.

"Mardi Gras," she explained with a tiny smile of amusement. "This is the Mardi Gras bedroom."

The room was a whimsical collage of purple, gold and green colors, all the colors of Mardi Gras. The headboard of the bed was gold and glittery and reminded him of a crown, a crown to represent Rex, King of Mardi Gras, he assumed. On the table beside the bed was a lamp, and the shade was made of rows and rows of Mardi Gras beads.

"Each room has its own air conditioner—a window unit," Leah continued. "In case you get hot," she added. "There's a kitchen at the end of the hall on the left and the living area is on the right. There's probably some bottled water in the kitchen if you're thirsty." Leah yawned again. "Make yourself at home, and I'll see you in the morning."

Hunter stood for several moments staring at the closed door that Leah had disappeared behind. Then, abruptly, the door opened again. "By the way," Leah said, "the sheets on the beds should be clean. Since the camp is rented out sometimes, it is always left clean and ready for the next occupants." After a slight hesitation, she finally said, "Good night," as she closed the door again.

Hunter shook his head. As if he cared about clean sheets, he thought as he turned and walked to the door she'd said was the bathroom. After all they had been through today, he could have slept on the ground if he thought it was safe from the people who were after them.

The moment Leah closed the bedroom door, she slipped off her loafers. She'd told Hunter that she was really tired, but tired didn't begin to describe how she felt. Every bone in her body ached, but her legs and feet were the worst.

After a brief glimpse at her puffy feet, she headed for the private bathroom attached to the bedroom. From experience, she knew that her swollen feet were simply a result of being on them too much and not anything to be overly concerned about.

In spite of being so tired that she could cry, she couldn't help smiling as she made use of the bathroom facilities then washed her hands and face. If Hunter thought the hallway was weird, just wait until he got a look at the main bathroom.

She dried her face and hands then headed straight for the small dresser in hopes of finding an old T-shirt to sleep in. Weird didn't begin to describe the decor in the main bathroom, she thought as she rummaged through the drawers.

Her grandmother's cousin had always had a wicked, irreverent sense of humor and plenty of money to indulge his wild imagination. When he'd rebuilt the camp after Hurricane Georges had destroyed it, he'd pulled out all of the stops and convention be damned. An avid collector of many things, he'd utilized his Second World War memorabilia in the bathroom. The light switch was a handgun, and the trigger had to be pulled for the light to come on. The walls were covered with camouflage material, and the sink was a steel helmet. The bathtub was shaped like a miniature Higgins landing craft, and the bathtub and the toilet were painted with the same camouflage look as the walls. When the toilet was flushed, "Taps" played from a tiny built-in speaker behind the tank.

As if just thinking about the song had conjured it up, Leah heard the muted sound of the melody. She paused and a silly grin pulled at her lips. Hunter had flushed the toilet. The grin turned into a fit of giggles. She'd give anything to see the look on his face right about now. Then, a moment later, the song ended, and so did the giggles as a rush of bone-deep fatigue washed over her.

Leah found an old worn Saints T-shirt in the third drawer she searched. She undressed by the bed, then slipped on the T-shirt. Once she'd pulled back the garish purple comforter, she climbed between the gold-colored sheets.

Leah groaned with sheer pleasure and relief as she stretched out and closed her eyes. Several moments passed, and she was on the verge of sleep when she felt the first small flutter in her abdomen. Her eyes popped open, and she splayed her hand across her stomach. Lying perfectly still and staring into the inky darkness, she waited to see if it would happen again.

Reminding herself that she needed to breathe, she took a deep breath. "Come on, baby, do it again," she whispered. "One more time for your mother." As if the baby had heard her, she felt the fluttery sensation again. Immediately, thoughts of calling out to Hunter flitted through her head. He should be there to share the experience of their baby's first movements. Then sudden tears filled her eyes. She couldn't call out to him, not now. He didn't know that she was pregnant, and she couldn't tell him, not until he regained his memory.

Leah sniffed and blinked back the tears. She was stuck between a rock and a hard place. Yet again she reminded herself that without any memory of their time together or the love they had shared, he would see it as just one more betrayal, most likely the ultimate betrayal that could cost her whatever future she hoped to have with him.

Leah awoke with a start the following morning, and for a moment, she felt disoriented as she glanced around the purple, green and gold room.

The camp. She was at the camp.

Then, like a kaleidoscope of nightmarish proportion, the events of the previous day came rushing back…Hunter, the federal agents, the men shooting at them, their hide-and-seek trek, and finally, their confrontation with one of the shooters.

With a shudder, she threw back the covers, pushed herself up and slid to the edge of the bed. What time was it? She glanced toward the double window in the room. Around the edges of the room-darkening shades, she saw daylight. With a frown, she switched on the lamp and reached for her watch on the bedside table. Ten o'clock.

Leah's frown deepened. So where was Hunter? Was he still sleeping? After a hasty trip to the bathroom, she opened the bedroom door and listened for any sound that would tell her whether he was awake. Opening the door a bit wider, she stuck her head out into the hall. When she saw that the other bedroom door was open, she tiptoed to it and peeked inside.

It was obvious from the disheveled covers that the bed had been slept in. Still frowning, she headed for the kitchen and living area. When she saw that Hunter wasn't in either room, she figured he was probably outside on the back deck.

Leah tried pushing open the back sliding glass door, but it was still locked. Shading her eyes against the eastern sun, she peered out the glass toward the back run and the deck area at the end, just to make sure. When she saw that Hunter wasn't there, she suddenly couldn't seem to breathe.

If he wasn't inside the house and he wasn't outside at the back, then… She pivoted and ran back up the hallway. Just as she reached for the front doorknob, out of the corner of her eye she caught sight of the house key still lying on the table where she'd left it. She glanced down at the doorknob. The button on the doorknob was pushed in, which meant that the door was locked. It could be opened from the inside without a key, but not from the outside. If Hunter had left and intended on coming back, wouldn't he have taken the key? But what if he didn't intend on coming back? What if—

Leah twisted the doorknob and flung open the door. At the sight of the strange man standing in the doorway, she screamed.

Chapter 8

"Hey, lady—"

Leah slammed the door closed. Her heart thumping against her rib cage, she braced herself against the door. Careless. She'd been careless and foolish to panic and open the door like that without checking through the peephole first. Letting her emotions override her brain was not a smart thing to do, and considering the circumstances, it was dangerous and could be deadly.

The sudden, sharp rap on the door accelerated her heartbeat.

"Hey in there," the man called out. "I didn't mean to scare you. My wife and I are renting the Summer Bliss down the way, and we heard some noise last night. Since we saw lights on over here, we wondered if everything was okay."

Leah's heartbeat slowed and she drew in a deep steadying breath. If the man was one of the shooters, he wouldn't have come alone, and he'd be trying to break down the door. The man was an innocent, just someone showing neighborly concern. She'd forgotten that people who lived in or rented the camps were like that.

Leah squeezed her eyes closed. *Think. Say something.* If she didn't say something and say it soon, he might conclude that they didn't belong and call the police, and the last thing they needed was for the police to show up.

Leah glanced down at the T-shirt she was wearing. *Not exactly the thing to wear when talking to a strange man.* Then, inspiration struck, and forcing a smile, she opened the door just enough to stick her head through it. "S-sorry about that. I wasn't expecting anyone to be standing at the door when I opened it."

The man nodded. "That's understandable. Like I said before, I didn't mean to scare you. Name's Henry, Henry Jones."

Henry Jones was dressed in typical camp attire: shorts, T-shirt and sandals. An older man with a head full of gray hair, Leah guessed that he was probably in his late fifties or early sixties.

"No harm done, Henry," she said. "I'd ask you inside but we got in pretty late last night, and I just woke up. Guess I didn't realize that anyone else would be renting nearby this late in the season. My cousin had assured me that we'd have the place to ourselves." Leah cast her eyes downward, feigning embarrassment. "We're on our honeymoon," she murmured.

A grin tugged at the man's lips.. "Well, I guess congratulations are in order. And don't you worry one bit. Me and the wife won't be making pests out of ourselves."

"Oh, I didn't mean—"

"Hey, no problem." He laughed. "We're not too old to remember how it was."

Leah was suddenly uncomfortable with the turn of the conversation, and not liking the sudden gleam in the older man's eye, she searched for some way to change the subject. Then, more inspiration struck, and Leah frowned. "We heard a noise last night, too. What do you think it was?"

The man shrugged. "No telling, and out here, sound travels, so it could have come from anywhere."

"Well, we appreciate you checking up on us." She left the sentence hanging and hoped that the man would take the hint and leave.

"No problem." He glanced down, and after a long moment of silence, he shrugged. "Guess I'll be moseying on back to the Summer Bliss. If y'all need anything, just holler."

Leah smiled. "Thanks again."

With another shrug, Henry turned, and hands in his pockets, he shuffled off down the run toward the levee.

Leah immediately closed the door and checked the button on the doorknob to make sure that the door was still locked. Then she peered through the peephole and watched until Henry disappeared out of sight. As soon as he was, Hunter once again filled her thoughts.

Turning her back to the door, she leaned against it and stared up at the ceiling. "Think," she muttered. "Use your brain." Just because Hunter wasn't there didn't mean he'd abandoned her. And though she was fairly certain he wouldn't abandon her, she didn't kid herself about the reasons he stayed. No matter how he felt about her, he needed her to fill in the blanks of his memory. And afterward, after he'd regained his memory, then what? Would he still want her? Would he remember that he'd loved her?

Leah shied away from further thoughts of what the future might bring. Best to concentrate on the present for now. Besides, there were lots of reasons Hunter might have left. Well...not lots of reasons, she decided, but at least one or two. Like food, for one. Though the camp might have a few basics, no one left food. Foods like eggs or milk would spoil, and stuff like bread and other commodities might attract rats and roaches. More than likely, he'd awakened hungry and had decided to go out to stock up on a few groceries. But if that were the case, wouldn't he have left a note? Leah grimaced. She'd been in such a panic that she hadn't bothered to even look for a note.

She shoved away from the door and headed down the hallway. If he had left a note, she figured he would have left it in the kitchen.

Once in the kitchen area, she glanced around. With a sigh of relief and a mental reprimand for panicking and jumping to conclusions, she walked over to where the coffeepot sat on the counter. There, in front of the empty coffeepot was a small notepad. She picked it up.

Leah, have gone to pick up a few groceries. The note was signed simply, *Hunter.*

As Hunter waited for an opening in the traffic so that he could cross Hayne Boulevard, he felt sweat trickle down his back. It was barely midmorning and already hot as blue blazes. He could stand the heat. New York was stifling in the summer time. But it was the humidity that was the killer. How on earth did these people stand it? he wondered as he reached up and wiped away the sweat from his forehead. If it was this hot and only midmorning, how hot would it be by high noon?

Hunter suddenly went still as he realized that the only way he could know about the heat in New York was if another piece of his memory had returned. Bits and pieces. Slowly but surely things were coming back.

Hunter grimaced. Way too slow to his liking, he thought as a large truck whizzed by and he savored the brief, hot breeze it stirred. He didn't need his memory to know that he wasn't a patient man.

Looking both ways, he jogged across the road. When the

grocery bags slapped against his thigh, he held them out away from his body. Along with the coffee and a variety of other staples, he'd bought eggs. At the rate he was going though, he'd be lucky if they weren't scrambled by the time he reached the camp.

Up ahead on the grassy levee he saw the Old Codger sign, and wondered if Leah had awakened yet. He'd debated on whether to wake her or let her sleep. Then he'd remembered how exhausted she'd been by the time they reached the camp and had decided to let her sleep.

Hunter swallowed hard. While he debated on whether to wake her, he'd made the mistake of looking in on her. He could still see her curled on her side, her hair splayed across the pillow. Glorious dark auburn hair that made a man want to run his fingers through it just to see if it was as soft as it looked. During the night she'd kicked off the sheet, and the thin, oversize T-shirt did little to cover the body beneath it. Not only could he see each curve of her body, but he'd had a full unobstructed view of her shapely bare legs, legs that he imagined wrapped around him.

The longer he'd stood there watching her, the more he understood why he'd been attracted to her. But when he felt the unexpected quickening in his loins, he'd tried to deny the strength of the desire he was feeling. How could he desire someone he couldn't trust?

Hunter grimaced. The answer was simple. Since the beginning of time men had been suckered in by love, ever since Eve had convinced Adam to eat the forbidden fruit, since Delilah and Sampson.

Denying his desire for her was impossible. But what he did about that desire now was a choice. He might not remember his past, but his gut told him that he was nobody's fool. He'd trusted her and she deceived him, but once was all it took. He wouldn't be misled so easily again. And though it hadn't been easy as he stood there watching her sleep, he'd quietly but firmly closed her bedroom door and left her a note.

With his free hand, Hunter automatically reached down and rubbed his thigh. Leah wasn't the only one who'd suffered from their day of hide-and-seek. All that running and walking had played havoc with his leg, and only now was the stiffness fading.

Hunter had just reached the Old Codger sign when he spotted the lone man at the top of the levee. He froze then tensed and eased the bags of groceries from his right hand to his left. With his right hand, he reached for the gun hidden beneath his shirt at the small of his back. He might not be able to fire the weapon, but if it came down to it, he could sure as hell bluff.

Hunter tensed even more, then slowly relaxed again when he realized that the man was simply out for a stroll and was headed down the levee away from him toward the next camp.

Definitely not one of the shooters, he decided. For one thing, the man was dressed in khaki shorts and a T-shirt, and he was wearing sandals. For another thing, the man wasn't paying the slightest bit of attention to him. Then, just as Hunter dismissed the man as a threat, he stopped and turned toward him.

Hunter tensed again, but the man just grinned and waved. Cupping his hand over his mouth, the man called out, "Good morning."

Hunter nodded and waved back.

"Have fun," the man called out again and then he laughed. "And don't do anything I wouldn't do." Still laughing, he turned away, and disappeared down the other side of the levee.

Now what the devil had he meant by that? Hunter wondered as he stared at the spot on top of the levee where the guy had disappeared.

Strange, he thought, almost as strange as the bathroom in

the Old Codger. Just thinking about the bizarre bathroom made him laugh, and with a shake of his head, he switched the grocery sack back to his right hand and began the climb up the levee.

By the time he was halfway down the run leading to the camp, he'd dismissed the man and his weird comments as easily as he'd disconnected the sound effects of the toilet the night before. "Taps," of all things. Hunter almost groaned out loud. What kind of weirdo would rig a toilet to play "Taps" when it was flushed?

Leah was dressing when she heard the soft knock at the front door. Sucking in her stomach, she snapped and zipped her jeans, and praying that Henry hadn't decided to return, she hurried to the front door.

Reminding herself to look before she opened the door, she peered through the peephole. Though his back was turned to the door, she immediately recognized the man as Hunter.

"You should have taken the key," she said as she opened the door.

Hunter shrugged. "I figured you'd be awake by the time I got back."

"I hope you've got milk in those bags," she said, closing the door and following him down the hall.

In the kitchen, Hunter hefted the bags onto the countertop, then began unloading them. "Coffee, sugar, milk, eggs, bread, margarine, lunch meat, mustard and chips," he said, naming each item as he took it out of the bags. "And for dessert—" He pulled the last two items out of the bag and held them up for her to see. "Honey buns—one for you and one for me." He motioned toward the grocery items on the counter. "I figured that would hold us for a while. We can wander out and get dinner this evening."

"Honey buns?" Leah whispered.

"You do like them, don't you?"

Leah nodded. "Yes—of course I do, but you *know* I do." When Hunter frowned, she explained. "Don't you see? You remembered. It was a standing joke between us—the only dessert that I knew how to fix."

Hunter shook his head. "Guess I don't remember that part."

Leah sighed. "I can cook a lot of things," she explained. "But I don't do desserts. I always kept honey buns on hand if I wanted something sweet."

Leah could tell from the blank look on Hunter's face that he still didn't understand, and worse, he didn't get the joke. "Never mind," she said, disappointed. "It's no big deal anyway."

Hunter shrugged. "Sorry." He grabbed the bag of coffee, opened it, and turned his back as he began preparing the coffeepot.

Hunter's movements were jerky and his shoulders were stiff. Instead of encouraging him, as she'd intended, all she'd done was remind him of his amnesia. Time for a change of subject, she decided. "We had a visitor while you were gone."

Hunter paused and turned to face her, his eyes narrow, his head tilted to one side. "Gray-haired man dressed in shorts?"

Leah nodded. "Name's Henry, Henry Jones," she drawled, attempting to mimic the older man's voice. "But how did you know?"

Hunter chuckled, his shoulders relaxed, and he resumed the task of spooning coffee into the drip basket of the pot. He closed the basket and turned on the switch. "I saw him walking along the top of the levee." He turned, crossed his arms and leaned against the counter. "Just what did he mean by 'have fun' and 'don't do anything I wouldn't do'?"

Leah felt her face grow warm. "I—ah—I kind of told him that we were on our honeymoon." When Hunter's expression turned taut and derisive, Leah grew defensive. "It was the only thing I could think of at the time," she stressed. "Well, it was," she retorted.

For long seconds the only sound in the room was the gurgling of the coffeepot as Hunter continued staring at her as if she'd just sprouted horns. Then, finally, he said, "And just why did you even open the door to begin with?"

There was no way she could tell him that she'd panicked when she couldn't find him, no way she could admit to how foolish or careless she'd been. "I had to tell him something so he wouldn't be nosing around."

"That's not what I asked. I asked—"

The sudden sound of reveille interrupted, and it took several moments for Leah and Hunter both to realize that the music was coming from the cell phone that Lance Martin had given to Hunter. At the same time, both turned to stare at the phone. It was on the table where Hunter had left it earlier that morning before he'd gone after groceries.

In two steps, Hunter was at the table. He snatched up the phone and clicked the talk button.

"Hunter? Is that you?"

Though the voice on the line was a bit hoarse, it sounded like Lance Martin, but Hunter wasn't totally convinced that it was. "Who wants to know?"

"This is Lance—Lance Martin."

"So you did survive."

"Yeah, but just barely," Martin answered. "I'm in the hospital, but I'll live."

"And what about your partner?"

"Ray wasn't so lucky."

"Sorry," Hunter said.

"Yeah, he was a good agent, a good partner, and a good friend. But that's not why I'm calling. I need to know where you are—your location—so we can send someone after you."

Hunter laughed. "You've got to be kidding."

"Hunter, this is serious. Dead serious."

"Don't I know it." He also knew there were ways of tracing a cell phone. What he didn't know—couldn't remember—was how long it took to get a fix on their location.

"Come on, Hunter," Lance cajoled. "You can run but you can't hide. Sooner or later we'll find you. Think of your wife."

Hunter felt his temper flare. "I am thinking of her. Gotta go now." He clicked the talk button to disconnect the call, and then he turned the phone off completely.

For several moments, he stood staring at the cell phone as the agent's words echoed through his head. *Think of your wife.* How could he not think of her? That's all he'd done since he'd had the first flashback when he'd been stuck in the hospital in Orlando. And it was just that—the thinking about her—that was driving him crazy.

She was his wife, so he must have loved her, but he didn't remember anything about her being his wife. That he desired her was a given. What man in his right mind wouldn't? But the sticking point was trust. Even if she could explain why she'd lied about their relationship and why she had made the phone call that alerted the feds, there was more. It was just a gut feeling, but he strongly suspected that she was still holding something back. And that proved that she couldn't be trusted,

His grip tightened on the phone. He'd been a fool to leave the damn phone in plain sight in the first place. What if Lance Martin had called while he'd been gone? Would she have told him where they were? Or what if she'd decided to call the police?

Hunter slipped the phone into his pants pocket. That was one mistake he wouldn't make again. From now on the cell phone went wherever he went.

He glanced up at the wall phone near the cabinet. He'd have to take that one out of action as well.

* * *

Leah was on pins and needles, waiting for Hunter to explain the phone call. She felt sure that the caller was one of the agents, which meant that one or both had survived, after all. But he seemed in no hurry to talk about the call as he just stood, staring at the cell phone.

Something was wrong, she decided. If the expression on his face was any gauge then something was definitely wrong. But what? And why wouldn't he say something?

When several more moments dragged by and he still hadn't said a word, Leah felt herself begin to lose patience. Then, abruptly, without a word, Hunter pocketed the cell phone. When he stepped back over to the coffeepot and picked up the decanter, she suddenly realized that he had no intention of saying anything at all about the call.

"Well?" she prompted as he poured two cups of coffee.

He handed her one of the cups and motioned toward the bag of sugar. "You'll have to open the sugar for your coffee."

"That's not what I meant and you know it." She glared at him. "Since the phone belongs to Lance Martin, I assume that the caller was either him or Ray Harris, which means that one or both survived. So which one was it?"

Hunter sighed and reached for the bag of sugar. But Leah was quicker and grabbed it first. "Forget the sugar," she snapped as her temper flared. "I want to know what's going on."

"It was Lance Martin," he finally explained, his tone a bit testy. "He's alive."

"What about Ray Harris?"

Hunter shook his head. "He didn't make it."

The news was sobering, and Leah shuddered inwardly as the image of the sandy-haired agent came to mind. "That's too bad," she murmured. "So what else?" she asked absently, still thinking about the death of the agent. When, after a moment, Hunter hadn't answered, she pressed harder. "What else did Lance Martin have to say?"

Hunter rolled his eyes. "Nothing, Leah. Nothing important."

Leah felt her temper rise. "If it's not important, why not tell me what he said? *What else did he say?*" she repeated, emphasizing each word.

Hunter narrowed his eyes. "If you have to know, he wanted me to tell him where we are so he can send more agents to pick us up."

"You've got to be kidding."

"That's what I told him," he said. "Now hand me the sugar and I'll open it for you."

Leah glared at him and lost the battle with her temper. "I can open it myself," she snapped as she ripped the top open. "I don't know why you couldn't have just told me that to begin with. The nerve of that man! After all we've been through, if he thinks we're going to just yell our location over the phone lines, then he can just think again."

When Hunter grinned and held out a spoon, Leah snatched the spoon from him and plunged it into the bag of sugar.

"My thoughts exactly," he said.

But his words only irritated her more as she measured out two heaping spoonfuls, dumping each in her coffee.

"Now," Hunter drawled, "about your friend, Henry Jones."

Leah stirred her coffee so vigorously that it sloshed over the sides of the cup.

Hunter leaned against the countertop. "You never did answer my question about him."

Leah was in no mood to be interrogated, and it took every bit of control she could muster to keep from throwing the spoon at him, but she carefully placed it on the countertop instead. "He is not my friend, thank you very much." And before he could grill her further, she picked up her coffee, dumped half of it in the sink, topped the cup off with milk and headed for the sliding glass door.

Hunter didn't follow her immediately, and Leah breathed a sigh of relief as she closed the door behind her. What she needed at the moment was space and time to get control of her emotions.

Though it was hot outside, it wasn't nearly as hot as Leah felt on the inside. She took a deep breath, and as she let it out slowly in an attempt to relax, she headed down the run.

A breeze kicked up off the lake. Savoring the brief respite from the heat, Leah squinted against the glare of the gray-blue water shimmering and sparkling under the midday sun.

Halfway down the run, her vision suddenly blurred, and she stopped and grabbed hold of the rail. Though she tried convincing herself that the tears were simply a result of the glare off the water and had nothing to do with Hunter or the topsy-turvy emotions of being pregnant, deep inside she knew better.

She'd been shot at, chased, and had to run for her life. She was tired and she was an emotional wreck. But it was Hunter's reticence about the phone call that had been the last straw. The way he'd acted had only confirmed what she already knew but hadn't wanted to face. The bottom line was that he didn't trust her. And if he didn't trust her now, how would he react when he found out that she was pregnant?

More tears filled her eyes and she squeezed her lids closed. If only she had someone to talk to, someone who could tell her what to do.

Leah shook her head. It pained her to admit it, but there was no one. With the exception of Christine, the one friend she felt she could rely on, all of the rest of her so-called friends were the people she worked with, and she had no close relatives, not since...

"Oh, Grandm'ere," she whispered. "Where are you when I need you?"

Then, unbidden, almost as if the breeze was whispering in her ear, she could hear her grandmother's voice in her head. *That's enough now, Leah, girl. Time to get off your pity pot. The good Lord gave you a brain, so use it and stop feeling sorry for yourself.*

Leah couldn't begin to count how many times her grandmother had told her those exact words, and just remembering them gave her a measure of comfort.

Swallowing against the ache in her throat, Leah sniffed and blinked back the tears. One way or another, Hunter would find out that she'd deceived him yet again. With each passing day he was remembering more and more. Sooner or later he'd remember that night in Orlando. He'd remember her birthday celebration, and he'd remember what happened afterward. Sooner or later he'd recall exactly why she'd sent him to the drugstore. And when he did find out, for the sake of their baby, she'd have to deal with it.

At the end of the run, the small deck was shaded and there were a couple of lawn chairs and a table. Leah seated herself in one of the chairs.

In the distance, she spotted a sailboat, and as she sipped her drink and watched the boat skimming over the water, she made up her mind that she had to tell Hunter about their baby. Telling him might be the one way she could redeem herself in his eyes, the one way she could regain his trust. Then again, telling him could also backfire. Telling him could be the beginning of the end; the end to any hope she had that Hunter would once again love her.

Leah tightened her grip on the coffee cup. She had to do it, had to take the chance.

Chapter 9

Leah headed back down the run toward the house, and with each step she took her resolve to tell Hunter about the baby weakened.

If only she could have just a little more time with him before she told him, time to once again establish the relationship between them. Her footsteps slowed. Even better, with a little more time, he might regain his memory. Surely once he regained his memory and remembered the love they had shared... Leah's footsteps slowed even more. How long though? How long should she wait?

By the time Leah came inside, Hunter had successfully sabotaged the wall phone and had begun making sandwiches.

"I'm starving," Leah told him, eyeing the stack of sandwiches. "But one, maybe even two, are more than enough for me. You've got enough there for an army."

Hunter's hands stilled as he realized that he'd been mindlessly making sandwiches as if he were working on an assembly line. But his thoughts had been elsewhere, mostly trying to figure out what his next move should be. He shrugged. "Guess I got a little carried away."

While Hunter put away the bread, the mustard and the few remaining slices of lunch meat, Leah took the plate of sandwiches and the bag of potato chips over to a small table that overlooked the lake.

"I forgot to buy soft drinks," he said, "so I guess we'll have to drink coffee or water."

"Water's fine with me," Leah said when Hunter poured himself another cup of coffee.

Once they were settled at the table, Hunter waited until they had both assuaged their initial hunger before he broached the subject that had occupied his mind during the time that Leah had been outside. "I've been thinking," he began. "This is a perfect place to hide out temporarily, but we can't stay here indefinitely. I haven't exactly figured out how, but I think I need to return to Orlando. I can't help but believe that if I retrace my steps there, if I go through the motions, it might spark my memory."

Leah nodded as she chewed then swallowed. "Makes sense, I guess, but we've got a problem of transportation. We can't use my car because they're watching the house. And if, by some miracle, we were able to get it without being caught, then they'll be watching for it. We can't rent a car either without a credit card. Like I said before, mine's charged to the limit."

Hunter stared past Leah out the window. "Yeah, and both the shooters and feds are probably watching the bus and train stations as well as the airport." He shrugged. "Guess I could always go back the way I got here."

Leah shook her head. "No way. Sorry, but I'm not into hitchhiking."

"I wasn't suggesting that *you* hitchhike."

Leah narrowed her eyes. "And just what were you suggesting then?"

"You would stay here."

"Okay," she drawled. "And if I stay here, just how are you going to know which hotel we stayed at in Orlando and what drugstore you went to?"

"I'll know because you'll tell me."

When Leah smiled, Hunter knew immediately that he'd backed himself into a corner.

"Uh-uh, sorry," she said. "Where you go, I go, but I'm not hitchhiking."

"Okay, Miss Know-it-all. What's your solution? Not that I'm agreeing that you come with me, mind you."

"I think we should stay here until your memory returns. Give it a few more days. Then—and only then—if it doesn't, we can always—"

Suddenly Leah's eyes widened, and when she said nothing more, Hunter frowned. "What? We can always what?"

Leah smacked her hand against her forehead. "Why didn't I think of it sooner?"

"Think of what?"

Her expression stilled and grew serious. She leaned forward. "The psychiatrist. One of the reasons that Martin and Harris wanted to get you back to Orlando was because they had a doctor there who thought he could help you regain your memory through hypnosis."

"Yeah, so?"

"So—Orlando's not the only city that has psychiatrists. In fact, I know one who might be willing to do the same thing. Dr. Ted Stone is one of the best psychiatrists in the state."

Hunter's gut reaction to Leah's suggestion was not just no, but hell no. But why? Why would he have such a negative reaction, especially if submitting to hypnosis might help get his memory back?

After several moments, the only reason he could come up with was that it had something to do with what had happened in New York. From what Leah had told him, he must have seen a psychiatrist, considering the nature of his problem with firing his weapon. Maybe his experience with the doctor there had been a bad one.

"I don't know," he finally said, shaking his head slowly.

"What's to know?" Leah argued. "If you ask me, it's a no-brainer. The worst that could happen is that the hypnosis wouldn't work. And the best that could happen is that you would regain your memory. Another thing to consider is that he would be bound by patient-doctor confidentiality, so we don't have to worry about him talking to the FBI or the police."

She had a point, and after a moment, he reluctantly nodded. "Okay. So how do we go about getting this doctor to see me?"

Suddenly Leah was all business. "The first thing we need to do is call Dr. Stone and see how soon he can fit you into his schedule. I'm just hoping that since he knows me, that will make a difference."

Leah suddenly frowned. She was staring at his shirt. Hunter glanced down. Maybe he had mustard on it. Then, she cast her eyes downward at herself, and her frown deepened.

"The next thing we need to do is buy some clothes," she murmured. "We can't just keep wearing the same ones over and over." She paused thoughtfully. "We can't go to the mall—too risky. Hmm…maybe—" Her mouth curved into a slow smile. "I know…we'll hit the Junior League."

"Ah, come again?"

"The Junior League Thrift Shop. You know—used clothes. No one would ever think to look for us there."

Hunter wrinkled his nose.

"Don't be such a snob," she scolded. "Most of the stuff

there has barely been worn. I've gotten some bargains for just pennies."

"I am not a snob," Hunter retorted, stung by her accusation. "At least I don't think I am."

"You're not," she confirmed. "So why the look?"

For an answer, Hunter simply shrugged.

"Well, never mind. First things first." She stood, then went into the kitchen.

When the sound of drawers being opened and closed reached his ears, Hunter stacked the plates and joined her in the kitchen. "What are you looking for?" He placed the plates in the sink.

Leah had begun opening the cabinet doors. "A phone directory. I'm sure they have one somewhere," she said as she opened another cupboard. Then, she paused. "You know, maybe I'll just call the hospital, instead. With everything that's happened I completely forgot about work, and while I'm making my excuses, I can ask for the number of Dr. Stone's office." She closed the cabinet and reached for the phone.

For several moments she listened to the receiver and jiggled the switch hook. "Great!" she muttered. "The line's dead." She hung up the receiver, then turned to Hunter and held out her hand. "I'll have to use the cell phone."

Hunter shook his head, and careful to keep a poker face, he said, "That's not a good idea. Not here. There are ways of tracking calls…" Hunter frowned and went stone still. "Tracking calls," he repeated thoughtfully.

Something that Lance Martin had said in their brief conversation nagged at him. *You can run but you can't hide. Sooner or later we'll find you.*

As the agent's words tumbled around in his brain like rocks in a polishing machine, each word heavy with innuendo, Hunter finally figured out that it wasn't so much what the agent had said but how he'd said it.

Hunter stared straight ahead with unseeing eyes. Lance Martin…the phone…suddenly, like pieces of a puzzle, everything fell into place. He muttered a curse, and Leah snapped her head around to stare at him.

"What's wrong?"

"Lance Martin," Hunter muttered. "It was all an act, all orchestrated. Lance Martin is the Bureau leak. That bastard was going to hand us up on a silver platter to the shooters and still come out smelling like a rose. Then it all went haywire. The shooters missed."

Hunter drew in a deep breath and let it out with a sigh. "Think about it. When we bailed, Ray Harris was still alive, so why would the shooters kill just Harris and not Martin? And Martin was the one who gave us the cell phone, the one who's made all the phone calls. How else did the shooters know we were in the coffeehouse yesterday? Remember? I had switched the phone back on and made that call to Jack, then we had our little disagreement. And a few minutes later the shooters showed up outside. The bastards have been tracking us with the damn phone."

Leah shivered. At first she'd thought that Hunter had finally gone too far with his conspiracy theories, that he really was a mental case after all. But by the time he'd finished explaining, all of it was beginning to make sense.

"Big Brother," she murmured and shivered again. Leah ground her teeth. "One thing's for certain. We've got to get rid of that phone."

"Yeah, and we've got to get out of here now."

Leah nodded, and on their way out, she grabbed her purse and the key to the front door. Once they were outside, she quickly locked the door and slipped the key back into the gargoyle. She turned just in time to see Hunter pull the cell phone out of his pocket, turn it on and punch in some numbers. Then, like a baseball pitcher winding up for a pitch, he reared back and hurled the phone out into the lake. "Let 'em track that," he drawled with satisfaction.

"What phone number did you dial?" Leah asked as they hurried down the run toward the levee.

"Beats me," Hunter answered with a shrug.

At the gate, Hunter wrapped the chain in such a fashion that it looked as if it had never been broken.

Just before they reached the top of the levee, Hunter muttered, "Wait here and let me check it out first." Bending low, he eased up the last few feet, and after a quick glance around, he signaled to her that all was clear.

Ever aware that the shooters could show up at any minute, Leah and Hunter jogged to the same spot where the city bus had dropped them the night before. Within mere minutes, both were drenched in sweat, and Hunter began pacing.

"I don't like this," he said, his eyes darting back and forth, searching up and down the road. "It's too open out here. We're sitting ducks."

He abruptly stopped in front of Leah. "How far is the stop before this one?"

Before Leah could answer, she spotted the bus coming down the road. She motioned toward it. "Here comes the bus now."

The bus was only about half-full, and Hunter and Leah sat near the front with Hunter on the window side. They had only gone about a mile when a black SUV streaked past them, driving in the direction of the camp.

"That was too close for comfort," Hunter muttered. "Too damn close."

Beside him Leah snickered, earning herself a glare from Hunter. "I was just thinking about them trying to track that cell phone," she explained.

Though Hunter didn't comment, she thought she saw a smile pull at his lips before he turned away to stare out the window.

* * *

Shopping with Leah proved to be an experience that Hunter knew he wouldn't soon forget.

He wasn't sure just what he'd expected, but the reality was a far cry from what he'd imagined. The thrift shop was clean and orderly and the people who were shopping in it looked like ordinary people. Not the homeless types or bums that he'd imagined would be there.

Leah had a shrewd, practical eye when it came to choosing clothes, and since Hunter didn't really care what he wore as long as it was comfortable, he let her do the shopping.

She'd already chosen each of them a couple of sets of clothes—jeans and pullovers for him, and a couple of knit pants she called capris, with matching shirts for herself—but she wanted each of them to have a dressier set. "Dressy casual," she called them.

"If you choose clothes all in the same color range then you can mix and match," she explained as she examined a pair of navy slacks. "You can also choose neutral colors that will go with anything," she added as she rejected the pants and pulled out a pair of khaki-colored slacks, instead.

Though they hadn't been in the store very long and the odds of either the shooters or the feds finding them was nil, Hunter was still wary and scrutinized every customer who came into the shop.

By the time they were ready to pay for their purchases, Hunter's arms were full. In addition to clothes, Leah had also made sure that they each had a pair of tennis shoes, a pair of loafers for him, and a pair of sandals for herself. She'd also found a couple of knapsacks that would hold all their purchases. Then she'd selected a cap for him, one with an LSU Tigers logo on the front. For herself, she'd found a floppy straw hat.

"Hats make good disguises," she'd told him.

Though he did agree that the hats might prove to be useful, she'd said it so seriously that he couldn't resist teasing her. "I think you've been reading too many mystery books or watching too much TV."

Not even his teasing had fazed her, though. She'd simply shrugged and kept shopping.

Hunter dumped the merchandise onto the counter. "Ah, just one thing," he said. "We didn't get any underwear."

Leah dumped her selections on the counter as well. Then she leaned closer, and shielding her mouth with her hand she whispered, "I draw the line at wearing someone else's old underwear."

It was all Hunter could do to keep a straight face, but Leah was too busy rifling through her purse to pay attention.

Hunter reached out and stilled her hand. "I'll pay for these," he told her. "It's only fair," he said in his best deadpan voice, reminding her where the money had come from.

After a moment a smile trembled over Leah's lips, and she nodded. "You're absolutely right. It is only fair."

Once they'd paid for the clothes, Leah stuffed them into the knapsacks, all except for the hats. "Put this on." She handed Hunter the LSU cap. Then she shoved the straw hat on top of her head and stuffed her hair up into the crown.

With each of them carrying a knapsack, they exited the store.

"About the underwear thing," Leah said once they were outside. "For now we'll just have to make do with washing out what we have each night, at least until we can get to a department store."

It was the serious look on her face that did it, and Hunter couldn't help laughing.

"Hey, laugh all you want," she told him. "Can I help it if my grandm'ere had a thing about clean underwear?" But even as she said the words, she began laughing, too.

A few minutes later, as they approached the bus stop, Leah said, "We need to find a phone so I can make those calls."

Hunter glanced around. "What we need is a pay phone."

"Yeah, well, good luck," Leah retorted. "With everyone carrying cell phones, it's hard to find an old-fashioned pay phone anymore."

"How about a gas station? I noticed several gas stations had pay phones when I was traveling from Orlando."

Leah nodded.

At the second gas station they checked, they found a pay phone that worked.

The first call Leah made was to her supervisor at the hospital, and as she waited to be connected, she thought again about her decision to tell Hunter about the baby. If only she could find the right time—

The phone clicked. "This is Margaret. How may I help you?"

"Hi, Margaret, this is Leah."

"Leah! Where in the devil have you been? I've been trying to reach you all day."

"Margaret, I'm so sorry. I should have called sooner, but I couldn't get to a phone right away. I'm having some problems that I can't go into and I need some time off."

"Is it the baby? You haven't miscarried, have you?"

Leah cut her eyes toward Hunter who was standing guard. She was tempted to lie and use the excuse that Margaret had just handed her, but she was far too superstitious to do so and far too afraid to tempt the powers that be in that way. "No, nothing like that."

"How much time are we talking about?"

"To be honest, I'm not sure, but I think I have some vacation time built up. Could I use those days for now?"

Though reluctantly, Margaret finally agreed. "You've got

ten days coming to you. After that, I can't guarantee anything."

"I understand," Leah told her. "And again I apologize, but just one more thing. Could you please give me the number to Dr. Stone's office?"

"Leah! What's going on? Why on earth would you need a shrink's number?"

"Ah…like I said, I'm having some problems, and I'd really rather not go into it, not right now."

There was a silence on the line for several moments before Margaret finally said, "Okay. Hold on a minute."

Though Margaret did finally give her the doctor's office number, Leah could tell she was not happy about the situation.

"Thanks, Margaret. I promise I'll explain everything when I see you again." Leah disconnected the call, dropped in the correct change then tapped in the number that Margaret had given her. It took some fast talking and a bit of pleading, but Leah was able to secure Hunter an appointment.

"They're going to work you in tomorrow morning," she told him as she hung up the receiver. "You won't see Dr. Stone, though. You'll see Jan Morgan, instead. She's an associate of Dr. Stone's, a licensed professional counselor who works closely with him. She specializes in hypnosis."

Hunter shrugged. "Whatever."

Leah scowled. "With that kind of attitude, we might as well forget it." Though she didn't know a lot about hypnotic regression, she did know that the patient needed to be willing. "If this is going to work, you can't just—"

Hunter threw up a hand. "I know, I know." He shook his head. "Look," he said stiffly, "I'll do what needs to be done when the time comes, but until then, I'd just as soon not think about it."

And that was that, Leah thought as she stared down at the ground. End of discussion. Then so be it.

In the distance thunder rolled, and Leah glanced up at the dark clouds forming in the distant sky. "Changing the subject here, but since we can't return to the camp, we need to find somewhere to stay tonight."

Hunter nodded. "My thoughts exactly. I hate to—mainly because doing so will eat up our money—but better to be broke than get caught out in the rain."

"Right now we're fairly close to Dr. Stone's office, and I'm pretty sure there are several hotels in this area."

"Okay, let's go," he said.

"I think there's one a couple of blocks over," Leah told him. "It's not fancy, but it's a lot cheaper than the ones on St. Charles Avenue."

Leah was right, Hunter thought as they entered the hotel room. The hotel wasn't fancy, but as far as he could tell, the room appeared to be clean and it was a lot cheaper than he'd expected.

Leah dropped her knapsack on the double bed that was closest to the bathroom. "The first thing I'm going to do is take a shower," she announced. She opened the knapsack and began to rummage through it. "I would have preferred to wash this stuff before wearing it," she grumbled.

Hunter dropped his knapsack on the other bed. "The hotel probably has a laundry service."

"Yeah, and they probably charge a fortune, too. Besides, no telling how long it would take." She chose a pair of capris and the knit pullover that matched. "We need toothbrushes and toothpaste," she said as she tried smoothing out the wrinkles of the pullover.

Hunter reached up and rubbed his stubbled jaw. "Yeah, and I could use a razor."

Leah frowned. "Did you happen to notice whether the hotel has a gift shop?"

"No, but there's one way to find out." He headed for the door.

"If they don't," Leah called out, "I think there's a drugstore just down the block. In fact, hold up."

Hunter paused at the door as Leah grabbed the pen and pad of paper from the bedside table near the phone.

"There are a couple of other things I need as well," she explained and began scribbling on the paper. "Toothbrush, toothpaste, hairbrush and..." She paused thoughtfully, then abruptly ripped off the top sheet of the pad and wadded it up. "Never mind about a list," she said. "I'm going, too." She dropped the paper into the wastebasket then joined him at the door. "Have you got the key?"

Hunter nodded.

The hotel didn't have a gift shop after all, but one of the women at the front desk gave them directions to the nearest drugstore.

When they exited the hotel, Leah looked up and frowned. "It's definitely going to rain," she said.

Hunter glanced up. Dark clouds were rolling in and a breeze had kicked up. "We'd better get a move on then," he suggested.

By the time they reached the drugstore, fat raindrops had begun to fall. "Probably just an afternoon thunderstorm," Leah murmured as they ducked inside. Above the door, a collection of bells jingled as they entered. "Maybe the storm will pass by the time we're finished in here," she added.

The man at the checkout counter overheard Leah's comments. "You folks tourists?"

Before Leah could answer, Hunter nodded. "Yeah, why?"

"I hate to be the one to tell you, but we're in for a tropical storm. One popped up in the Gulf yesterday, due south of the city."

"Oh, great!" Leah muttered. "That's just peachy, just what we need."

"It's been all over the local news," the man said.

Hunter grimaced. "We haven't exactly been keeping up with the news or the weather for a couple of days." The weather had been the last thing they'd been concerned about. "So when's it supposed to hit?" he asked.

"Tonight, around midnight," the man answered. He waved his hand toward the doorway. "This is just the outer bands—just the beginning. It's fast moving, though, or so they say. According to the weatherman it should move on through by noon tomorrow, and it's not supposed to be too bad. Just some wind and a lot of rain."

"Guess things could be worse," Leah grumbled. "Better a tropical storm than a hurricane."

The man laughed. "You've got that right."

Leah forced a smile for the man behind the counter and pulled a shopping buggy loose from the line near the register. "Guess we'd better hurry," she told Hunter.

Hunter grimaced. "I don't think it's going to matter one way or another." He motioned toward the glass door. Outside, it was pouring rain. "Either way, we're going to get wet."

We're going to get wet...we're going to get wet...

Hunter's words echoed through Leah's mind as she pushed the cart down the aisle containing toothpaste and toothbrushes. Hunter didn't remember, but once before they'd been caught in the rain and gotten soaked. They had been out on one of the many sight-seeing jaunts that Hunter liked to take. She had warned him before they'd left that a cold front, preceded by rain, was supposed to come through later that day, but Hunter had laughed and told her that neither of them would melt.

By the time they had returned home that afternoon, they had both gotten soaked and were shivering from the cold. Hunter had given her a look that she'd come to recognize and had suggested that a hot shower was just the thing they needed. Sharing a shower with Hunter had been the first time she'd ever showered with a man or made love with a man in the shower, and even now, she could still remember the sensual, exotic experience.

Too bad *he* didn't remember, Leah thought as she blinked furiously against the sudden tears building in her eyes.

"What's wrong?" Hunter asked as he dropped the toothbrush he'd selected into the shopping cart.

Leah shook her head. "Nothing," she lied. "Nothing's wrong. I think I've got something in my eye. That's all."

"Want me to take a look?"

Leah shook her head. "No!" she objected, taking a step backward. When Hunter gave her a puzzled look, she realized that her objection had been more strident than she'd intended. "But thanks anyway," she quickly added, and with a shrug gave him what she hoped passed for a smile.

The last thing she wanted or needed at the moment was Hunter to get that close. She blinked several times and swallowed the ache in her throat. If he so much as even touched her now, she was afraid she'd fall apart completely. "I think it's better now," she explained, and blinked several times for good measure. "But I think we should add sunglasses to the list."

She could tell that he was still puzzled by her odd behavior, but he seemed to sense that she couldn't or didn't want to explain. And after a moment, he finally nodded then turned away.

Once they had selected the items they needed, Leah added an umbrella, and since they had left the shooter's flashlight at the camp, Hunter picked out a flashlight and batteries.

"Guess that's all for now," Leah said.

"No use in rushing out," Hunter responded as he stared toward the glass front door.

Thunder rumbled in the distance, and following Hunter's

gaze, Leah shuddered. Outside, the rain was coming down in sheets. "My thoughts exactly," she agreed.

By an unspoken agreement, they roamed the aisles of the drugstore in hopes that the downpour would let up. They were headed down the next to last aisle when Leah suddenly rushed ahead to the middle.

"Hunter, come see! Can you believe it?"

When Hunter approached, she pointed at the small rack of men's and women's packaged underwear, then immediately began examining the different sizes and types of panties. She'd just spotted the size she was looking for when she heard a low choking sound coming from Hunter.

She glanced over at him, and when she saw the amused look on his face and realized that he was doing his best to keep from laughing, a smile began pulling at her own lips. Then Hunter threw back his head and roared with laughter.

"Hey, laugh all you want," Leah told him, trying her best to keep a straight face. "But right now, new, clean underwear is a luxury." She selected the right size panties and dropped the package into the shopping cart.

When Hunter laughed even harder, Leah glared at him. But Hunter's laughter was infectious and before long, she found herself laughing along with him.

"I swear," he said, still chuckling. "You do have a thing about underwear, don't you?"

Leah giggled and waved toward the rack. "Which do you prefer?" she teased. "Boxers or briefs?" But as she stared up into Hunter's blue eyes, a sudden vision of the first time she'd seen him in just his underwear flashed through her head, and she felt her cheeks grow warm. The pair of white briefs he'd been wearing had been stretched to the limit due to him being fully aroused.

"Hmm, boxers or briefs…" Hunter repeated, his words drawing her back to the question she'd asked. Hunter rolled his eyes then teasingly waggled his eyebrows. "Neither," he answered. "I'm not wearing any now, so why bother?"

Leah giggled. "Just for that, you get briefs." She pulled a package off the rack and dropped it into the shopping cart. "Size medium should be about right."

They were both still snickering when Leah turned the shopping cart around and headed toward the checkout counter.

She'd only gone a couple of steps when Hunter grabbed the cart, spun it around, then grabbed her by the wrist.

"Cops!" he whispered, pushing the cart and pulling her quickly toward the end of the aisle. "Just pulled up outside," he explained as they ducked behind the end of the aisle.

Chapter 10

The end of the aisle that Hunter dragged her to was the aisle farthest from the front entrance of the store. Leah's heart raced. Hunter still had a firm hold on her hand, but he was staring at the surveillance mirror mounted on the wall near the end of the last aisle.

"Keep your back to that mirror," he whispered, finally releasing her hand. "Pretend you're still shopping. If worst comes to worst, head for that exit." He nodded toward a door near the back of the store. "And go straight to the hotel." The bells jingled over the front entrance. With trembling fingers, Leah picked up the first thing she saw, a container of body lotion. She turned her back to the mirror, and with unseeing eyes, she stared at the list of ingredients written on the back of the container.

"Hey, Jake," she heard the man at the counter say. "What's happening?"

"You name it, and it's happening," the officer responded.

"It ain't a fit day out there for man or beast." He laughed. "Just us cops and the bad guys." He laughed again. "And it's only going to get worse."

"Yeah, I'm already dreading the drive home."

"Nothing's flooding, yet," Jake said. "Probably will be though by the time you close up."

"So what can I do you for?" the counterman asked.

"Give me a pack of cigarettes, will ya?"

"Thought you'd quit smoking."

"Yeah, well, I keep trying."

"Your usual brand?"

"Yeah," the officer answered.

"Here you go. That'll be three-fifty."

"Damn!" the policeman muttered. "Guess I'd better start trying harder."

The man behind the counter chuckled. "Yeah, you and everyone else. Here you go, here's your change, and you take care now."

"And you be careful driving home tonight," the policeman called out, and within moments the bells above the door jingled.

Several minutes passed, and Leah had to remind herself to breathe. Only when Hunter finally whispered, "It's okay now—he's gone," did she stop shaking.

"Time for us to go, too," Hunter told her as he pushed the cart toward the front counter.

"Past time," Leah agreed.

In spite of the umbrella, by the time Leah and Hunter reached the hotel, their shoes and pant legs were soaked.

When they entered the air-conditioned hotel, Leah shivered from the cooler air. "Now for sure I need a good hot shower."

Once in their room, the first thing she did was pull off her shoes, and Hunter did the same. "These things are soaked through and through," she said, leaving the shoes by the door.

"If you'll give me the drugstore bag, I'll put that stuff in the bathroom." She held out her hand for the plastic shopping bag he was holding.

When Hunter handed her the bag, she removed the packages of underwear, the flashlight and the batteries, and dropped them on the bed. Then she gathered up the capris and shirt that she'd laid out earlier, and headed for the bathroom.

Once inside, she started to close the door, but then hesitated.

Taking a deep breath, she firmly shut the door. Breathe deeply and don't think about it, she kept telling herself. There's plenty of light.

From the other side of the door, she heard the sound of the television. From the little she could hear, she guessed that Hunter was watching the weather channel.

Just as she'd unloaded the bag onto the countertop, there was a light rap on the door.

Leah opened it.

Hunter motioned toward the metal towel rack on the wall near the bathtub. "Toss me a towel, will you? I'm dripping on everything."

"You can shower first if you want," Leah offered. "I can wait."

Hunter smiled but shook his head. "No, you go ahead. Just a towel will be fine for now."

Leah pulled out one of the towels and handed it to Hunter.

"Thanks," he told her.

Once Leah had closed the door, she turned on the shower and quickly undressed. As she examined the array of toiletries provided by the hotel, she wondered just how bad the storm would get. Since they were on the third floor, she didn't worry too much about flooding, but she did worry about the wind. Thank goodness they hadn't returned to the camp for the night. Being in the camp, out over the water was the worst possible place they could sit out the storm.

Leah peeled the wrapper off a bar of soap. It was going to be a long night, one she wasn't especially looking forward to.

She picked a small bottle of shampoo then stepped into the shower. The hot water felt like heaven as it sluiced over her head and body. She'd just lathered up her hair when she suddenly froze.

Of all the things they had purchased that day, the one thing she'd forgotten to buy was a nightgown... She'd started to buy one when she'd been picking out clothes, but she'd figured she'd just continue wearing the T-shirt and save a few pennies. She groaned. Of course at the time she hadn't planned on having to share a room with Hunter.

Leah rinsed out the shampoo. The thought of sharing a room with Hunter shouldn't bother her. After all, they were married, and they'd shared much more than just a room and a bed.

Leah lathered up her hair a second time. So why did it bother her? But even as she asked the question, she already knew the answer. With Hunter being unable to remember anything about their short married life, sharing a room with him would be like sharing it with a stranger.

While Leah was in the shower, Hunter stood by the window, the towel slung around his neck, and stared out at the dark sky and pouring rain. Their room was on the front side of the hotel, and in spite of a couple of oaks, he still had an unobstructed view of the street below. The street was filling with water fast and what little traffic was out had slowed to a crawl. Tree branches whipped and swayed from the force of the wind, and a trash can had blown over and was rolling down the sidewalk.

With one last look at the street below, he walked over to the bed and picked up the package of batteries. He had a funny, uneasy feeling that before this night was over, they were going to need a good flashlight.

He heard the shower cut off, and a few minutes later the whir of the hair dryer. While Leah dried her hair, Hunter put batteries in the flashlight, watched the weather at least three times and checked the street below more times than he cared to count. And still that restless, uneasy feeling persisted.

So what was the problem? Why couldn't he sit still longer than a couple of minutes at a time? And why did he feel as if any minute he was going to jump out of his skin.

Hunter stared at the two double beds. The one Leah had claimed was still neat, the bedspread smooth, with only her knapsack on top. The cover on the one he'd claimed was wrinkled, the pillows bunched up, and all his stuff strewn on top.

He walked back to the window. The mess on his bed wasn't what was bothering him though, he finally admitted as he stared at the rising water in the street. And though he was concerned about the storm, it wasn't the root of his problem either. It was what would happen later, once it was bedtime, that was eating away at him.

Visions of Leah asleep that morning, wearing nothing but a T-shirt, played through his head. Then he thought of the other visions he'd had of her, the ones while he was being held prisoner in the hospital.

Hunter began pacing the length of the hotel room. He might not remember their time together as man and wife, and he might not want to admit that he desired Leah because of the lies she'd told him, but just the thought of sleeping in the same room with her was driving him crazy.

Like it or not, he did desire her. And like it or not, he was beginning to have a healthy respect for her in spite of her secrets. She was intelligent and easy to talk to. She had also proved to be resourceful and thrifty. And except for mentioning that her feet were swollen and the one time she'd admitted to being tired, she'd been a real trooper, considering the circumstances.

Hunter heard the dryer cut off, and he gathered up a clean set of clothes. Maybe a cold shower would put things in prospective. Maybe, but it was doubtful. A cold shower was only a temporary fix for what was bothering him, a mere Band-Aid for what he feared was a mortal wound that could bleed him dry.

When Leah emerged from the bathroom, Hunter was standing near the window, staring out at the swaying trees and blinding rain beyond.

"Your turn," she said. She walked over to the window. "It will be dark soon. If it's okay with you, I think I'll order up room service now, just in case the electricity goes off later."

When Hunter turned away from the window and faced her, she was keenly aware of his scrutiny and the look of approval in his eyes. She didn't need Hunter's approval, but knowing he did approve made her glad that she'd taken extra time to fix her hair.

Then, without warning, almost as if he'd turned off the switch to his emotions, his expression changed and a look of withdrawal came over his face. "I think ordering some food is a good idea," he said evenly.

"Any preferences?" she asked.

Hunter shook his head and headed for the bathroom. "Not really," he called over his shoulder. "A hamburger, fries and a soda are fine with me, but feel free to order whatever you want." Hunter went inside the bathroom and closed the door.

A moment later, Leah heard water running from the sink. For the short time she'd known Hunter she'd learned he was a creature of habit when it came to personal hygiene. Rarely did his routine vary. First he brushed his teeth. After brushing his teeth, he shaved. And only after he'd shaved did he finally shower and dress.

From the familiar noises coming from the bathroom, she was fairly sure that he still followed the same routine. That he did so was a small thing, a silly thing to even think about, but Leah found a bit of comfort and hope in it, knowing that his loss of memory hadn't affected this one particular area of his life.

With her ears still tuned to the sounds from the bathroom, Leah draped her damp clothes over a chair, then went to the phone and placed their room-service order—hamburgers, fries, a soft drink for Hunter, and a glass of milk for herself.

As she hung up the receiver, she glanced around the room. The top of Hunter's bed was a mess. She stepped over to the bed, and though she had intentions of straightening it, she hesitated.

Would he mind? she wondered. Or would he view her actions as an invasion of his space, his privacy? Before his so-called death, there had been only a few times that she'd had to clean up after him, mostly because during those first few weeks, he'd taken on the role of cleaning since she was the one working. But the few times she had cleaned up after him, he'd never complained.

This Hunter might be different though, she reminded herself. This Hunter didn't remember those times, and he might not like her straightening up his belongings.

Deciding against disturbing his stuff, she walked over to the window. What little daylight left was fading fast. Below, a car had stalled, and the driver, with the help of a couple of men, was trying to push the vehicle up onto the sidewalk.

Leah stepped back and eyed the small window. The wind was blowing hard, and though the possibility of anything flying through the window was remote since they were up on the third floor, she pulled the curtain closed anyway. The curtain wouldn't provide much protection, but she figured it was best to take as many precautions as possible.

From the bathroom the sound of the shower being turned on reached Leah's ears. Sudden memories of another time, another place filled her mind, and a delicious and all too familiar surge of longing rippled through her at the thought of Hunter naked with only a door separating them.

Leah stared up at the ceiling. Hindsight might have made her doubt the sanity of marrying Hunter after only knowing him for such a short time, but she'd never once doubted her desire for him.

She'd had a couple of long-term relationships before Hunter, but her feelings for neither of the men had come close to what she'd felt for Hunter. At times, it was as if she were on a runaway train with no way off. All he had to do was look at her in a certain way or touch her...

She squeezed her eyes tightly shut, willing the erotic images to disappear. But closing her eyes only made things worse, made the images even more vivid. Best to get her mind on something else, but what?

She opened her eyes and glanced around the room. When her gaze landed on the television, she snatched up the remote as if it were a lifeline. Settling at the bottom edge of her bed, she flipped through the channels in hopes of finding something—anything—that would take her mind off the overwhelming need to feel Hunter's arms around her, to feel the strength and warmth of his flesh against her own.

She was still channel surfing when she heard the shower stop. Expecting Hunter to emerge at any moment, Leah turned to stare at the bathroom door. She was still staring when the loud rap on the hotel-room door vibrated throughout the room. Leah jumped, and with her heart pounding, she jerked her head around toward the sound.

"Room service," a muffled voice called out from the other side of the door.

Of course, just room service. Leah released her pent-up

breath and pushed herself off the bed. She was almost to the door when Hunter stuck his head out of the bathroom.

"Don't answer that!"

Leah shrugged. "It's just room service."

"You don't know that for sure." He pushed the bathroom door open, and securing the towel wrapped around his hips, he stepped into the bedroom.

"The door—" Leah's breath caught in her throat at the sight of him. Her erotic memories of him were nothing compared to the real thing. He truly was a beautiful specimen of a man from his bare muscular chest down to his feet.

She cleared her throat. "Th-the door has a peephole. I intended to check before I opened it."

"Like you checked before you opened the door to your buddy Henry at the camp?"

Leah felt her face suddenly grow warm with embarrassment. "But—h-how did you know?" she sputtered.

Hunter's expression held a note of mockery. "I didn't know—not for certain—not until just now," he said as he headed straight for the small lamp table that was positioned between the beds. "You gave it away when you wouldn't talk about it," he added. He pulled open the drawer at the top of the table and removed the gun.

"Go into the bathroom and close the door," he ordered. With both hands holding the weapon in front of him, Hunter eased over to the door. He jerked his head forward, toward the bathroom. *"Now!"* he mouthed.

Leah did as he'd asked, but she didn't like it. For one thing, he couldn't pull the trigger on the gun even if he needed to. The most he could do was bluff—bluff and get himself killed. For another thing, she didn't like the fact that he was being so paranoid. First the policeman at the drugstore, and now this.

She entered the bathroom, closed the door and leaned

against it. She also didn't like the fact that he was ordering her around as if she didn't have the sense that God gave a goose.

The bathroom was still steamy from Hunter's shower, and it smelled of soap and his own unique scent. His clothes were folded and stacked on the countertop, a stark reminder that he had on nothing but a towel.

Then she heard muffled voices coming from the room, the clink of dishes, more voices, and finally the sound of a door closing.

A minute later the soft knock on the bathroom door made her jump.

"You can come out now," Hunter told her.

Still miffed about the whole incident, Leah pushed away from the door. Just as she turned and reached for the doorknob, a clap of thunder rumbled through the heavens outside and seemed to go on and on. The whole room felt as if it was vibrating from the force.

Leah froze and fear streaked through her veins. "Tornado," she whispered. Then the lights went out.

Chapter 11

"Leah, just keep still," Hunter called out. "I'll get the flashlight."

Leah had to force herself to answer. "Okay," she said as she stared into the inky darkness, her heart racing. Though the eerie sound was muffled, she could hear sirens, and goose bumps chased up her arms.

Leah breathed deeply to ward off the panicky feeling building within. Her grandmother had told her it was because of the accident that had killed her parents.

Only later, when she was older, had she found out the complete truth about the horrors of that night. While her parents lay dying in the front seat of the smashed car, Leah, only five at the time, had been trapped in the back seat. She'd had to lie there for what seemed like forever—lie there listening to the sirens of the approaching emergency vehicles while firefighters worked furiously, trying to get her and her parents out of the wrecked automobile.

"Open the door and step back," Hunter told her.

Hunter's words jerked her out of the past, but her legs were still trembling when she opened the door and the beam from the flashlight hit her in the face. With the door open, the sirens were even louder.

Leah held her hand up to shade her eyes against the glare of the light.

"Are you okay?"

Hunter's voice sounded strange to her ears, a bit unsteady, as he lowered the beam, but then the sirens grew louder, and all Leah wanted was for the sirens to stop.

"Leah?"

The piercing sounds finally began to fade. "I'm okay," she whispered.

"Here." He handed her the flashlight. He had obviously pulled on a pair of jeans after answering the door. "Shine it over at the table, and I'll get our food. For now, until we find out what's going on, I figure we'll be better off in the bathroom. No windows."

Hunter left but returned within seconds with the food tray. Then he left again to quickly gather up pillows and a blanket off one of the beds.

"Do—do you think it was a tornado?" Leah asked as she tried to steady the beam of light while Hunter arranged the pillows, blanket and tray of food.

"I don't think so," he answered. "But we can't know for sure."

"Too bad we didn't think to buy a battery-operated radio when we bought the flashlight." Leah sat down on one of the pillows then jumped right back up again. "I think there's a way of getting more light," she murmured, staring at the countertop and the mirror on the wall behind it. "Mirror's reflect light." She placed the flashlight on the counter with the beam directed toward the mirror.

"There, that's better, isn't it?"

"Good idea," Hunter agreed.

Concentrating on the light and trying not to think about being closed up in the small room, Leah lowered herself to the pillow. "Maybe we should try to get downstairs, instead of staying here," she suggested.

"Maybe, but why don't we wait a few more minutes and see what happens? I also think we should go ahead and eat before the food gets too cold."

"Ah, I think I'll wait," she hedged, unable to hide her disgust at the thought of eating in the bathroom.

"Suit yourself." He uncovered the tray. "It may not be the best place in the world to eat, but I've seen people eat in worse."

Leah went still as Hunter's words sank in. "You've 'seen people eat in worse places'?" Sudden excitement, like a live wire, raced through Leah. "You've remembered something else!" she exclaimed. "What? Tell me."

Hunter wasn't sure he could tell her. At first the memory had been just a flash, just a brief glimpse of the past. Then, when he'd shone the flashlight on Leah and he'd seen the look of sheer terror in her eyes, the full-blown memory had come rushing back with a vengeance.

For long moments Hunter simply stared at Leah. At least now she had more color in her cheeks and wasn't as pale as before. Having a healthy fear of storms was one thing, but Leah's reaction had been over the top.

"Come on, Hunter," Leah urged. "Maybe if you talk about it, you'll remember other things as well."

Hunter gave her a shrewd look. "If you talk, I will," he responded. "You show me yours, and I'll show you mine."

"Talk about what?" Leah shrugged, and unable to hold his gaze, she cast her eyes downward.

She was stalling. "Come on, Leah. You were scared out of your mind a few minutes ago."

Still she hesitated. Then, finally she took a deep breath and began to talk. When she'd finished telling him about the night her parents died, his insides felt as if he'd swallowed and digested broken glass.

"Is this the first time you've told me about your parents?"

"No," she murmured. "I told you not long after we met."

Hunter's face fell. "And I just made you relive it all again." He shook his head. "I'm sorry."

"It's okay." She shrugged. "You didn't know. But now, it's your turn," she challenged.

Hunter lowered his gaze to the food tray, but he no longer had an appetite. He finally said, "It was that loud clap of thunder that did it. I was a soldier in the first Gulf War. That's all," he lied.

"Not fair," she protested.

Hunter shrugged. "Life's not fair."

Leah's look of raw disappointment weighed heavily on Hunter's conscience, especially after she'd bared her soul to him, not once, but twice now, counting the time he didn't remember. He felt like a heel, but even knowing he'd hurt her, there was no way he could tell her all of what he'd remembered, no way he could talk about that day, not now and maybe not ever.

He'd killed that day, and men around him had been killed. His convoy had been ambushed on their way through one of the many small towns near the Kuwait border. They'd taken out the bad guys, killed every one of the sons of bitches, but it was afterward, after the battle was over, that they found a group of locals, mostly women and children. The bedraggled group had been penned up like animals in a cage made of barbwire. From the looks of them, they were being starved. But it was a particular woman and her baby that had really got to Hunter. The woman had several nasty, festering cuts on her forearm. From the interpreter, he'd learned that she had been cutting herself and letting her baby suck her blood for nourishment to keep the baby alive.

Overhead, the light suddenly flickered, and Hunter gladly relegated the inhuman memories back to the darkest recesses of his mind.

"Come on, baby," he muttered, staring up at the light fixture. "'Let there be light.'"

A moment passed, the lights flickered again, and then the fixture glowed steady, bathing the small bathroom in light. Outside, only the muted sound of the blowing wind and driving rain could be heard.

For several seconds neither of them moved or said a word.

"Thank goodness," Leah finally whispered, blinking to adjust her eyes, and before Hunter could stop her, she sprang up from the pillow and fled to the other room.

Leah immediately turned on the television, and as she clicked through the channels to find a local station, grief and despair tore at her heart. After baring her own soul, something she didn't do lightly, Hunter's refusal to share what he'd remembered hurt. Despite all they'd been through in the last two days, he still didn't trust her. He couldn't have made it clearer if he'd shouted it from the rooftops.

Leah finally found a local station that was giving an update on the storm. "It was a tornado," she murmured as she watched the news camera pan an area that used to be a neighborhood.

Hunter walked out of the bathroom, and Leah glanced his way. Except for his bare feet, he'd finished dressing, she noted, and he was carrying the tray.

"Did you say something?" he asked as he set it on the small table near the windows.

"I said it was a tornado," she told him. "But it didn't touch down. At least not in the city," she added. "Just look at that." She pointed at the television screen. "It touched down on the West Bank before it went over us, and they're saying that it's headed across Lake Pontchartrain for the North Shore."

When the phone suddenly rang, both Hunter and Leah jerked their heads around to stare at it. Since Hunter was closest, he picked up the receiver.

"Hello?" he said, and after a moment, he nodded. "Yeah, we're fine, and the lights are back on now." He listened a moment more, then said, "Yeah, thanks," and hung up the receiver. "Management," he informed her. "They're just checking to make sure everyone is okay."

The hamburgers and fries were cold, and with each passing moment, Leah felt the gulf between her and Hunter widening as they ate and watched the news update.

The storm had moved across the city more quickly than had been predicted, and according to Doppler radar, the brunt of the storm was now hitting the North Shore.

Leah had to force herself to eat. For the baby's sake, she kept telling herself as she fought to keep from gagging with each bite she took.

Hunter motioned at his plate. "Well, I've had better," he grumbled as he polished off the last fry.

Leah had only eaten half of her hamburger and had hardly touched the fries, but she shoved her plate away. "I agree," she said. "I've had enough." She yawned. "I'm going to bed."

Leaving Hunter still sitting at the table, she got up and walked over to the bed. Once she'd pulled back the covers, she glanced over at Hunter.

"Do you mind if I switch off the lamp?"

When Hunter shook his head, she turned off the lamp,

plunging the room into semidarkness except for the glow from the television.

Aware that Hunter was still watching her and feeling as if she was doing a striptease, she turned her back to him and pulled off the capris. The panties she'd bought were full-size and showed even less skin than a bathing suit would have. At least that's what she kept telling herself as she folded the capris and placed them at the foot of the bed.

For a moment Leah paused as she debated what to do about removing her bra. She was so tired that the bathroom seemed like the other side of the world. There was no way she was going to strip half-naked in front of Hunter, but there was no way she was going to sleep in the bra either, she decided.

Feeling more self-conscious with each passing second and glad that Hunter couldn't see her flushed face, she reached up beneath the back of her knit shirt and undid the clasp of the bra. By pulling the straps over her arms through the sleeves of the knit shirt, she was able to divest herself of the garment without ever taking off her top. Throwing the underthing on top of the folded capris, she climbed into bed, crawled beneath the covers and closed her eyes.

As Leah lay there, her eyes closed, she prayed for blessed, oblivious sleep. Outside, the wind had died down and the rain had eased. But inside, even with the drone of noise from the television, she heard every move that Hunter made…the clink of the dishes as he stacked them onto the tray…the rustling noises he made as he cleared his bed…the rasping of his pants zipper as he stripped off his clothes. And finally, the sound of the mattress giving as he climbed into bed.

"Are you asleep, yet?" he asked.

For a moment she was tempted to pretend that she was, but she decided that was childish. "No," she answered. "Not yet."

"Will the television bother you if I leave it on for a while?"

"No," she answered as she snuggled down deeper beneath the covers, searching for the sleep her body craved. Leah heard the exact moment that Hunter began breathing deeply and evenly, a sure sign that he had finally dropped off to sleep.

Knowing that he was asleep, she felt the tension ease from her body, bit by bit, and she was finally able to relax and drift off herself.

For a moment, Leah was disoriented when she awakened in the strange, dark room. Someone else was here with her. Then, just before she panicked, she remembered. She was in a hotel room and Hunter was asleep in the other bed.

Leah frowned. When she'd fallen asleep, the television was still on. Now it was off. Since she didn't remember turning it off during the night, Hunter must have done so.

What time was it? She eased up so that she could see the digital clock on the bedside table. Seven o'clock. Then why was the room still dark? She glanced over at the window. The drapes she'd drawn the night before had to be the room-darkening kind.

Leah slid to the side of the bed nearest the bathroom. If she could just find her pants and bra and get dressed without waking Hunter…she felt around the bottom of the bed until she found the clothes. Although she wasn't showing her pregnancy a lot yet, if he looked close enough, he might realize…

Leah shook her head. She was being paranoid. While her stomach was a bit rounder than normal, the only way he would suspect that she might be pregnant would be if he regained his memory and remembered the night in Orlando, the night of his so-called death. Even so, there was no use tempting fate.

Dismissing the fear, she closed her eyes and tried to form a mental picture of the room. Then she stood and felt her way to the bathroom.

Once inside, she eased the door shut. When the latch clicked, Leah cringed at the loud noise it made. Sending up a prayer that the noise hadn't awakened Hunter, she switched on the light.

Hunter sat straight up in bed, his nerves at full stretch. Straining his eyes and ears for the least movement or sound, he tried to detect the source of the noise. Then he saw the thin line of light beneath the bathroom door.

With a sigh, he released his pent-up breath. Leah. The noise had been made by Leah. With a shake of his head and a sudden craving for a cup of hot coffee, he reached over and switched on the lamp.

Strange, he thought as his gaze landed on the foot of Leah's bed at the empty space where she'd placed her clothes the night before. If they were married, why was she suddenly so shy about dressing and undressing in front of him?

"Women," he muttered. Who could figure them out?

Dragging himself to the edge of the bed, he reached down and grabbed the jeans he'd left on the floor. He stood up, stepped into the jeans and pulled them on. He fastened them, zipped them, then went still. Today was the day he would see Jan Morgan, the LPC.

After a moment, he reached down, snagged his T-shirt and pulled it over his head. Then he walked over to the window and pulled back the curtains.

Daylight flooded the room, and as he stood staring out, once again he tried to analyze why he had such an aversion to seeing someone who might be able to help him. Again he thought about the incident in New York. And again, all he could come up with was that his aversion had to have something to do with that particular time in his life.

Even so, he'd told Leah that he would do what he had to do, and like it or not, he would. As she'd pointed out, the worst that could happen would be that the hypnosis wouldn't work.

The bathroom door opened. "Sorry I woke you," Leah said. "I tried to be quiet."

Hunter shrugged. "No problem." Just as he'd suspected, she was completely dressed. "Right now though I need to get in there." He motioned toward the bathroom. "Then I need a cup of coffee. Some breakfast would taste pretty good, too."

Leah stepped out of the path to the bathroom and Hunter brushed past her. "Do you want me to order room service again?"

Hunter paused at the bathroom door and faced her. "I don't know about you, but I'd rather have my food hot this time. I think it would be safe enough for us to try out that fast-food restaurant near the drugstore we went to yesterday."

Leah nodded. "Sounds good to me, but I'd better call and make sure it's open for business this morning."

Hunter entered the bathroom, and as he'd done the night before when she'd called room service, he listened at the door for a moment until he was sure she was calling the restaurant and not the feds or the police.

He wanted to trust her, but something kept nagging at him. It was just a gut feeling, but he couldn't shake it. *Fool me once, shame on you. Fool me twice, shame on me.* The old saying popped into his mind. She'd lied to him about their relationship, and by trying to check up on him, she'd inadvertently betrayed him. And again there was that constant feeling that there was something else, something he couldn't put his finger on.

Though the sun was shining outside and the streets were no longer flooded, there were leftover reminders of the fierce storm. Broken limbs littered the sidewalk, abandoned and flooded vehicles were being towed away, and several business owners were out cleaning up the trash from in front of their stores.

"What time do we have to be at the doctor's office?" Hunter asked, adjusting his cap and slipping on his sunglasses.

"The office opens at nine." Leah stopped, twisted her hair then shoved it up under her straw hat. Once she'd slipped on her sunglasses they detoured around a huge limb blocking the sidewalk. "I figure that by the time we eat, we can head that way."

The restaurant was more crowded than Leah would have guessed for a weekday morning, and a sudden queasy feeling began building in the pit of her stomach from the smells that assaulted her as they headed toward the counter.

Once they were in line, Hunter turned to Leah. "What do you want to eat?"

Though it didn't happen often, not nearly as often now as the first three months of Leah's pregnancy, at times just a certain smell could trigger a bought of nausea. Had to be the fried hash-browns smell, she decided as she studied the menu above the counter in an attempt to find something that she thought she might keep down.

"Leah," Hunter prompted.

"A small caffeine-free Coke, an order of pancakes and a glass of milk."

Hunter frowned. "A Coke?"

Leah nodded. "An old habit," she lied. "The sugar gets me going," she said, further compounding the lie. The truth was, before she got pregnant, she'd been a coffee fiend. Morning, noon or night, it didn't matter. Now the smell of it before mid-morning could make her gag.

Giving her a strange look, Hunter turned toward the woman behind the counter and placed their order.

An hour later, they were back out on the street.

Hunter wasn't exactly sure what he'd expected, but the huge old house wasn't at all what he'd envisioned. Inside, as

Leah talked to the receptionist, Hunter removed his sunglasses and glanced around the room as he slipped them into his pocket. Though the house was probably close to a hundred years old, the furnishings were contemporary—a couple of sofas and several upholstered chairs.

Hunter eyed the only two other patients in the room, a man and a woman. He dismissed the woman immediately, but something about the man set off a funny tingle at the nape of his neck.

Impossible, he thought. He was just being paranoid. With one last wary look at the man, he turned his attention back to Leah and the receptionist.

The receptionist smiled at Hunter. "I'll need you to fill out these forms." She handed him a clipboard with a pen attached. "Return it to me once you've finished."

With another glance at the man who was thumbing through a magazine, Hunter guided Leah to the opposite side of the room from where the man was sitting. Once they were seated, Hunter stared down at the form, and a sinking feeling of despair settled in his gut. Then, like a kettle building steam, a slow-mounting rage took hold. "Hmmph, this won't take long," he muttered. "Let's see now," he said, keeping his voice low. "Name, Hunter Davis." He wrote his name. "Date of birth. Unknown." He scribbled the word. "Address. Unknown." Again he scribbled the word. "Occupation— hey—" He glance up at Leah. "I can actually put something there. How does wacko, unemployed policeman sound?"

Leah's insides quivered with anger. "Give me that." She snatched the clipboard from him. Hearing him call himself a wacko was too potent a reminder of her own doubts and mistrust, and of her lies. "I'll do it," she snapped. "And don't you ever say something like that again."

Hunter's blue eyes darkened. "But that's what *you* thought, wasn't it?" His voice was quiet, but cold with contempt.

Trying to ignore Hunter, Leah began scribbling down the information needed on the form, supplying her address, phone number and insurance information. But ignoring Hunter was like denying that the sun rose in the east.

"I'm sorry," she whispered, the pen stilling in her hand. "I made a mistake."

"Several," Hunter confirmed.

"Mr. Davis?" the receptionist called out. "If you're through filling out that form, you can go in now," she told him.

Leah grabbed at the chance to end the discussion. "I'll give this to the receptionist," she said as she got to her feet. Without waiting for Hunter's response, she hurried over to the desk and handed the clipboard to the woman.

"Just go through that door into the hall, Mr. Davis," the receptionist instructed as Hunter approached the desk. "Turn to your right, and Ms. Morgan's office is the third one on the left."

Leah had assumed that Hunter would go in alone and that she would wait in the reception area. As she turned to head back to her seat though, Hunter blocked her path.

"I want you to come in with me," he said.

Leah frowned. "I'm not sure they will let me."

"Either they let you or we walk out. Besides, you *are* my wife, aren't you?"

Leah nodded slowly. She wanted to ask why he was insisting that she go with him, but deep down she already knew why. The sad and painful truth was that he didn't trust her out of his sight.

Not wanting anyone to overhear her, Leah lowered her voice. "I know you don't trust me," she told him. "But if I was going to betray you, I could have already done it several times. I could have easily sneaked out that night at the camp, or even last night, once you went to sleep."

Hunter's steely gaze was unwavering. "You just think you could have sneaked out."

His soft words sent a chill down her spine.

"Now, are you coming, or do we leave?"

"I'm coming," she whispered, aware once again that she was in a lose-lose situation. If he regained his memory, he would remember the night in Orlando and the pregnancy test he'd gone to the drugstore to buy. But then he'd also know that she'd lied again. Either way she could lose him forever.

Jan Morgan was a tall, slim woman who, Leah guessed, was probably in her midforties. Though not beautiful, she was an attractive woman with a kind face.

She shook Leah's hand then she shook Hunter's hand. "Hi, I'm Jan Morgan."

Her voice was soft and melodic, easy on the ears, and Leah could easily believe that she could use that voice to hypnotize.

"I take it that you want your wife to sit in on our session," the counselor said, directing her remarks to Hunter.

When Hunter nodded, she smiled. "Okay, then let's get started." She motioned toward a chair that resembled an overstuffed recliner. "Why don't you sit there, Hunter?" She turned to Leah. "And you can sit over there." She motioned toward a sofa alongside a wall behind the recliner.

"Why don't we begin by you telling me why you're here and what you hope to gain?"

When Hunter hesitated, she said, "Just take your time."

Hunter sighed. "I have to tell you right up front that I have my doubts about this whole thing."

The counselor nodded. "That's understandable. Many of my patients feel the same way in the beginning. And I'll be honest with you, hypnosis therapy isn't an exact science. It may or may not have the results you're looking for. But there's only one way to find out."

Hunter stared at her thoughtfully, then finally nodded. "I

like that you're at least honest and not trying to pull my chains."

Jan laughed. "I've found that honesty is always best. It's the most important part of any relationship, especially a counselor-patient relationship."

Leah felt her cheeks suddenly grow warm. Along with love and trust, honesty was also one of the most important elements of a marriage. Maybe if she'd been honest to begin with… She lowered her gaze and stared at her hands. *Too late now. Too late…too late…*and as the silent, condemning words echoed through her mind, Hunter finally began talking.

But Hunter's words were a blur. While he gave the counselor an abbreviated version of what had happened to him, leaving out the part where he thought he'd been held prisoner in the hospital, Leah swallowed hard and fought against the threat of tears that stung her eyes.

By the time Hunter had finished, she felt a bit more in control again. The counselor was talking, explaining exactly what she intended on doing during the rest of the session, and Leah listened with fascination and interest.

"What I'm hoping will work for you is called present-life regression. That simply means that once you're under hypnosis, we will try to go back to a point in your life we can use as a reference, preferably a more pleasant time. However, I will caution you that it's possible that you won't see anything during this first session. Some describe the session as observing themselves as if they were watching television, and others describe it as if they are actually living in the experience.

"The first thing we need to do is get you to relax."

Leah watched Hunter closely as Jan took him through a breathing exercise, then a visualization exercise. When she began asking Hunter questions though, to Leah's acute disappointment, he didn't answer. But still, the counselor persisted in her soft soothing voice for several more minutes. And still, Hunter remained unresponsive.

"Now, Hunter, I don't want you to be discouraged," the counselor told him as they prepared to leave. "Your memory will return—I'm sure of it. It's just going to take time. I'd like to see you again in about a week. You can make an appointment with the receptionist on your way out."

So much for hypnotherapy, Leah thought as she forced a smile, murmured "thanks" and shook the counselor's hand. Hunter had agreed, albeit begrudgingly, to this one session, and it was highly unlikely that he'd ever agree to another one.

Leah walked into the hallway, and behind her, Hunter pulled the office door closed. When she turned to go back to the reception area, Hunter quickly stepped in front of her.

"Wait."

Leah frowned. "What's wrong?"

"I think we should find another way out," he said.

The look in Hunter's eyes sent a sudden wave of fear sweeping through her. If she'd learned nothing else over the past two days, she'd learned that Hunter's instincts were, for the most part, right on.

Leah nodded. "But how?" she whispered as she followed him down the hall, away from the reception area. "How did they find us, and how did you know?"

"There's got to be a back door to this place," he muttered, ignoring her question. He turned down another hallway. "There—" He pointed to the Exit sign two doors down. But when they reached the door, he grabbed her arm and stepped between her and the door. "Hold up a minute," he told her. "If they've got the front staked out, there's no way they'd leave the back door open."

Leah held her breath as Hunter eased the door open just

wide enough to get a peek outside. "Dammit to hell," he said, quickly pulling the door shut again.

"What? What's wrong?"

"We're trapped," he said.

Chapter 12

"Do you think it's the shooters or the FBI?"

"Since there's a big black SUV parked out there, my guess is that it's the shooters."

Leah's stomach knotted. "You never did say how you knew they were there in the first place."

Hunter shrugged. "It was just a feeling. Something about that man in the reception area. He was wearing a sports coat, but it had a conspicuous bulge near his arm that made me think he was packing. Regardless, right now, we've got to find a way out."

"Maybe there's another exit," Leah offered. "There are several doctors in this building. Maybe one of them has a private entrance."

"Maybe," he said. "But there's no way to know for sure. I say we find a nice big window to climb out of. Either that or find a hiding place to hole up in till they get tired of waiting. Of course, I could try and bluff our way out."

When Hunter reached behind his back beneath his shirt,

Leah grabbed his arm before he could pull out the gun he'd tucked away in the waistband of his jeans.

"Don't," she said. "I'd rather climb out a window." She paused, and as Hunter slowly lowered his arm, her mind raced as she tried to think of other possibilities.

"Maybe," she finally murmured as one particular idea began to take shape. "Just maybe there's another way."

"Okay, let's hear it, because I'm fresh out."

"How many men did you see out back?"

"Only one," he answered. "But there could be more," he added.

"Yeah, well, even if there are more, my plan might still work. What if Ms. Morgan placed a call to the police to complain about a man lurking out back who's making her patients uncomfortable? And once the police show up—"

"And began questioning him," Hunter interrupted, finishing her thought, "we could walk out and there would be nothing he could do about it with the cops there." He nodded. "That just might work. So, are you up to playing Ms. Morgan?"

"Oh, shoot!" Leah frowned.

"Now what?"

"Wouldn't the cops come in first to talk to the counselor?"

A slow smile pulled at Hunter's lips. "Probably, but not if you told them—not if *she* told them that she had to leave for some reason. And not if she told them to just get the man off the property."

Leah nodded. "Okay. Now all we need is a phone."

Hunter narrowed his eyes. "I think I saw an empty office down the other hall. Let's try that one first."

Moments later they cautiously stepped inside the empty office. "Wonder who this one belongs to?" Leah said.

"Doesn't look like it belongs to anyone," Hunter commented as he closed the door and switched on the overhead light. "Except for the phone, that desk is as clean as a whistle. Let's just hope the phone works." He walked over to the desk and picked up the receiver. "It's got a dial tone." He dropped the receiver back onto the phone.

Leah began opening drawers in the desk. "If there's a phone there's got to be a phone directory." She finally located the directory in the bottom drawer. "Okay," she murmured as she thumbed through it until she found what she was looking for.

She drew in a deep breath. "Here goes nothing." She picked up the receiver and tapped out the number to the Sixth Precinct police station. When the call was answered, she said, "Hi, this is Jan Morgan. I'm an associate of Dr. Ted Stone, and we've got a problem over here at his offices."

As Hunter listened to Leah pretending to be Jan Morgan, he had to wonder how many other lies she'd told. She was certainly good at it. If he didn't know better, he'd be inclined to believe she was the real deal on the phone. But he did know better.

He wanted to trust her, wanted to believe in her, but he still couldn't shake the feeling that there was something that she hadn't told him, something important that she'd held back.

"Okay, that should do it," Leah said as she hung up.

Hunter tilted his head toward the door. "Let's go take a look."

Back at the exit, Hunter checked, waited a few minutes then checked again. The third time he sneaked a look outside, a patrol car pulled into the back parking lot. "The cops are here," he said. "But let's give it a minute more."

After a moment, he looked at Leah. "Ready?"

When she nodded, he said, "Stay close, and keep walking. We're going to head in the opposite direction, away from the hotel, then we'll double back. And if things go south and we get separated, then stay low and run like hell. We'll meet back at the hotel."

Two policemen were questioning the shooter when Hunter and Leah stepped out the door. Hunter slipped on his sunglasses, and when he placed his hand at the small of Leah's back, he could feel her shivering with fright. "Easy now," he murmured. "Just take it nice and easy."

The shooter was facing them and the two policemen only gave them a brief glance. Hunter made sure that they kept their distance, but as they walked behind the policemen, the shooter glared at them, his face a picture of disbelief, rage and frustration.

When Hunter glanced over his shoulder and saw that the shooter was still glaring at them, he couldn't resist. He lowered his left arm behind his back, and fisting all his fingers except the middle one, he flipped the shooter the bird.

Hunter didn't think that Leah had noticed what he'd done until she suddenly elbowed him hard in the side. "Hey, what's that for?"

She glanced up at him and rolled her eyes. "As if you didn't know," she retorted. "My grandm'ere always told me that you never taunt a tiger in a cage 'cause he might find a way out and eat you."

Hunter grinned. "Sounds like good advice, but—"

"Yeah, yeah, I know," she scoffed, a trace of laughter in her voice. "But you just couldn't resist."

With each step that took them farther away from the doctor's office, Leah felt the tight knot in her stomach loosen. They had kept a steady pace, fast-walking down the street in front of the old house, and then they had cut over a block and doubled back toward the hotel.

As they walked along in silence, Leah tried to puzzle out the situation they had just escaped from. Just as they approached the hotel entrance, she finally gave up. "How did they find us? I figure it had to have something to do with the calls I made."

"You're probably right. They must have put a tap on your supervisor's phone, just in case you called in. Once you asked for your doctor friend's number, I guess they put two and two together then staked out the place to wait for us to show up."

Leah shivered. "It's enough to make a person want to crawl in a hole somewhere and never come out."

Hunter held the door for Leah, and they entered the hotel. "No way I'm crawling in a hole," he vowed. "Like I said before, I think the answers and the key to my memory are back in Orlando."

Leah swallowed hard as they waited for the elevator. "If you go, I go."

When they stepped inside the car and Hunter released a huge sigh, Leah knew that she had her work cut out for her if she was going to convince Hunter that she should go with him. She could either go with him or tell him about the baby, but she knew deep in her gut that she couldn't have it both ways. Once he learned she was pregnant, there was no way he'd let her go with him. He would think it way too dangerous.

"Looks like the maid came while we were gone," Leah murmured, noting that the beds had been made.

"Yeah, well, I want us to be out of here before checkout time," Hunter said as he began shoving his stuff into his knapsack. "So pack your things."

Knowing the battle had begun Leah faced Hunter and placed her hands on her hips. "And then what?"

Hunter zipped the duffel bag. "Then we need to think of somewhere you can stay for a while, just until I get this mess straightened out."

"No!" She shook her head emphatically.

Hunter snapped his head up and glared at her. "What do you mean 'no'?" he said, an edge to his voice.

"I mean no. What part of it don't you understand? Be reasonable. Don't you think if I had somewhere to go, I would have said so before now? I can't go to any of my friends. I can't put them in danger like that. And I can't go to any relatives for the same reason. Besides, I don't have any relatives that are all that close."

Leah swallowed hard and stiffened her spine with determination. Whining was not her style, and neither was begging, but she'd do both if she had to. "I have nowhere to go, Hunter. Nowhere, but with you. Or back to my house."

For long seconds Hunter stared at her with an expression that told her nothing about what he was thinking or feeling. Determined to wait him out, she braced herself and stared right back at him.

Long seconds went by as the tension between them stretched even tighter. Finally, with a sigh, Hunter's lips thinned into a hard line, he closed his eyes, and bowed his head. "You win." He ground the words out between his teeth. After a moment, he opened his eyes and slowly raised his head. "This time," he added with a silken thread of warning in his voice.

Leah released her breath with a whoosh. She'd won, but at what cost? And what did he mean, "this time"?

"I'll get the stuff out of the bathroom," she offered, glad to have an excuse to flee from the dangerous look in his eyes if only for a few minutes.

In the bathroom, Leah took her time gathering the few things they'd purchased at the drugstore. Then, after only a moment's hesitation, she added the new soaps, shampoos and lotions that the maid had left. Arms full, reentered the bedroom. She dumped the stuff on the bed, then, as she picked up Hunter's toothbrush, deodorant and razor, she said, "Guess you'd better keep these with your things." She dropped them beside his knapsack, then turned and began packing the rest with her belongings.

"What? I don't get any shampoo or soap?"

With her cheeks burning, she picked out a bar of soap and a bottle of shampoo, but before she could hand them over, he began laughing. "I was just kidding."

The man was an enigma, a chameleon. "Ha, ha," she told him as she dropped the soap and shampoo on his bed then turned and finished packing.

Hunter picked up the items. "I figure the first thing we need is transportation," he said, slipping the toiletries into a side pocket of his knapsack.

Leah zipped up her knapsack. "I'm not hitchhiking," she said, turning to face him.

"Okay, so any ideas?"

Leah thought a moment, the slowly began to nod. "Maybe." She frowned, her mind racing. "What if we took the bus, but caught it at a station outside of the city? Surely they can't have every bus station between New Orleans and Orlando covered."

Hunter shook his head. "Tricky. I bet they have all the main routes covered. If they were smart they would just have someone riding the route, back and forth. Our taking the bus is too obvious."

Leah grimaced. "So much for that idea." Then, after a moment more, she smiled. "What if I was able to persuade someone to rent a car for us?"

Hunter's dark eyebrows slanted in a suspicious frown. "Who?"

"Christine—Christine Brady. She's a friend of mine who's a nurse, too. We work together."

Leah could tell from Hunter's expression that he was skeptical. She could also tell that he had no recollection of Christine.

"What makes you think this so-called friend of yours would be willing to rent you a car?" he drawled. "And what makes you think she can be trusted?"

Hunter's remarks stung, and Leah stared at him for long seconds trying to decide if he was being sarcastic or if she was simply being overly sensitive because of her guilt about lying to him. Probably because of her own guilt, she decided as grief and despair washed over her. "Because Christine is my friend," she finally answered. Inside, she felt a flutter. Yet another reminder of her duplicity, she thought as she automatically touched her stomach.

"Are you sick?" Hunter stared pointedly at her hand.

Sick at heart, she thought, but she swallowed hard and shook her head. "No. Just hungry I guess." Yet another lie. Eager to divert Hunter's attention from her stomach, she reached for the phone. "Unless you object, I'm calling Christine."

When Hunter offered no response, she tapped out her friend's home phone number. She was pretty sure that Christine was working the graveyard shift and should be home.

On the fourth ring, Christine answered with a sleepy. "Hello."

Leah cleared her throat. "Christine, I need a big favor."

"Leah? For Pete's sake, where have you been, girl? Margaret's been throwing hissy fits trying to get in touch with you."

"I know, I know," Leah murmured. "I talked to her earlier and I'm really sorry about this, but I'm in a bind."

"Sounds serious. Are you okay? The baby okay?"

At the mention of her baby, Leah glanced at Hunter and felt her cheeks grow warm. "Everything's okay," she answered, avoiding any specific reference. "I've just got a problem that I can't go into at the moment. What I need is to rent a car, but my credit card is maxed out. I've got the money—cash—but I can't rent a car without a credit card."

"What's wrong with your car? You didn't have a wreck, did you?"

"No—nothing like that. Oh, Christine, it's a long story that I can't go into right now, but I promise, I'll fill you in as soon as I can."

"Listen, girl, you're scare'n me. Are you in some kind of trouble?"

Leah hesitated, unsure how much would be safe to tell her friend. Then she thought of the shooters and the dirty FBI agent. "Nothing I can talk about right now, but if you could rent a car for me, I would be forever grateful."

For long seconds there was only the hum of the telephone line in Leah's ear. Then, finally, she heard Christine sigh. "Okay, but just promise me you aren't in any kind of trouble."

"I'm not." Yet another lie, thought Leah, but a necessary one. The less Christine knew, the better off and the safer her friend would be. "How soon could you do it?" she asked.

"Not until tomorrow morning. I'm working a double shift tonight."

Leah glanced over at Hunter. "Not until tomorrow morning," she repeated for Hunter's information. When Hunter rolled his eyes and then shrugged, Leah said, "Guess that will have to do, and thanks." Leah paused. She didn't want to tell her friend about the FBI or the shooters, but she did need to warn her some way. "Ah, one more thing. Please don't tell anyone that you talked to me. No one," she emphasized.

"I knew it! I just knew it. You *are* in trouble."

"Like I said, nothing that I can talk about right now. And nothing I can't handle," she added.

"Sounds like big trouble to me."

"Please," Leah whispered. "Just trust me on this."

"I don't like this. No siree, I don't like the sounds of this one bit."

Leah slowly began to relax. From the tone of Christine's voice, she could tell that her friend was giving in. "Please," she whispered.

"Oh, okay. Why not? But I'd better not end up in jail because of this."

Words of reassurance stuck in Leah's throat and guilt washed through her. If the shooters found out that Christine had helped them, jail would be the least of her problems. Leah willed herself to keep calm. "It's nothing illegal, I promise. Now could you bring the car to the zoo?"

After Leah and Christine had agreed on a time, Leah hung up. "We're supposed to meet her in front of the zoo around ten tomorrow morning." Leah eyed the knapsacks they had packed. "Guess that means we stay here another night."

Hunter glanced at the knapsacks, then at the clock on the bedside table. When his gaze strayed back to the knapsacks and the bed that Leah was sitting on, the same restless feeling he'd experienced the night before came over him with a vengeance, the same sensation that made him feel as if he was going to jump out of his skin. But this time he knew the source of his unrest, and he also knew that there was no way he could stay pinned up in the small hotel room all afternoon and all night with Leah, not without going out of his mind. He needed to get out, to get away from her, if only for a little while.

His eyes caught and held hers. "You said you were hungry?"

Leah nodded.

"How about something to eat?"

Leah shifted on the bed. "You want to order room service again?"

Hunter shook his head. "No, I thought I'd go out and get us something."

Leah suddenly looked uncomfortable, and when she

shifted on the bed again, for a disappointing moment he feared that she was going to insist on going with him. "And I don't have to go?"

"No, not unless you want to."

"I don't."

"Okay, so what do you want?"

"What I'd really like is an oyster po'boy—dressed."

Hunter frowned. "Dressed?"

A smile pulled at her lips. "All that means is that I want all the fixings—lettuce, tomatoes and mayonnaise."

"I take it that a po'boy is some kind of sandwich then."

"Yes, but instead of regular bread or a bun, it's made with French bread."

"An oyster po'boy dressed," he repeated. "Anything else? Something to drink?"

Leah hesitated then nodded. "Milk to drink, and bread pudding for dessert."

"Any suggestions where I should go?"

When Leah's lips curled into a grin, and a devilish look sparkled in her eyes, Hunter knew he'd made a mistake. He held up a hand. "Don't answer that." Then, because he couldn't help himself, because the look on her face was doing funny things to his insides, he laughed.

"Left yourself wide open with that one," Leah snickered.

"Okay, so where is a good place to get the food?"

Still smiling, Leah said, "When you leave the hotel, go right about two blocks. I can't remember the name offhand, but there's a small diner along there that makes a pretty good po'boy."

Hunter nodded, pulled on his cap and headed for the door, then hesitated. What if something happened to him? What if, for some reason, the shooters caught up with him? He shoved his hand down inside his pants pocket and pulled out the roll of money he'd taken from the shooter.

Hunter counted out half the money, walked back to Leah, then held out the money.. "Take this," he said. "Just in case something happens and I can't get back."

Leah jerked backward as if she'd been slapped, then she shook her head violently. "No!" she said between clenched teeth. "Nothing is going to happen."

The desperation in her voice, along with the look of terror in her eyes, brought him up short. And for the first time since he'd found out that she'd lied to him about their relationship, that she'd made the call that had brought the feds down on him, he wondered if he'd been mistaken about her. Maybe she really did care what happened to him. But if she cared, why not tell him everything? Hunter sighed with frustration. "I'll be back. I promise." He dropped the money on the bed, then turned and left the room.

At first Leah was too stunned to move as she watched Hunter walk out the door and pull it shut behind him. But the finality of the automatic lock clicking into place spurred her into action. She couldn't let him go. If she let him go it would happen all over again.

She jumped off the bed and ran to the door. But hesitated as she reached for the knob. *You're overreacting,* a tiny voice of reason whispered in her ear. *Just because Hunter had said the same words the night he'd left her in the Orlando hotel room didn't mean that he wouldn't come back this time.*

Still, Leah took several deep breaths, then forced herself to turn around and walk back to the bed. "He will come back," she murmured. "He will come back."

With a trembling hand, she yanked back the bedcovers and climbed in between them, and pulled them up to her chin. Beneath the covers, she curled into a fetal position and shivered. Cold, she was so cold.

Though she kept telling herself that Hunter didn't realize

what he had done, what he'd said, she still couldn't shake the feeling of déjà vu.

Leah squeezed her eyes tightly shut as if doing so would vanquish the terror of that night four months ago. Just before he'd left to go to the drugstore, he had divided the money in his pocket, handed it to her and had said, "Just in case." Then, just as he'd walked out the door, he said, "I'll be back."

Leah opened her eyes. But he hadn't come back.

This time would be different though, she kept trying to re-assure herself. This time he would come back. This time he wouldn't die. So why couldn't she stop shivering?

Ten minutes later, Leah was still hovering beneath the covers and staring at the digital clock. At least she'd finally stopped shivering. Another minute went by, and again she told herself that nothing would happen to him this time. Hunter would come back. But in a trance, she watched each agonizing minute flick by on the clock.

She had estimated that it would take Hunter about five minutes at the most to walk to the diner, another fifteen minutes or so to order and receive the food, then five minutes to walk back to the hotel.

The numbers on the clock changed again, the slight click sounding way too loud in the silent room. Thirty minutes had passed, plenty of time for Hunter to walk to the diner, purchase the food and return to the hotel. So where was he? Why wasn't he back yet?

She'd give him five more minutes, she decided.

Then what?

Leah suddenly threw back the covers and climbed out of bed. "Then what?" she muttered mockingly. "Not this time," she whispered fiercely. This time she wouldn't sit around and wait for the knock on the door, for the police to come and tell her that he'd had an accident, that he was dead. This time she'd go looking for him.

Leah began pacing the bedroom. Two more minutes passed…three minutes…four minutes.

"Enough," she whispered, and snatching up her purse, she stomped toward the door. Just as she reached for the knob, a loud knock sounded. Leah yanked her hand back as if she'd just touched a hot iron.

It was happening again…Hunter leaving…the knock on the door…the police… Just like the last time.

"No," she whispered, shaking her head from side to side. "Please, no."

Chapter 13

"Leah, let me in."

A moment passed before it registered that the muffled voice on the other side of the door was Hunter and not the police. Leah took a deep breath, then let it out. Ever so slowly, the built-up tension drained out of her.

The knock sounded again, and she jumped.

"Leah, open the door."

Her hand trembling, Leah grabbed the doorknob, twisted, and opened the door.

"I forgot my room key," Hunter said. In his arms was a large paper sack.

Leah stepped back and Hunter entered the room. The moment the smell of fried seafood reached her nostrils, her traitorous stomach rebelled. She shoved the door shut and fled to the bathroom. Once inside, she dropped her purse on the floor, eyed the toilet, then turned on the faucet and splashed cold water on her face.

The last thing she needed or wanted was to throw up. Being pregnant had heightened all her senses. Not only did certain smells set her off, but her emotions were off balance as well, and the two combined were a sure recipe for disaster.

Leah swallowed back the bile that kept rising in her throat and continued splashing cold water on her face.

"My God, you're as pale as a ghost. Are you okay?"

She glanced toward the doorway where Hunter was standing, staring at her, his expression one of worry and concern. "Upset stomach after all," she managed to mumble, then splashed more water on her face. "Probably a virus. Or all of this stress." Not a total lie, she thought, cringing.

Leah heard movement behind her. "Here." Hunter handed her a washcloth.

"Thanks," she whispered. Once she'd wet the washcloth and wrung it out, she held it over her face. Even without seeing Hunter, she could feel his presence next to her.

"When I first came out of the coma," he said, "I stayed nauseated a lot. The nurses would put wet washcloths over my throat. They said doing so would help sometimes. But I guess you already know that."

Leah nodded.

"Maybe if you would just lie down for a while…" His voice trailed away.

"I—I think I will," Leah said as she lowered the washcloth. Wetting it one more time, she turned off the faucet and wrung out the washcloth.

"Here, let me help you."

Before she realized what was happening, Hunter turned her toward him and swung her up into his arms. She probably should protest, she thought, but the sympathetic tone of his voice, added to the warmth and strength of his arms, had paralyzed her tongue, and for the life of her, she couldn't utter a sound.

Leah closed her eyes and savored the feel of being wrapped in Hunter's arms, savored the sound of his strong heartbeat next to her ear. There had been too many long lonely nights when she had ached for his touch, ached for the comforting feel of his body next to hers.

Too soon, the brief contact was broken as he gently lowered her onto the bed. Leah gripped the washcloth tighter to keep from reaching out and pulling him down beside her.

"Just take it easy for a while," he said soothingly as he pulled the washcloth out of her hands and placed it on her neck.

"Thanks," she whispered hoarsely staring up at him. His eyes had darkened almost to navy, a sure sign that their closeness had effected him as well.

There was still hope, she thought as she closed her eyes.

Shifting onto her side, Leah pulled her knees up against her stomach. And as she lay there, listening to him moving around the room, all she wanted was to escape, to sink into the blessed oblivion of sleep, so she wouldn't have to think about the pain of the last four months, and the possibility of a future without Hunter.

As quietly as he could, Hunter pulled the wrapped sandwiches, his soft drink, Leah's milk and the disposable container full of bread pudding from the sack. Once he'd washed his hands in the bathroom, he settled near the window and unwrapped his sandwich.

As he bit into the oyster po'boy and chewed, his gaze rested on Leah as he thought back over everything that had happened during the last two hours. Something was wrong. To say the least, her reaction had been strange, even before he'd left.

One minute they had been laughing and joking around, and the next...Hunter grimaced and swallowed as he recalled the sudden desperation in her voice, the terror in her eyes. But why? What had caused that desperation and terror?

He took another bite of the sandwich and chewed slowly as he went over everything he'd said and done. All he'd said was...

Hunter suddenly stopped chewing as scenes of another time, another hotel room, flashed through his head. He squeezed his eyes tightly and tried to hold on to the fleeting flashes of memory. But were the scenes actual memories, or were they just imagination?

He swallowed the food in his mouth, and when he felt it sticking in his throat, he grabbed his cola and took several long drinks. The scenes had to be actual memories, he decided. In the scenes, he and Leah had been laughing and joking, just as they had been doing earlier. And in those memory scenes, just as he had done earlier, he'd counted out the money in his pocket and left half of it with Leah.

Just in case...I'll be back.

He'd said the same words to her then that he'd said today. But he hadn't come back then. Hunter sighed heavily, and for the first time since he'd returned to New Orleans, he thought about how Leah must have felt that night in Orlando, thought about the confusion and agony she must have endured when he hadn't returned. No wonder she'd freaked out earlier. No wonder she'd been so upset.

When Leah awoke, the hotel room was dark and quiet except for the muffled sounds of the traffic on the street below. After a moment she realized that she was alone. So where was Hunter?

She eased herself up and glanced at the illuminated dial of the digital clock. It read nine, and Leah frowned. She couldn't believe she'd slept so long.

She reached over and switched on the bedside lamp. Beside the lamp was a note written on a hotel notepad, and she immediately recognized Hunter's scrawled handwriting. She picked up the notepad and read the note.

Leah, have gone down to the hotel bar for a nightcap. Your milk is in the ice bucket, and your sandwich and bread pudding are on the table.

Leah placed the notepad back onto the table, and for long moments she sat staring at Hunter's empty bed. Unbidden, a twinge of irritation swept through her that he'd left her alone in the room. How long had he been gone? she wondered.

Leah slowly climbed out of bed, and guilt quickly replaced the irritation. Instead of being aggravated, she should be grateful that he'd been thoughtful enough to realize that she needed to sleep and not be disturbed. She'd slept for hours, and it would be ridiculous to expect him to just sit there, quietly staring at the four walls. At least down in the bar, he could watch TV.

Leah made a hasty trip to the bathroom, and when she came out, she walked over to the table where Hunter had left her sandwich and bread pudding. Wrinkling her nose, she set the sandwich aside. There was nothing worse than a soggy, cold oyster po'boy. Besides, she had always been wary about food that contained mayonnaise sitting out for any length of time without being refrigerated.

Next to the sandwich was the ice bucket, and inside, a carton of milk floated in a mixture of water and ice. There wasn't much Hunter could have done about preserving the sandwich, but at least he'd had the forethought to make sure that the milk didn't sour.

She pulled out the carton of milk, opened it and took a long drink. Then she eyed the container of bread pudding. The sandwich was probably ruined, but the bread pudding was a different matter.

While she ate the dessert and drank her milk, Leah turned on the television and watched the news. There were more film clips of the devastation left by the storm, but most of the local news centered on a scandal involving a prominent Louisiana politician and his connection to the gambling industry.

"Boring," Leah murmured as she switched the channel and finished the last bite of bread pudding. Once she'd deposited the leftovers in the trash, she channel surfed for several minutes. While flipping through the channels, she thought about joining Hunter in the hotel bar, then changed her mind. Except for an occasional glass of wine, she never had liked to drink that much anyway. Besides, alcohol wasn't good for the baby.

With a shrug, she resumed channel surfing, and after a few minutes, she found a movie that looked as if it might hold her interest.

Leah shifted in the chair. Not the most comfortable type of chair to relax and watch TV, she thought, eyeing her bed. And why not be comfortable?

She walked to the bed then paused and glanced down at the clothes she was wearing. She'd already slept in them once, and since they were wrinkled beyond help anyway, why not use them as pajamas?

"Everything, but the bra," she muttered. Along with her stomach, her breasts were getting larger, too. The moment she unhooked the binding bra, she sighed with relief. Once she removed it, she climbed into bed. First chance she got, she really needed to buy a couple of new bras.

The movie proved to be less interesting than she'd hoped, and as she lay in bed and tried to follow the plot, Leah felt herself growing sleepy again.

As she drifted off, she was vaguely aware of the sound of the door opening and the rustle of clothes as Hunter undressed. Knowing that Hunter was back, safe and sound, she relaxed even more. The last thing she remembered before sleep overcame her was Hunter switching off the television.

When Leah heard the moans coming from Hunter's bed, she was so groggy from sleep that she wasn't sure if they were real or if she was having a nightmare.

Then the moans grew louder, and she realized that they had to be real, that something was wrong. Feeling as if she were swimming against the currents in a river of fog, she fought her way back from sleep to consciousness.

"Jack!" Hunter suddenly cried out. "No! Oh, God, no!" he moaned.

Leah's eyes popped wide open. This was no nightmare, at least not her nightmare. She could hear Hunter thrashing about in the other bed. She forced herself up on one elbow, then reached out and switched on the light. After a moment, her eyes began to adjust.

Hunter moaned again, and as he came into focus, Leah drew in a quick breath. His face was contorted, beads of sweat had popped up on his forehead, and he was jerking his head from side to side.

Leah frowned and scrambled off the bed. Maybe she'd been mistaken. Instead of having a nightmare, maybe he was sick or in pain. All of her nurse instincts kicked into high gear as she eased over to the side of his bed, bent over him and cautiously felt of his forehead. She expected to feel heat from fever and was surprised that he felt cold and clammy to the touch.

She moved her hand down to his wrist and checked his pulse. Too fast. Way too fast. His pulse was racing as if he'd just run a three-minute mile. Leah grabbed hold of his shoulder and shook him. "Hunter, wake up! You're having a nightmare."

He groaned again and jerked his head from side to side as if denying whatever terror he was experiencing.

"Hunter!" she called out. "Wake up!"

Hunter suddenly tensed beneath her grip, gasped for breath, and his eyes snapped open. "What—what's happening?" As he stared up at her, for a moment he had the same blank look in his eyes that she'd seen when she'd found him sleeping on her porch.

"Hunter, it's me, it's Leah," she told him gently. "You were having a nightmare."

The blank look in his eyes slowly faded, and she could tell that he had finally recognized her.

"Leah?" he whispered.

She nodded.

"A nightmare?"

Leah nodded again. "Just a nightmare," she said softly.

Hunter squeezed his eyes shut and shook his head. "Sorry about that."

"No, no, it's okay," she soothed, relieved that he was awake, but even more relieved that he had recognized her. "Would you like to talk about it?"

Her hand was still on his shoulder, and she felt him shudder. Leah's voice softened. "Talking out a nightmare sometimes helps get rid of it once and for all."

"If only that were true," he whispered hoarsely and shuddered again. "Do you think that the same holds true for a memory?"

Leah swallowed hard. He'd said a "memory," but which memory? she wondered. Had the session with Jan Morgan been successful after all?

A feeling of dread washed through Leah, and she couldn't shake the fear that her time with Hunter was running out. Too soon, he would remember everything and her secrets would catch up to her. And she had no guarantee how he would react

You should be ashamed, the tiny voice of her conscience whispered in her ear. In spite of the personal repercussions, for Hunter's sake and for the safety of them both, as well as the safety of their unborn child, he needed to regain his memory. He needed to remember everything.

"I honestly don't know if the same holds true for a memory," she finally answered. "But what I do know is that sharing a memory, whether bad or good, sometimes helps."

As Hunter stared into Leah's dark brown eyes, he detected a glimmer of fear. Though he wondered about the fear, he also saw sympathy and compassion, and he felt it in the gentleness of her touch.

Maybe she was right. Maybe talking about the nightmare to someone like her, someone who seemed genuinely concerned, would help.

"It all started the night I shot that little girl." Hunter's insides shriveled. "Afterward, I—I—" Suddenly unable to put words to the emotions he'd experienced, he shook his head. There were no words strong enough to describe how he'd felt then or how he still felt now. Afterward, when he'd realized what he'd done, he'd broken down and cried like a baby.

Hunter willed the memory to the farthest corner of his brain. "Let's just say I had a hard time with the whole thing."

When Leah eased down and sat on the edge of the bed beside him, he held his breath. Would she remove her hand? Would she sever the contact? He hoped not. He couldn't explain it, but just her touch gave him the courage to keep talking.

Once she'd settled on the bed, she eased the grip she'd had on his shoulder, but left her hand resting there.

Assured that she wouldn't break the contact, Hunter finally breathed again. "Anyway," he continued, "there was an inquiry by Internal Affairs. Thanks to my partner and my captain and after days of endless questions, the rat squad finally exonerated me."

He paused, remembering how Jack had backed him up, and how his captain had raised holy hell until IA had finally given in and closed their investigation. Hunter sighed and went on with the story. "Standard procedure in something like that requires that the officer see a police psychiatrist before he can return to the job."

Hunter grimaced. "Just my luck I drew the one doctor who happened to have a little girl the same age as the one I'd shot."

Hunter's temper suddenly flared just thinking about the woman doctor, but he took a deep breath and willed it under control.

"It didn't take me long to see the writing on the wall and to realize that my doctor had her own agenda." He reached up and pinched the bridge of his nose. "Funny—" he dropped his hand "—before then I'd always thought that head doctors were supposed to be neutral—you know—not biased one way or another. Well, I'm here to tell you it just ain't so. They're just as human as the rest of us. Anyway, I knew enough to complain. But instead of making me see another shrink right away, I was allowed to go back to the job since my squad was shorthanded."

Hunter swallowed hard. "A few days later, Jack and I were called out on a liquor-store robbery. The perp was still in the store when we got there. There was a firefight, and that's when the bottom fell out again. That was the night I found out that I couldn't fire my weapon."

Leah murmured a sound of sympathy, and Hunter continued. "Jack caught a bullet, and the perp got away." Hunter's temper flared again, and he cursed. "All because I couldn't return fire."

He bit off the words, then looked directly into Leah's eyes and willed her to understand. "In my nightmare, I was there again," he said. "Watching everything happen and unable to do a damn thing about it until it was too late. Because of me, my partner almost died that night. After that incident, I requested time off."

Even in the dim lamplight, Hunter knew that the sudden sheen in Leah's eyes was tears; yet another sign of her compassion. The pressure from her hand on his shoulder increased.

"No wonder you didn't want to go to a psychiatrist," she whispered. "You didn't remember then, but your subconscious remembered. And no wonder your session with Jan Morgan didn't work." Leah paused thoughtfully. "Or did it?" she murmured. "Hunter, don't you see? Maybe this nightmare is the beginning of you regaining your memory."

Her enthusiasm was infectious, and Hunter wanted to believe, could almost believe that he was on the verge of gaining back all of his memory. But he'd thought the same thing before and only bits and pieces had returned. "Maybe," he cautiously conceded, and because she seemed so eager for it to be true, he suddenly didn't want to disappoint her.

"You were right about one thing," he said.

When Leah frowned in puzzlement, he explained. "Talking about it did help."

"Oh, Hunter, I'm so glad."

The pleased tone of her voice was so heartfelt and genuine that he felt the barrier of doubt that he'd erected deep inside break loose. He stared into her eyes, trying to convey his sincerity. "Thanks for listening."

She gave him a smile that set his pulse racing. "You're welcome. Anytime."

Hunter sensed that she was about to remove her hand from his shoulder, but the thought of her breaking off even that slight physical contact unsettled him. Before he could change his mind, he reached up and covered her hand with his. "No," he said. "Don't."

A confused look crossed her face, and he shook his head. "Don't go," he whispered. "Not yet," he added. "Stay."

For long, tension-filled moments, neither of them moved, and neither dared to breathe. An array of emotions flitted across Leah's face: surprise followed by wariness, then fear mingled with desire and indecision.

When Leah finally slid her hand up to his cheek and caressed him with a touch that was as light as a butterfly, an aching heaviness settled in his groin. He might not remember most things, but some things a man never forgot.

Again, the vision of her lying naked beneath him flashed through his head, a vision that had been so powerful, he'd risked everything to find her. And yet, he hesitated, torn between his desire for her and the uncertainties that gnawed at his gut.

She leaned closer toward him so close that he could see the tiny flecks of green embedded in the brown depths of her eyes. "Hunter," she whispered, her breath warm against his lips. "I've missed you. Kiss me."

Hunter's heart slammed against his chest. There was no mistaking the blatant invitation in her eyes or the yearning in her voice.

She pulled away from him, reached for the bottom of her T-shirt, then in one bold movement, she took hold of the hem and pulled the garment up over her head. She dropped the shirt on the floor beside the bed, and for a moment, he couldn't move, couldn't breathe as he stared at her.

Her ivory breasts were budded at the tips with pink, and in the soft lamplight they seemed to glow, as if beckoning him. "Beautiful," he whispered hoarsely. "You're so beautiful."

With a ghost of a knowing, satisfied smile tugging at the corners of her lips, she reached for his hand and leaned closer. "Touch me," she whispered again. Her voice invited and pleaded as she guided his hand to her breast.

She was soft, so soft and full beneath his fingers, and as he tested the weight of her breasts then squeezed gently, he groaned deeply in his throat. Her nipple was taut and ripe as he rubbed his thumb back and forth over it, and he couldn't resist. The need to taste her was overpowering. As if she'd read his mind, she arched her back and leaned closer.

His lips grazed the upper swell of her breasts, then moved lower. He flicked his tongue over her nipple, back and forth, until it hardened to a pebble. She tasted sweet and smelled of musky womanhood.

Leah's soft groan of approval made him bolder. He opened his mouth around the tip of her breast and sucked slowly, deeply. Her hands caressed and pulled against the back of his head as she moved away and twisted, urging him to give equal time to her other breast as well. He complied gladly.

"Yes," she moaned. "Oh, yes." She buried her face in his hair and her fingers tightened.

Long moments later, Hunter released her and drew in a ragged breath. Plunging both fingers into her thick hair, he cupped the back of her head and pulled her down toward him, closing the scant few inches that separated them. When his hungry mouth claimed hers, her lips were soft, warm and more responsive than he could have imagined. The taste of her was as sweet as honey. Then she moaned and arched toward him, and his iron control snapped.

Quickly but gently, he reversed their positions until she was the one lying in the bed and he was sitting beside her. Giving her small nipping kisses from her earlobe down to her neck, he tugged off her panties. Then Hunter stood, and as he slid off his shorts, his eyes devoured her. Her hair was a fiery halo spread out against the white pillowcase. Her breasts heaved with every breath she drew. His gaze traveled farther down over the slightly round mound of her stomach to the apex of her legs. Farther down, her legs were shapely and moved restlessly against the sheet.

Leisurely, savoring the way her eyes followed his every move, Hunter lowered himself to the bed beside her. Ever so gently, he tantalized and teased her with his fingers, sliding them over her breasts, down her stomach and farther. She was warm and moist and ready.

When he tasted her sweet mouth again, she moaned out her need and arched upward toward him. Her hands clawed at him, pulling, begging. Unable to deny either of them any longer, he moved quickly over her, and with one sure surge buried himself deep within her.

For agonizing seconds he held back. Then she wrapped her legs around him, drawing him in deeper. Her restless hands moved down his back, pressing against his buttocks. She pushed upward with her hips, urging him to complete what he'd started.

Hunter had no choice; he lost control. His hungry mouth claimed hers as he withdrew and thrust deeply. A moan of mutual satisfaction vibrated between them. He thrust again and again, building and building more momentum like the flames of a raging fire devouring everything in its path until nothing was left but warm, glowing embers.

Afterward, Leah was still trembling but too spent to move as Hunter eased off her and lay beside her. But the moment was bittersweet as she listened to Hunter's heavy breathing. Consciously, he still didn't remember her or how it had been between them, didn't remember the love they had shared. But she took solace in the fact that his subconscious remembered…and her own body had remembered as well.

Leah closed her eyes and savored the boneless, satiated feeling. All too soon she would have to face the reality of their situation. But for now, for just a little while longer, she wanted to pretend that the last four months had never happened. She wanted to pretend that men weren't trying to hunt them down to kill them, and she wanted to pretend that they were still in love, still looking forward to a bright future together.

"Was it like that before?"

Hunter's question jerked her back to reality. Leah was pretty sure that she knew exactly what he was asking. But she wanted to make certain. "Was what like that?" she asked.

"The sex," he answered. "Was it always so—so intense?"

"Yes…always," she whispered. "Every time."

As Leah waited for him to say more, she tensed. When the silence between them stretched over several moments, she began to feel the chill of the air-conditioned room on her naked body, and her misgivings increased with each passing minute.

Uneasiness and confusion seeped in the longer he kept silent, and she suddenly wasn't sure what to do next. Maybe he was expecting her to say more, but what more could she say? Or maybe he was waiting for her to move to the other bed. Earlier he'd asked her to stay. Did he still want her in his bed?

There was only one way to find out, she decided. With every intention of moving to the other bed, she turned over onto her side. But just as she was about to push herself up, Hunter reached out and pulled her back against him, then covered them both with the sheet and blanket.

With her back against his warm chest and his arms around her, Leah sighed contentedly. Actions spoke louder than words, didn't they? Tomorrow, with all of its worries and dangers would come all too soon, but for tonight, she would pretend just a little bit longer.

Once Leah had settled back into his arms, Hunter breathed in the musky scent of her. He could feel her soft hair against his cheek, her silky skin beneath his fingers. But as he stared into the darkness, her answer kept echoing throughout his mind... Always... Every time...

Could he believe her? Had she been telling the truth, or had she simply told him what she thought he wanted to hear? Without his memory she could tell him anything, and there was no way of proving or disproving what she said.

Lord help him, he wanted to believe her, wanted to believe that everything she'd done from the beginning was justified. With every ounce of his being he wanted to trust her. But still there was that gut feeling that she was holding something back?

Hunter squeezed his eyes tightly shut and silently cursed his traitorous body for asking her to stay, for making love to her, and for being unable to let her return to the other bed.

He didn't know what or who to believe anymore. But he did know that he'd just made a huge mistake. It would have been better all around if he'd kept his distance.

Leah moved slightly, and Hunter sighed. With her warm body pressed against his, it was hard to even think straight. He'd worry about the rest tomorrow.

When Leah awoke, she immediately sensed that she was alone in the bed. Had it all been a dream? Had she really made love to Hunter, then slept in his arms throughout the night?

Though she could hear the shower running, all of her uncertainties and fears returned with a vengeance. For weeks after she'd returned home from Orlando, her dreams had been filled with Hunter. In her dreams, he'd made love to her, had held her throughout the night. Then, with the harsh daylight of the morning, cold reality would return. Once again she would have to face the fact that she was alone.

As if to reassure herself that this wasn't a dream, she reached out beside her. The bed was still warm from Hunter's body.

Leah pushed herself up and smiled as her muscles protested. Not only was the bed still warm, but she had other physical proof as well.

What she needed was a good hot shower. She glanced at the clock. They had a couple of hours before they were to meet Christine, plenty of time for a shower and breakfast. And for a change, she was hungry.

In the bathroom the shower cut off, and Leah was suddenly self-consciously aware of being naked, and pregnant. Making love in the pale lamplight during the middle of the night was one thing. Hunter had been so caught up in their love-making that she doubted he'd even noticed her stomach at all. And if he had, there was no way he would have known that the roundness was because she was pregnant, especially since he didn't remember how thin she'd been before his accident. But Hunter looking at her nude body in broad daylight was something else altogether. He wasn't a stupid man. Far from it.

Leah stared uneasily at the bathroom door, and no matter how hard she tried, she couldn't shake the feeling that her secret was about to blow up in her face.

Chapter 14

Hunter switched off the shower and wondered if Leah was awake yet. In spite of his doubts about her and in spite of being unable to remember her, he couldn't deny that making love to her had been an incredible experience.

He grabbed a towel and dried himself off. It had felt right, felt familiar somehow, so why the hell couldn't he remember her or their brief marriage?

Hunter frowned as he slung the towel over the shower-curtain rod and reached for his jeans. He was certain that the nagging feeling in the pit of his gut was because he'd missed something, something important about Leah that was tied to their marriage.

Paranoia, he decided as he stepped into his jeans, then snapped and zipped them. He was being paranoid, but after all that had happened to him, how could he not be paranoid?

Hunter grabbed the knit shirt and pulled it over his head. Once he got to Orlando, and retraced his steps there, he'd remember what had happened. Then he'd know why someone wanted him dead. And maybe, just maybe, he'd also remember Leah and what it was about her that kept nagging at him.

Hunter combed his hair then gathered his toothbrush and razor. Right now, though, he had to get through the first few awkward minutes of coming face-to-face with her in broad daylight.

When Hunter came out of the bathroom, Leah was standing near the window, staring out at the street below. He frowned. Why the devil was she wrapped up like a mummy in the bedsheet?

Leah turned away from the window and faced him. When she saw him staring at the sheet, she shrugged. "I was cold," she explained, answering his unspoken question. "And I didn't want to dress without taking a shower first."

She walked to the bed and picked up a stack of neatly folded clothes. As she walked past him, she paused and tilted her head upward. "And by the way, good morning." Without waiting for a response, she continued to the bathroom, but instead of closing the door completely, she left it open a few inches.

So much for awkward moments, he thought, staring at the partially open door. With a sigh, he turned away and tried not to think of Leah unwrapping the sheet, tried not to think of her naked, in the shower, lathering soap all over her body.

When Hunter felt the familiar hardening in his groin, he snatched up the remote control and switched on the television. Anything to divert his attention. Anything to drown out the sounds coming from the bathroom.

Over the next two hours, they checked out of the hotel, and with hats and sunglasses firmly in place, headed for the closest fast-food restaurant and had breakfast.

After breakfast, they donned the hats and sunglasses again and caught the streetcar. When the streetcar reached the

Audubon Park area, they got off and walked the rest of the way to the zoo.

Within minutes after Hunter and Leah had reached the entrance to the zoo, a gray midsize car pulled up several feet from where they were standing.

"It's Christine," Leah said as sudden apprehension coursed through her. Everyone Leah knew, including Christine, thought that Hunter was dead. But Christine was one of the few people who had actually met Hunter, one of the few who would recognize him. What she needed right now was some way to warn her friend not to say anything about Hunter. But even more urgent, she needed to warn Christine not to say anything about her pregnancy.

"Just wait here," Leah told Hunter in an attempt to buy some time. "Give me a minute to explain who you are. Okay?"

Hunter gave her an odd look, and she tensed. When he finally nodded, she took a deep breath and rushed over to the driver's side of the car before Hunter could change his mind. Leah got there just as her friend opened the door and stepped out.

Christine was still wearing her nurse's uniform. A tall woman, she was willowy thin with skin the color of mocha, and eyes so dark they were almost black. Though she didn't look a day over thirty, Leah knew that Christine was, in fact, almost forty.

Christine glanced at Hunter, then did a double take.

"Don't say a word," Leah cautioned in a low voice. When a look of confused recognition pass over her friend's face, Leah added, "Please—especially about me being pregnant," she added.

Christine narrowed her dark eyes and glared at Leah. "Girl, what in the devil is going on here? Unless my eyes deceive me, that man standing over there is your dead husband."

Leah nodded. "Yes, he is, but as you can see, he's not dead." Leah rushed on before Christine could say anything more. "I promise I can explain, and I will explain *everything*, but just not right now. For now I need you to trust me."

Leah swallowed hard. "And one more thing," she added. "For your own sake, for your safety, I also need you to promise you'll keep quiet about seeing Hunter and me. If anyone— anyone at all—asks, you haven't seen or talked to me for days, and as far as you know, Hunter Davis is dead. And that includes the police or any men who claim to be FBI agents."

For long moments, Christine stared at her, and Leah grew afraid that she'd just made a huge mistake. She was asking a lot of their friendship, and she could hardly blame Christine if she refused to go along.

Finally though, Christine slowly nodded. "Okay, but I have to tell you, I don't like the sound of any of this." She shook her head. "Not any of it. Are you sure that man hasn't kidnapped you or something?"

"No—nothing like that. I promise. I know you don't understand," Leah murmured. "And I'm sorry. But right now I can't explain and I don't have a choice."

When Leah went through the ruse of introducing her friend to Hunter, to Christine's credit, she acted as if she were meeting him for the first time.

Since Hunter didn't have a driver's license with him and didn't know the ins and outs of the city, Leah drove. Traffic was light, and within fifteen minutes, Leah pulled in front of a parking lot near Charity Hospital where Christine had left her car.

Christine got out then walked around to the driver's side of the car. "The gas tank is full, and I was told this model gets really good mileage. You be careful now," she cautioned Leah. Then she leaned into Leah's window and hugged her neck. "I'll expect to hear from you in a couple of days—call me."

When Christine pulled away, she narrowed her eyes and shook her finger at Hunter. "And you—you'd better take good care of my friend here, or you'll answer to me."

Hunter simply nodded. Then, with a tiny wave of good-bye to Christine, Leah checked the rearview mirror and pulled out into traffic.

During the time it took Leah to reach the interstate ramp, Hunter didn't say a word but simply stared out the passenger window. He was too quiet, she decided.

"Is something wrong?" she asked as she merged into the traffic on I-10, heading east.

At first she didn't think he was going to answer, but after a moment he sighed heavily and turned to face her. "I've changed my mind."

"About what? Going to Orlando?"

"No, *I'm* going to Orlando, but I think you—"

Leah interrupted. "But you think I should stay here." She shook her head firmly. "Sorry, but that's not an option. Besides, we've already had this discussion."

"Wasn't much of a discussion as I recall. You sidetracked me with that psychiatrist business the first time, and the next time we discussed it, you led me to believe that you had nowhere to go…"

You win… This time. Hunter's words came back to her. Now she knew what he'd meant. He'd given in, but only for the moment. Once more Leah firmly shook her head. "I don't have anywhere to go or stay, so there's no use talking about it again."

"What about your friend Christine?"

"Look—" She spared him a quick, pointed glance. "Getting her to rent a car for me is one thing. As long as she doesn't let on that she's seen or talked to me, I figure she'll be safe enough. But if I stayed with her—" A third time she shook her head. "I just can't take that chance. I can't put her in danger like that."

Several tense moments passed, and she could feel Hunter staring a hole through her. "Yeah," he finally agreed. "You're right. I just thought—" He shrugged. "Hell, I don't know what I thought. Never mind." He abruptly reached down and adjusted his seat into a reclining position. Then he pulled the bill of his cap down over his eyes. "I'm taking a nap," he grumbled. "Wake me when we get to Mississippi, then I'll drive." He shifted away from her and leaned back against the seat.

An hour later when Leah drove past the Mississippi state line, Hunter was still sleeping. She really needed a rest stop, but she dreaded having to wake him. While he slept, she didn't have to worry about saying the wrong thing or about him asking her questions. Deciding that she could wait a while longer, she kept driving.

By the time she approached Gulfport, she was more than ready to stop for a few minutes and began searching in earnest for a good place to exit the interstate. Being pregnant had its drawbacks, but the worst was having to go to the bathroom so frequently.

Leah spotted what appeared to be a good exit, one that advertised several fast-food restaurants, and she switched on the blinker. A few minutes later she pulled into a restaurant. The minute she turned off the engine, Hunter immediately sat up.

"Where are we?" he asked, yawning as he pushed the brim of his hat out of his eyes.

"Near Gulfport." Leah pulled the keys out of the ignition. Just in case Hunter got some hare-brained idea about leaving her, she didn't intend on making it easy for him. "Gotta go," she said. "Nature calls." Without waiting for a reply or for Hunter to follow, she grabbed her purse and slipped the keys inside. She shoved open the door, climbed out, slammed it shut then hurried toward the restaurant.

When she came out of the rest room, Hunter was waiting

for her. "I don't know about you, but I'm hungry. Since we're here and it's past lunchtime—" he shrugged "—we might as well eat."

"Sure," Leah replied.

"What do you want?" Hunter asked as they studied the menu above the counter.

Leah silently apologized to her baby and promised she'd eat more healthy foods next time, then said, "A large hamburger—no mayo and add mustard—a small fry and a large skim milk."

"You sure do like milk," Hunter commented.

Leah felt her face grow warm. Ordinarily she would have ordered a soft drink. The milk was for the baby. She forced a smile. "Milk is good for you," she said.

Though Hunter gave her a strange look, he shrugged again. "If you say so." Then he placed an identical order, all except the milk. Instead, he ordered coffee. "I figure I'm going to need the caffeine to stay awake," he said as if he needed to explain.

After they'd finished eating, Hunter decided that they might as well top off the gas tank.

Once they were on the road again, it wasn't long until Leah felt her eyes grow heavy. As Hunter had done, she adjusted the passenger seat into a reclining position. Then she pulled off her hat, and as she shook loose her hair, she dropped the hat on the floor. Leaning back into the seat, she propped her head against the door and closed her eyes.

When Leah awoke, she sat up and glanced around. Hunter had exited off the interstate and was parked beside a gas pump at a service station. "Where are we?" she asked.

"We're about halfway between Mobile and Tallahassee."

Leah made a face. "I never was all that good at geography."

Hunter nodded tiredly. "Me, neither, but according to

this—" he tapped a folded map that he'd wedged between the visor and the ceiling of the car "—I figure we're about halfway to Orlando. I'm hoping that if we continue to make good time we'll get there around midnight."

Leah groaned. "Too bad we couldn't have flown. We would have already been there by now." She shrugged. "Oh, well, I might as well go make use of the pit stop."

"Yeah, me too, just as soon as I fill up the gas tank."

The minute Leah climbed out of the car and stood up, a sharp pain jabbed her in the stomach. With one hand she grabbed her stomach and with her other hand she kept a tight grip on the door.

"Is something wrong?"

The pain eased and Leah shook her head. "No, I'm just stiff from riding." At least she hoped that was the problem. "I'll be fine once I walk around a bit."

But as Leah walked away, she silently called herself all kinds of names that weren't fit to say out loud. She knew better, knew that when a pregnant woman took a long trip, she needed to stop every hour or so and walk around. Promising herself that she would make a point of asking Hunter to stop more often, Leah entered the small building.

The air inside smelled of freshly brewed coffee, and her mouth watered at just the thought. Rolling her eyes at her pregnancy-dictated caffeine deprivation, she continued to the rest room.

Using a map of Orlando that they had picked up at a tourist center, they only got lost once before finally locating the right hotel.

It was well past midnight when Hunter pulled into the hotel parking lot. Once he switched off the engine, he gave a huge sigh of relief.

"Thank you, dear Lord," Leah murmured as she shoved

open her door, eased out of the seat and stood. Though she felt a bit stiff, the pain she'd had earlier was gone.

"Amen to that," Hunter added, folding the map and shoving it between the visor and the ceiling of the car. He climbed out of the vehicle and glanced around. "At least there's someplace to eat close by." He motioned toward a restaurant next door to the hotel then walked around to the trunk.

While Hunter retrieved their knapsacks from the trunk, Leah glanced toward the restaurant, then quickly returned her gaze to the hotel.

As she stood staring at the small building, a raw primitive grief overwhelmed her, and she couldn't shake the dull ache of foreboding. Hunter might not remember the hotel or their honeymoon, but she remembered it all. She remembered every detail from the beginning to the end. When they had first arrived, she'd been a bride filled with love and joy, but when she had finally been allowed to leave, she'd left a heartbroken widow filled with sorrow and guilt.

Not wanting to dredge up all the sad, miserable feelings she'd experienced when she had boarded the airplane alone to return to New Orleans, Leah swallowed the ache building in the back of her throat. Would this trip be the same? If and when Hunter remembered it all, would she once again return to New Orleans alone? Dear Lord, she hoped not, prayed not.

As they entered the hotel lobby, Hunter's steps slowed. Did he recognize any of it? Leah wondered as she watched him study the reception area. She couldn't tell from the noncommittal expression on his face. Within seconds though, his shoulders dropped ever so slightly, and disappointment knifed through her.

Knowing that nothing looked familiar to him, Leah turned away. For Hunter's sake she wanted him to remember, but at the same time, the return of his memory could be the end for her…again.

"Guess no one's at home," she said to cover up her own misgivings. Spying a small bell on the long reception desk, she walked over to it and tapped it several times.

After a moment, a side door opened, and a rumpled, sleepy-eye man entered the room. "Can I help you folks?"

Leah nodded. "We need a room."

Nodding, the man walked to a computer monitor. "You're in luck. We just had a whole group check out this afternoon—a real-estate convention." He tapped several keys on the keyboard. "Single or double?" he asked.

"Would suite 230 happen to be available?"

The man glanced up and gave her a curious look.

"We've been here before," Leah hurriedly explained. "On our honeymoon," she added. "And—well—you see, we'd kind of like to have the same suite again."

A small smile pulled at the man's lips and he nodded knowingly. Turning his attention back to the computer screen, he tapped the keys again. "Well, looks like your luck's holding. Suite 230 it is. So how long will you be here?"

Leah shrugged. "We're not sure. Probably a couple of days at least."

He nodded then looked up expectantly. "Credit card?"

Hunter stepped closer. "No credit card. We'd prefer to pay cash. How much?" He pulled the roll of money from his pocket.

Though the man behind the counter gave Hunter a suspicious look, the look disappeared when he saw the thick roll of money in Hunter's hand. "Four hundred and fifty," he said. "That includes tax but it doesn't include any phone calls."

Hunter raised his eyebrows, but he counted out the money and handed it to the man.

The suite was made up of a bedroom with a king-size bed, a large bathroom complete with Jacuzzi, and a living area and dining area. Off to the side of the dining area were a row of cabinets that contained a microwave and a small refrigerator.

As they entered the suite, once again Leah kept a wary eye on Hunter for a sign of recognition.

Hunter walked to the doorway leading into the bedroom and stared at the bed. Leah held her breath. Would he remember the passion they had shared in that bed?

When Hunter shifted his gaze from the bed to her, his eyes darkened to navy, and the smoldering look he gave her sent an unbidden surge of excitement and anticipation rushing through her. Was it possible? she wondered as hope soared. Had he remembered?

Then, as quickly as the look had come, it was gone.

"You take the bed," he told her, "and I'll sleep on the sofa."

Leah stiffened with shock. Of all the things she'd expected him to say, separate sleeping arrangements wasn't one of them.

"Why?" she asked, totally confused.

Hunter shrugged as if it was no big deal. "Caffeine overload. I'd probably just keep you awake. Besides, no use in both of us missing out on a good night's sleep."

Leah's face grew hot with humiliation, and without warning she felt her temper flare. His excuse was flimsy at best, and as a war raged inside, she fought to keep control of her emotions. Then raw hurt welled within, and tears threatened. It was obvious that he regretted last night, regretted making love with her.

"Fine!" she retorted in a low voice, taut with hurt. "But for your information, I'm too tired to do anything but sleep anyway." With one last icy look to mask the pain she felt, she grabbed her knapsack, pivoted and marched into the bedroom.

Once inside, she slammed the door then threw herself on the bed. Wrestling a pillow from beneath the bedspread, she buried her face in it to smother the sound of her sobs.

In the small living room, Hunter stared at the closed door

then shoved his fingers through his hair. "Great!" he muttered. "Just great!"

In his feeble attempt to be considerate, he'd gone and hurt her feelings. No, not just hurt her feelings. More like made her mad enough to chew nails. He turned to stare at the sofa. Although he was still pumped on caffeine, he knew that all he had to do was lie down and close his eyes, and he'd be out like a light…if he slept alone.

And if he slept with Leah. Well, he wouldn't be able to keep his hands off her and neither one of them would get much rest.

Hunter closed his eyes and shook his head. He'd been tempted though, oh, so tempted. But all it had taken was one look at her to realize that she was so exhausted she could hardly walk, and he knew he couldn't do it.

She'd get over being angry, he told himself as he walked over to the sofa, lifted a cushion and examined it more closely. Just as he'd figured, the sofa made out into a bed.

Hunter pulled off all the cushions and again told himself that Leah would get over it. So why did he feel as if he'd just plucked the wings off a helpless butterfly? He unfolded the thin mattress and springs, and picked up the set of sheets that had been folded within the mattress.

In the bedroom, Leah's sobs had subsided into an occasional hiccup, and her anger disappeared as quickly as it had come, leaving only regret and embarrassment in its wake. Thanks to her pregnancy and her unpredictable emotions, she'd overreacted and made a fool of herself. The more she thought about the whole incident, the hotter her cheeks burned with embarrassment.

She'd acted like a two-year-old throwing a tantrum, and all because Hunter had tried to be considerate. Poor man. He hadn't a clue. Right now he was probably regretting ever getting involved with her, probably hoped he never got his memory of her back.

Leah put aside the pillow then went into the bathroom. There, she blew her nose and splashed cold water on her face. As she blotted it dry, she knew she wouldn't sleep a wink until she made things right with Hunter.

In the other room, Hunter had just finished making up the sofa bed with the sheets and was trying to decide how to apologize to Leah, when the bedroom door opened. He turned in time to see her step into the room. In her arms was a pillow.

"You'll need this," she said, holding out the pillow. "I'm sorry for acting like a spoiled brat."

Guilt pangs stabbed Hunter. From the looks of her red-rimmed eyes and the slight flush to her cheeks, he strongly suspected that she'd been crying.

He walked over and took the pillow from her. "Thanks," he said. She nodded, but when she started to turn to go back into the bedroom, Hunter reached out and touched her arm. "Wait. About a few minutes ago, about what I said, I—"

"It's okay," she said softly as twin spots of crimson darkened her cheeks. "I—I overreacted. Just tired I guess."

"Not your fault," Hunter objected. "We're both tired." Then, because he couldn't help himself, couldn't stand being that close to her without touching her again, he reached up and brushed a stray tendril of her silky hair away from her face. "I should have explained myself better. If we share a bed, I don't think either of us will get much sleep."

She offered him a surprised small shy smile. "You're probably right," she said. Then, before he realized her intentions, she stood on tiptoe, lifted her head and kissed him on the bottom edge his cheek. "Good night," she whispered. Then she was gone.

Long after Leah closed the bedroom door and Hunter had undressed, then crawled onto the sofa bed, he kept running his forefinger back and forth over the small place where Leah had kissed him.

Even after just one night with her, one night that he actually remembered, he missed feeling her body next to his.

Hunter turned onto his stomach and readjusted the pillow she'd given him. Funny, he thought. She had yet to ask him if anything had seemed familiar. Not that it mattered, since so far, nothing had caused even a spark in his memory.

Maybe tomorrow, he thought as he shifted onto his back again. Maybe once he retraced his steps, he would remember his life before he'd awakened in the hospital, and he would finally know why both the shooters and the FBI were after him. And maybe then, both he and Leah would be out of danger.

But what if he didn't remember? What if none of it made a difference?

Chapter 15

He was trapped in the crush of the raucous crowd and there was no way out. When the crowd surged forward he had no choice but to be swept along with them. There were too many of them, and the noise was deafening.

Suddenly the people around him raised their arms and began waving and shouting, jostling him one way then another. Out of the corner of his eye, he spotted the reason for their excitement as he struggled to keep his balance. A monstrous alligator the size of a tanker floated across the top of the crowd toward them. On top of the alligator were men in garish costumes and masks. Lights glittered and flashed around the alligator and the men. The alligator was both terrible and beautiful in a surreal sort of way, and the closer it came, the louder the crowd shouted.

Somewhere a band began to play a rousing rendition of a Sousa march, and around him the crowd began chanting, "Throw me something, throw me something." Then the

masked men began throwing shiny beads and sparkling dou-
bloons, and a shower of purple, green and gold rained down
on his head.

Hunter awoke with a start, his heart still pounding. A
dream, he thought. Just a dream.

He blinked several times, and as he stared up at the ceiling for several moments, the pounding in his chest began to
slow back to a steady thud.

But was it a dream or a memory?

Hunter yawned and stretched then glanced at his wrist-
watch. The watch showed that it was almost noon. He tilted
his head and listened closely for any sign that Leah was awake
in the next room. Nothing, not a sound.

He sat up and stretched, his stiff muscles protesting. He
reached down and massaged his leg. He hated to, but he'd have
to wake Leah. They'd slept later than he'd planned, and it was
time to get moving, time to see if he could help jog his memory.

"Was I dreaming?" Hunter asked Leah an hour later as they
sat in a booth at the restaurant next to the hotel. He felt like
a fool for even asking, but he had to know.

Leah chewed the bite of roll that she had just taken and
then swallowed. "Yes and no," she finally answered. "You
were dreaming, but you were dreaming of a memory." Then
she explained. "Do you remember me telling you that you
came to New Orleans to see Mardi Gras?"

Hunter nodded.

"What you were dreaming about was the Mardi Gras parade we went to. One of the signature floats in the Bacchus
parade is called the Baccagator. It's a huge float that looks
like an alligator."

Hunter frowned. "You said 'we,' so you and I went together
to see this Bacchus?"

She cast her eyes downward, but not before he saw them

darken with pain. "Yes, we went together," she whispered. "That was the first day we met."

Unsure how to react, Hunter decided that it was time to change the subject. "To trace my steps the night of the accident, I think I need to start at the hotel, drive to the drugstore then take the shortest route to the accident site."

Leah nodded, pinched off another bite of the roll and popped it into her mouth.

"We know where the hotel is," Hunter continued, "and I'm assuming you know which pharmacy I went to that night. The only place left is the accident site. So, where did the accident take place?"

Leah felt as if she was on an emotional merry-go-round, up one minute with happy memories, and down the next with heart-wrenching ones.

"I don't really know where it happened," she finally replied. "All I was told was that there had been an accident, and that you had been killed. After they told me that, it never entered my mind to question the location. At the time, it didn't seem important."

Leah focused on the glass of orange juice by her plate. At the time, nothing had seemed important, nothing but her pain and grief. With her forefinger, she drew a circle in the condensation on the side of the glass, and glanced up at Hunter. "I guess I just assumed the accident happened between the hotel and the pharmacy."

A pensive look on his face, Hunter drummed his fingers against the tabletop. "We need to find out." He sighed heavily. "Can't find out from the cops or the hospital. Nobody knows we're here, and I'd just as soon keep it that way. If we could—"

"What about a newspaper?" Leah interrupted, leaning forward. "Surely an accident of that size, with a fatality, would have been reported in the newspaper."

Hunter shook his head. "Can't take a chance on asking questions, especially at a newspaper office."

Leah sighed. "Guess not," she murmured as frustration began to build. "We can't ask the cops, can't go to the hospital, not the newspaper office. So where?" She paused, her mind racing and discarding other ideas. Then suddenly, the perfect solution came to her. "What's to keep us from checking at a library? Most libraries archive newspapers, and since we know the date we're looking for, that would narrow it down."

After a moment Hunter slowly began to nod. "That just might work."

Hunter had long cleaned his plate, but she'd only eaten a small portion of what she'd ordered. Truth was, she was so nervous that she'd had to force herself to eat that.

"Take your time," Hunter said, "but when you're finished, we'll check with the hotel about directions to the nearest library."

Hunter's body language belied his words. He shifted in his chair, then he began drumming his fingers on the tabletop again, a sure sign of impatience. But who could blame him? If their positions were reversed, she'd be just as impatient to get on with it, especially if there was a ghost of a chance that doing so would help get her memory back.

Leah swallowed the bite of roll then washed it down with the remainder of her juice. She set the empty glass on the table, blotted her mouth with her napkin, then she picked up her purse. "Okay, I'm ready. Let's go."

The look of relief on Hunter's face was almost comical, and Leah couldn't help smiling.

"You're sure?" he asked, glancing at her plate. "You didn't eat much."

Leah shrugged. "I've had enough."

A different clerk was working behind the front desk at the hotel, and the cheery, older woman seemed more than happy to give them the information they were looking for when Hunter asked for the location of the nearest library.

"You want the Orlando Public Library," she told him. "Yes, siree, that's the one you want." She leaned down and fumbled beneath the desk. "It's the largest public library in the state." When she straightened again, she held up a map that looked similar to the one they had picked up at the tourist center the night before.

She unfolded the map then smoothed it out over the countertop. "Here we are." She tapped a spot on the map. She picked up a black marker and placed an X on the location of the hotel. "And here's the library." She tapped another spot on the map. "It's located on Central Boulevard between Rosalind Avenue and Magnolia." She drew another X where the library was located. "It's not far at all," she said, tracing a route on the map with the marker from the hotel X to the library X. "It's a pretty straightforward route to follow. Across the street from the library there's a parking garage. You can either park in there or there's metered parking on Rosalind. You shouldn't have a bit of trouble."

The clerk was right, Leah thought as mere minutes later Hunter approached the tall, concrete building that housed the library. The route had been easy to follow, and they'd had no trouble at all finding it.

"Think I'll park in the parking garage," Hunter said. "I don't like having to worry about feeding a parking meter."

Once they entered the library, they headed straight for the information desk. While Hunter asked for directions to where the archived newspapers were kept, Leah glanced around at the art on display.

"We need to go to the fourth floor," Hunter told her a minute later.

On the fourth floor they approached another information desk. Once Hunter told the lady behind the desk what he wanted, she motioned to the left at several metal file cabinets that contained microfilm for the *Orlando Sentinel*. Each of the small drawers in the file cabinets was dated. Near the cabinets was a row of microfilm machines. Each machine had its own desk and printer.

While Leah searched for the file that contained the three days following the date of the accident, Hunter got instructions on how to use the machine.

"I'll be damned," he muttered a few minutes after he'd loaded the microfilm for the newspaper dated the day after the accident. "Here it is—a front-page article no less." Hunter gave a low whistle. "They've even got a picture of me." Hunter zoomed in on the picture. "Where in hell did they get that?"

Leah was standing just behind Hunter, and she swallowed hard as she stared at the picture of him in the policeman's uniform.

As Hunter stared at his image all decked out in uniform, something suddenly clicked within his mind. That particular picture had been taken on the day he'd graduated from the academy.

A surge of adrenaline rushed through his veins. The only way he could know when the picture had been taken was if he'd remembered it. If he could remember that much, maybe he could remember more.

Hunter closed his eyes and tried to clear his head and concentrate. But when he tried to recall more, he came up blank. Sighing with frustration, he opened his eyes. "The accident happened late at night. Somebody somewhere had to really hustle to get a copy of this picture and make sure that write-up appeared the very next day."

Leah nodded. "At least now we know that part of what Lance Martin said was true, the part about them wanting to get the word out that you'd been killed."

Hunter looked up at Leah. "But why, dammit? Why me? What did I see that night that was so all-fired important?"

Leah's heart ached for Hunter. She was plenty frustrated herself, and she couldn't begin to imagine how frustrated he had to be.

"I want a copy of this page," Hunter told Leah as he adjusted the zoom. Reaching in his pants pocket, he pulled out some change, then he dropped two quarters in a box on the left of the desk. When the print button lit up green, he pushed the button. Moments later he pulled the copy from the printer under the desk.

Once he had a copy, he motioned toward a table. "Let's sit over there. I want to go over this more closely."

Seated side by side, they both read the article from beginning to end.

The front-page story contained a blow-by-blow account of the fiery accident, a head-on collision between a car and an eighteen-wheeler hauling gasoline. According to the article, the driver of the car had been identified as Hunter Davis, an off-duty New York policeman who was on vacation. He'd been speeding, lost control of his vehicle, and had crossed over into the oncoming path of the eighteen-wheeler. The driver of the eighteen-wheeler was also identified.

Both vehicles had burst into flames on impact, and, according to the newspaper, both drivers had died instantly. The blaze was so hot and the fumes from the gasoline were so toxic that firefighters had trouble putting it out. Traffic had been backed up for miles and the surrounding buildings had to be evacuated. By the time firefighters got the fire under control, it had consumed both vehicles and the drivers.

When Hunter had finished reading the article, he continued staring at the paper, lost in thought as his eyes scanned the other articles that had rated front-page coverage. His gaze skimmed over the latest reports about the war in Iraq. Farther down the page, beneath the article about the accident, a headline caught his attention: Murder Count Rises. Beneath the headline was a small color picture of the chalked outline of the spot where a man had been murdered. Beside the picture was the story about the murder.

Lost in thought, Hunter was absently skimming the first few lines of the article that accompanied the picture when Leah interrupted. "Are you finished?" she asked as she pulled out the map of Orlando that the hotel clerk had given them.

Knowing that she was referring to the accident article, Hunter nodded.

She unfolded the map then placed it on top of the copy of the newspaper page. After she'd studied it for several minutes, she pointed to a particular spot. "Here it is. According to the newspaper, the accident happened here. Over here is the hotel." She pointed at the X that marked the hotel.

"Now all we need is the address of the pharmacy," Hunter added. He turned to stare at Leah. "Well?"

Leah closed her eyes. Then, after a moment, she took a deep breath and opened them again. "I'm not sure," she admitted. "I think I must have blocked out a lot about that trip."

"You're not sure?" He grimaced. "Well, aren't we a sorry pair? I can't remember, and you've blocked it all out."

"It's only the actual name of the place that I don't remember," she retorted, ignoring his words. "What I do recall though is that when our plane landed, we rented a car and drove to the hotel. Later, when I got sick, I remembered that we had passed a pharmacy along the way." She lowered her gaze to stare at the map.

When they'd passed the drugstore, she'd almost asked Hunter to turn around and go back. If only she had, maybe everything would have turned out differently. If she'd just… Leah winced. All of the if onlys in the world couldn't change things now, and beating herself up out of guilt couldn't change things, either. What was done was done.

She looked up at Hunter again. "The one thing I do remember is that the name of the drugstore was different, unusual—you know, not one of the chains. More like privately owned."

"Well, at least that's something," Hunter commented. "Something we can work with," he added. He stared at the Orlando map. "Guess we need to backtrack. Looks like we go this way toward the airport from the hotel."

Leah followed his forefinger as he slid it along a route that led to the airport.

"Look at it good," he told her and tapped the map, "'cause you're going to have to guide me."

Leah silently repeated the names of the streets several times, and after a moment, she finally nodded. "I've got it."

"Then what's say let's do it?" Hunter folded the copy of the newspaper page, stood, and tucked it into his back pocket. "We'll start from the hotel and head for the airport."

Leah folded the map and stood. "Okay." Now if only she could recognize the name when she saw it.

A few minutes later they were on the road again. Leah could see the hotel in the distance, and she smoothed out the map in her lap.

"Now tell me again why I went out that night."

Leah froze and her hand doubled into a fist. Her lies had come back to haunt her. Just what had she told him? Her mind raced as she tried to remember exactly what she'd said. "Ah, I—I was sick—an upset stomach, and you went to get me something for the nausea."

Hunter nodded. "Yeah, that's what you said."

As if mentioning being sick made it so, Leah's stomach knotted. If he remembered what she said, then why had he asked? *Because he knows you're hiding something.*

She swallowed hard and tried to ignore the raw grief that threatened to overwhelm her.

* * *

After they passed the hotel, and Leah began calling out street names and giving directions, she felt a bit more in control again. They'd only driven a few blocks when she spotted a building that looked familiar. When they got close enough for her to read the name on the sign above it, a wave of excitement mixed with relief washed through her.

"That's it," she cried. "Godwin's Pharmaceutical! Up there on the right. I'm almost positive that's the one I saw."

Hunter flicked on the blinker and braked to a slower speed. "See anyplace to park?"

Leah searched both sides of the street. "Up there." She pointed to a small parking lot half a block down from the drugstore. "Maybe there's room in there."

Hunter slowed the car even more and turned into the tiny parking lot. The only space available was tight, but with some maneuvering, he was able to squeeze the car in between the two cars on either side.

Hunter switched off the engine, then glanced around for several moments.

Unable to stand the suspense, Leah asked, "Does anything look familiar to you?"

After a moment, Hunter shook his head. "Not really."

Her excitement died a quick death. "Maybe once we're inside the drugstore," she suggested hopefully.

"Maybe," he repeated, but to Leah he didn't sound very optimistic.

"Have you got room to get out on that side?" he asked.

"Just barely," Leah groaned as she squeezed out between the narrow opening of the door. Good thing she wasn't further along with her pregnancy, she thought.

Hunter met her at the back of the car, and together they walked back up the block toward the drugstore.

The pharmacy was just one of several specialty stores on

the block. They passed one that sold only kitchen utensils, one that advertised antiques, and a small grocery that specialized in Cuban foodstuffs. On the other side of the drugstore was a florist shop. Narrow service alleys separated each shop.

Leah's footsteps slowed as they walked past one store in particular. In one window was a display of baby furniture and baby clothes, and in the other window were several mannequins dressed in maternity clothes.

"Is something wrong?" Hunter asked.

Leah raised her eyes to find him watching her. "No," she said quickly. "Why?"

He dropped his gaze to where her hand was splayed across her stomach. "You keep holding your stomach, and you didn't eat much breakfast."

Leah felt her face grow warm, and nervous sweat trickled down her back. She hadn't realized that she'd been holding her stomach. Hoping that her cheeks weren't as flushed as they felt, she forced a tiny smile and shrugged. "It's the heat. I never have had much of an appetite in the summer." She slowly lowered her hand and shrugged again.

Though Hunter gave her a curious look, thankfully they had reached the front of the drugstore, so he didn't pursue the subject.

Hunter held the door open for her and the blast of cooler air was a welcome relief from the late-afternoon heat outside. Leah glanced around. Though small, the store was clean and orderly. There was one small checkout counter at the front, several rows of merchandise that ran the length of the store, and a larger counter for prescription drugs in the back that stretched across the width of the store. Except for her and Hunter and the two women waiting near the back counter, the only other person in the store was the pharmacist.

Leah studied several items on the shelves. Unlike the larger drugstore chains that offered almost anything and everything for sale, most of the merchandise here was strictly drug related.

For several minutes Hunter stood gazing around, a strained look of concentration on his face, and Leah held her breath. When he finally sighed and shook his head, she released her pent-up breath, and disappointment mixed with relief settled in the depths of her stomach.

"Can I help you folks?" the pharmacist called out from the back.

"I hope so," Hunter answered. With Leah following him, he headed down one of the aisles and approached the back counter. He motioned toward the two women who were standing nearby. "I can wait until you're finished with your customers."

The pharmacist, an older, balding man who wore wire-rimmed glasses, narrowed his eyes and stared at Hunter. "I'll be with you in just a minute," he said.

Hunter nodded and backed away. Only when the women had paid for their prescriptions and were walking out the front door did he finally approach the pharmacist again.

"What can I do for you?" the man asked.

"Do you recognize me?"

The old man hesitated, a suspicious look on his face as he studied Hunter for several moments.

"Do I look even vaguely familiar to you?"

The old man narrowed his eyes. "Mind if I ask why?"

Hunter shook his head. "Not in the least. I think I was in your store about four months ago, and I was hoping you could confirm that."

"Hmm, let's see now…four months ago. That's a pretty long time for an old man like me to remember. That would make it back in April." The man frowned and stared at Hunter for several seconds. "Naw," he muttered, shaking his head.

"Couldn't be." He stared at Hunter several seconds more. Then, suddenly, the old man paled and his eyes grew wide. "Lord God almighty, it is you."

"Then you do recognize me?"

"But—but—I thought—I mean, they said—" The man shook his head. "They said you were dead."

Blood roared in Hunter's ears, and he felt as if every nerve in his body was standing on end. "Then you do remember me?"

The man nodded. "You bet. You saved my life that night you came in. If it hadn't been for you, those thugs might have killed me, too, just like they killed that poor man in the alley."

For long seconds Hunter simply stared at him, his insides churning. "Wait a minute. Are you saying a man was killed that night?"

The pharmacist nodded. "Right out there in the alley." He motioned toward the left side of the store.

You're a material witness to a murder committed in Orlando.

The words of the FBI agent swirled in Hunter's mind. Was it possible? Could this be the murder the agents had been talking about? Hunter's heart began to pound. It had to be.

Hunter stared at the old man. "Tell me. Tell me exactly what happened."

The old man frowned at Hunter over the top of his glasses. "You don't remember?"

"No." Hunter shook his head. "I didn't die in that accident, but as a result of it, I have amnesia."

The man's eyes suddenly lit up with curiosity. "Amnesia, huh. I never met anybody that had amnesia."

"Well, you have now."

"Yep, guess I have."

"So?" Hunter prompted, growing impatient.

"Oh, yeah, well, after you left out of here, I went up to the front of the store to close out the register. In no time at all though, you came running back in, looking as if the hounds of hell were chasing you. Had me plenty scared, I tell you. Well, you took one look at me then shoved me down on the floor behind the counter. Told me to stay there if I knew what was good for me. Then I heard you run out that exit over there." He pointed at a side exit door.

The pharmacist laughed. "It's a good thing I'm an old man and can't get up too fast, because just seconds after you ran out the exit, there was a commotion out front, and two men ran through. They were so busy yelling at each other and trying to catch you that they didn't even see me. Once I got to my feet I called 911, and the next thing I know, there were cops everywhere. Then the next morning when I picked up my newspaper, I saw your picture on the front page saying that you got killed in an accident with an eighteen-wheeler."

The pharmacist paused and pursed his lips. "So why did they say you got killed?" He motioned toward Hunter. "Unless you have a twin, you look pretty alive to me. And another thing, why were those hoodlums chasing you? You didn't kill that fella in the alley, did you?"

"No." Hunter shook his head. "Nothing like that. It's a long story—a mistake," he fabricated. "But getting back to the man who was murdered. What do you know about him?"

"Nothing much. I just figured he got mugged. A lot of that happening lately."

Something niggled at the back of Hunter's mind. "Anything else?" he asked.

The man's forehead wrinkled in concentration and he stared up at the ceiling for several moments. Then he shook his head. "Sorry, that's about all I can recall."

Disappointment ripped through Hunter when he realized that he wouldn't get any more out of the man. He felt like putting his fist through a wall. Taking a deep breath and un-clenching his fist, he tried to stay calm. The last thing he needed was to make a scene or scare the old guy.

Hunter breathed deeply again. "Thanks. I appreciate the information." He held out his hand. "You've been a big help."

The old man grabbed Hunter's hand and shook it. "My pleasure. It's the least I could do for the man who saved my life."

With a curt nod, Hunter turned to Leah. "Let's go."

"Good luck with that amnesia," the pharmacist called out.

Without turning around, Hunter gave him a backhanded wave as they walked toward the store entrance.

As Leah followed Hunter, she felt as if she'd just been rung out to dry.

Now tell me again why I went out that night?

Leah's stomach knotted as Hunter's words echoed through her head again. She'd expected him to ask the old man what he'd purchased, especially after he'd made a point to question her about it earlier. To her immense relief, he hadn't asked though. She'd like to think that he hadn't asked because she'd been wrong, because he really did trust her after all. But she knew better. She'd seen the excitement on Hunter's face when the pharmacist had admitted that he recognized Hunter, and once the old man had begun talking, there had been more important questions to ask.

They reached the entrance door, and Hunter pushed it open and held it for her as she stepped outside.

Like Hunter, she'd listened to the man, and had been equally excited and frustrated at what he'd said. At least now they knew *where* Hunter had witnessed the murder. But even as she'd tried to force the pieces of the deadly puzzle to fit, there were still too many pieces missing to solve it.

Outside the drugstore, Hunter paused at the alley on the back-exit side of the store. The alley was dark though and there wasn't much to see. After a moment, he pivoted and walked to the other alley. "It had to have happened in this alley," he said, glancing around. "Besides, the other one's too dark for me to have seen anything." He motioned toward a light pole. "This one has a streetlight shining on it."

Hoping to jog his memory, he studied the alley several seconds more. Other than some graffiti on the wall of the drugstore and several trash cans, there wasn't a whole lot to see.

He finally shook his head. "Doesn't make sense. If the parking lot is down there, why would I have come this way to begin with? And why would I go back inside the drugstore and risk getting that old man killed?"

Leah thought about it for a minute, then said, "Maybe you didn't park in the parking lot that night. Maybe you parked somewhere farther down the street the other way."

Hunter slowly nodded. "Hmm, guess that's possible," he finally murmured.

"And maybe you risked the old man because you knew he'd call 911," she added. "But you really didn't risk him. He said that you pushed him beneath the counter and told him to stay there."

Hunter shoved his fingers through his hair. "Yeah, I guess it could have happened that way." With one last look at the alley, he took hold of Leah's hand and tugged. "Let's go," he said. "Right now I want to drive the route to where the accident happened. Maybe that will jog my memory."

Once back inside the car, Hunter eased the car out of the parking space then pulled out onto the street. With Leah giving him directions, he drove slowly toward the accident site.

The pharmacist had said that two men were chasing him, and the newspaper article had reported that he'd been speeding when his car had gone out of control.

You're a material witness to a murder committed in Orlando.

The words of the FBI agent kept swirling in Hunter's mind. At least now he knew what murder he'd witnessed, but why was that particular murder so damn important? And why did he get the feeling that there was more to it, that he'd missed something, some vital clue that was on the edge of his brain? But what?

Hunter's grip tightened on the steering wheel as once again frustration threatened to overpower his control. It seemed that the harder he tried to remember, the less he could remember. He was on the verge of getting his memory back. He could feel it. Like a vise tightening around his head, the pressure kept building.

And then there was Leah, yet another pressure added to the mix. He didn't have to look to know that she was watching him, watching him and waiting for any sign that his memory was returning. He could feel her eyes on him.

Hunter wasn't sure why, but the thought of disappointing her bothered him almost as much as the fact that nothing he'd seen so far had made a bit of difference. It was true that bit by bit, he was gathering more facts, but what good were the facts when his memory and his life was still a deep dark empty hole.

Leah leaned forward in the seat beside him. "I think that's the accident site up ahead." She pointed at a traffic light. "Near that intersection as best as I can figure."

Forcing back his frustration, Hunter tapped the brakes and slowed the car to a crawl. Ignoring the horn blaring from the car behind him, he stared at the stretch of highway Leah was pointing to. He wasn't sure what he had expected to see, but nothing looked even vaguely familiar.

"Dammit," he muttered as he drove past the intersection. So what the hell was he supposed to do now?

As Hunter searched for a place to turn around, an idea began to form. He might not remember anything about that night, but there were other ways of finding out what had happened and why he'd been targeted. There had to be. He just had to figure out what those other ways were.

On the way to the hotel, they pulled into the drive-through of a McDonald's and ordered some food to take back to the hotel with them. At the hotel, they took the elevator to the second floor. Once inside the room, they ate the food in silence.

Afterward Hunter pulled the newspaper article from his pocket, and settled on the sofa. He figured if he studied the story long enough, he'd eventually figure out what he needed to do next.

As he unfolded the clipping and smoothed out the crease lines, out of the corner of his eye he noticed that Leah had wandered over to the window. The look of longing on her face as she stared down at something on the ground stirred his curiosity.

"A penny for your thoughts," he said.

Leah simply shrugged as she continued staring out the window. "I was just wishing that I had bought a bathing suit," she said. "There's a really nice pool down there, and right now, I could stand to swim some laps."

"Didn't we pass a shop of some kind in the lobby? Maybe it has bathing suits."

"Yeah, it does, but the shop was closed."

Hunter was tempted to tell her to go out and buy herself a bathing suit, but then he thought better of it. For one thing, he didn't trust that somehow, someway, the shooters or the feds wouldn't trace them to Orlando. Besides, the mental image of her wearing a bathing suit was distraction enough without the real thing.

Better all around if they stayed together and kept out of sight as much as possible. Anyway, it was getting dark outside, and he didn't need his memory to know that driving around in the dark through a strange city wasn't the smartest or safest thing to do. Their present predicament was proof of that.

He lowered his gaze once again to the newspaper article and read it again. Many more times reading it, and he would have it memorized, he thought as his gaze strayed to the article and picture he'd started to read in the library about a murder.

He was staring at the photo of the chalked outline of the spot where the man had been murdered when he suddenly realized that something about the picture looked familiar. At first he thought it was because he'd looked at it back at the library. Then Hunter froze.

"That's it!" he exclaimed, his heart pounding.

Leah whirled. "What?"

"Here, look at this."

She hurried over to the sofa.

"I knew it—" he tapped the picture "—knew there was something I was missing." He smacked himself on the forehead with the heel of his hand. "When the old man mentioned the murder, for some reason, it just didn't connect right then."

Leah looked down at the picture he'd pointed to, and suddenly her eyes grew wide. "Why that's—"

Hunter nodded eagerly and tapped the picture again. "The alley by the drugstore. See here—" He pointed at the side of the picture with his forefinger. "Same graffiti on the wall."

Leah's eyes grew wide. "That means that—"

Hunter nodded again. "It means that this has to be the murder the feds said I witnessed."

Chapter 16

Excitement vibrated through Leah as she dropped onto the sofa beside Hunter and they both pored over the article beneath the picture. When they had finished reading it, Hunter tapped the article with his forefinger. "That's got to be it," he said as if to convince himself once and for all. "The date, the timing, everything. And I'd swear that's the same alley by that drugstore."

"I think you're right," Leah concurred. "I know you're right," she said more firmly.

A sense of urgency pulsated through Hunter, and he couldn't shake the feeling that time was running out. When he shifted on the sofa to face Leah, his mind went blank for a moment. Just a few inches separated them. A ripple of desire shot through him. All he had to do was move a few inches forward...

Hunter blinked and forced himself to remember what he'd meant to say, and again, a sense of urgency came over him.

He cleared his throat. "We need to make another trip to the library. According to the article, Neil Turner was the murdered man's name, so if there is anything more written up about him somewhere we can find it. I want to know just why he's so damn important."

Leah nodded. "I agree." Then, as if she'd sensed the same urgency that Hunter had felt, she said, "No time like the present."

Hunter glanced at his watch and groaned. "How late does that library stay open?"

"Why? What time is it?"

"Half past nine."

"Uh-oh." Leah grimaced. "If it's like most libraries, it's already closed…" Her voice trailed away and she frowned. "By the way, what day is it?" Since the morning that Hunter had turned up on her porch, time had ceased to exist.

Lines of concentration furrowed along Hunter's eyebrows. "I think it's Friday." He shrugged. "But I wouldn't swear to it."

Leah thought for a moment. "Yeah, Friday. I think you're right. Now to find out what time the library opens and closes." She walked over to the bedside table and took a phone directory out of the drawer. Once she'd found the listing for the library, she tapped out the number. She listened for several moments then hung up the phone.

"Guess it really doesn't matter what day it is," she murmured. "According to the automated answering service, the library is closed. It will open again at nine in the morning." Leah yawned. "Just as well," she said. "I'm tired." She pushed up off the sofa. "Guess I need to call Christine before calling it a night." Hunter's eyes narrowed suspiciously. "Just to let her know I'm okay," she added. "Then I'm going to bed."

As Leah tapped out her friend's phone number, Hunter glanced back down to the newspaper article and tried not to think about all the things he could do to her in bed.

Christine answered on the third ring.

"Hey, it's me," Leah said.

"Leah, where are you? And what the hell is going on?"

Leah frowned at the desperate tone in Christine's voice. "Christine, just calm down and tell me what's wrong."

"I—I'm not sure. All I know is that I'm scared."

"Hold on a minute." Leah muffled the receiver against her breasts. "Hunter!"

He glanced up from the article and she motioned for him to come to where she was standing. "You'd better come listen to this."

Once Hunter was beside her, he leaned down and Leah positioned the receiver so that he could hear the conversation as well.

"Okay, Christine, explain," Leah told her friend.

"Remember what you said about men claiming to be FBI agents? Well, two men came to my house—showed me badges and everything. They asked a lot of questions about you and Hunter. But just so you know, I didn't tell them anything. Anyway, I think they've been following me."

Without warning, Hunter reached down and depressed the switch hook, disconnecting the call.

A dial tone buzzed in Leah's ear. "Hey!" she cried. "Why did you do that? I didn't finish talking."

"They could be tracing that call."

Hunter's words quickly deflated Leah's righteous indignation. "Yeah, you're right." She slowly lowered the receiver then placed it on top of the phone. "I just hope Christine will be okay. If anything happened to her because of me—"

"It won't," Hunter retorted. "She's going to be just fine."

"I hope so," Leah whispered as she turned toward the bedroom.

"Where are you going?"

Leah paused then turned to face Hunter. "I'm going to get my stuff together. I just assumed that we would have to move to another hotel."

The new hotel they moved to was farther away from the library, but was almost a carbon copy of the old one. They were able to get a two-room suite that was almost identical to the one they had left, and there was an all-night diner right next door.

The minute they stepped inside their suite, Leah headed straight for the bedroom. "I'm going to bed," she announced. Once inside the bedroom, she closed the door.

Hunter closed the door leading out into the hotel hallway, and for long moments he simply stared at the bedroom door. The temptation to join Leah was strong, and it took every bit of willpower he could muster to turn away and fold out the sofa bed instead. Making love to her only complicated things and only confused him more than he already was. Yes, they were married, but he didn't remember her or their marriage. Until he did remember, it was safer to keep his distance.

In the bedroom, Leah curled up beneath the covers and stared into the darkened room. Would Hunter join her in bed or would he choose to sleep in the other room? Leah adjusted her pillow. She could hear the muffled noise from traffic outside, and somewhere in the night, she heard a siren.

Leah shivered and took deep even breaths and the sound of the siren faded. Then she heard another sound—the television. With a sigh, Leah closed her eyes and prayed for sleep.

The following morning after breakfast, Hunter drove them to the library. As they walked from the parking garage to the library, Hunter said, "If this Neil Turner was a material witness, there should be something about him in previous newspapers. The problem is how far back do we need to go?"

Leah glanced up at him. "The only thing we can do is start, say, in January, and work our way forward. If we don't find something in that batch, we'll have to start further back."

Within minutes of approaching the front entrance to the library, a woman appeared and unlocked the doors.

Inside, they took the elevator to the fourth floor. "I'll take the first three months," Hunter told Leah. "And you take the next three months, from June to April."

Two hours later, after scanning every newspaper for the month of January, Hunter clicked on the newspaper for the first day in February. As he skimmed the front page, a strange excitement filled him.

According to the article, Neil Turner had been the right-hand man of Carlos Lorio, reputed to be the crime boss for the entire southeastern section of the United States, Lorio was responsible for a ring of crime that included everything from illegal drugs to money laundering and prostitution. It was alleged that Lorio also had some key politicians in his back pocket as well. But Neil Turner had begun to notice that Lorio was acting strangely, taking unnecessary dangerous risks, and Turner began to fear for his life. He'd gone to the police, the FBI had been called in, and after a plea-bargaining session, Turner had agreed to testify against Lorio. Turner's testimony would have put Lorio on death row, plus it could have busted Lorio's entire operation wide open.

"This is it," Hunter whispered when he'd finished reading the article. He glanced over to the desk next to him where Leah was sitting. "Leah." He motioned for her to come closer. "Look at this."

Leah moved her chair closer to Hunter and read the article. The scent of her filled Hunter's nostrils, and he breathed deeper.

"You're right," she cried when she'd finished. Her dark eyes sparkled with excitement. "No wonder Neil Turner's murder was such a big deal," she said, her voice vibrating with intensity. Then she quickly sobered. "I wonder…" Her voice trailed away.

"What?" Hunter prompted.

"There still has to be more," she said. "Something that would connect this Lorio character directly to the murder."

Hunter began nodding. "The only way would be if Lorio offed Turner himself. I must have seen Lorio kill Turner."

Leah glanced down at the article again. "One more thing." She tapped Carlos Lorio's name with her forefinger. "Why does that name seem so familiar?"

Hunter glanced at the name, and at the same moment, they looked up at each other, and in unison, they said, "The man with the gun at my house." "That creep with the gun at your house."

Before Hunter realized what he had done, he reached for Leah at the same time she reached out for him. Elated by their discovery, he hugged her close and she wrapped her arms around his neck. "The man's name was Lorio—*Tony* Lorio," he said against her ear.

"And wasn't he from Orlando, too?"

Her warm breath on his skin sent goose bumps chasing up his arms, and Hunter nodded. With her soft breasts molded against his chest, he felt every breath she took, every word she spoke, and too late he realized that he never should have touched her.

Then she began to tremble, the same way she'd trembled in his arms when they had made love. Just thinking about that night set off waves of desire, and now, as he had then, he felt himself growing hard.

Keeping her firmly pressed against him, Hunter pulled his head back just enough to see her face. "What would you think about getting a copy of the article and taking it back to the hotel?"

"I think that's the best idea I've heard, yet," she murmured. "Besides—" she slid her eyes sideways "—I think we've got an audience."

Hunter turned his head in the direction that she'd indicated with her eyes and saw two little girls who looked to be about eight seated at a nearby table. Both girls were staring at them with wide eyes, and both were giggling.

Hunter chuckled and reluctantly released Leah.

A moment later, he folded the copy of the article and shoved it into his back pants pocket. On their way to the elevator, they passed by the table where the two little girls were seated, and Hunter couldn't resist.

"Bye, girls," he said with a wink and wave.

When both girls squealed and ducked beneath the table, Hunter laughed.

"Shame on you," Leah told him, but she was laughing, too.

The drive back to the hotel reminded Leah of the drive from the airport the first time they had come to Orlando. Every chance he got, Hunter would reach over and touch her as if to reassure himself that she was real. And each look he gave her smoldered with desire.

By the time Hunter unlocked their hotel room, the article, Carlos Lorio and the giggling little girls were the last things on their minds.

The moment they stepped inside the suite and Hunter closed the door, he pulled her into his arms and kissed her with a passion that made her tingle from head to toe.

This is how it should be, she thought, savoring each nipping kiss that he trailed down her neck as they moved slowly toward the bedroom.

By the time they reached the bed, they had left a trail of discarded clothes that stretched from the outside door through the small living area to the foot of the bed in the bedroom.

When Hunter finally lowered Leah onto the bed, there was nothing left between them but bare skin.

Leah awoke first and eased out from within Hunter's arms. Though he groaned in protest, he shifted, and continued sleeping.

Collecting her clothes as she went along, she tiptoed out of the bedroom and pulled the door closed behind her.

Making love to Hunter again had been bittersweet. She separated her clothes and pulled on her underwear then the knit pants.

Though satisfying in every respect, there was still something missing. She fastened her bra and slipped the knit T-shirt over her head, but a little voice in her head kept whispering for her to take what she could get, to enjoy and savor each moment she had with him, because it could be the last.

Yet another voice argued that he still didn't remember her or their marriage, and he still didn't know that she was carrying his child. Until he did, she was living on borrowed time. Hunter might well consider it the last straw once he learned that she hadn't told him about her pregnancy.

Her stomach growled, and though she wasn't really hungry, she knew she needed to eat something for the baby's sake. With a sigh, she walked over to the desk phone and tapped out the number for room service. After she'd ordered a house salad for herself and a hamburger with fries for Hunter, she slowly hung up the phone.

Maybe once she'd eaten something nourishing and good for her, she'd be able to function better. And maybe, just maybe, once Hunter had rested and had eaten, he'd be more receptive when she told him about the baby.

And tell him she would, she decided. It was time. Deceiving him was taking its toll on both her mind and emotions, not to mention her appetite. And now that they knew why they were being hunted, there was no real reason in delaying her confession any longer.

Leah suddenly tensed when she heard a noise from the bedroom. Hunter was awake. Gathering her courage, she turned toward the door.

When the door opened, Hunter emerged fully dressed. Even from across the room, the furious expression on his face sent chills down her spine.

He stalked farther into the room, his angry eyes never leaving hers. "I've had another memory flash," he announced, still glaring at her. "I knew there was something you were keeping from me. I knew it!" He pointed an accusing finger at her. "You lied to me about why I went to the drugstore that night. I went to buy a pregnancy test." His gaze slid down and he stared pointedly at her stomach. "To see if you were pregnant with our child."

Without realizing it, Leah splayed her hand protectively over her abdomen.

"Well?" he demanded. "Are you pregnant with my child?"

All she could do was nod, and if she lived to be a hundred, she knew that she would never forget the look of betrayal on Hunter's face.

"Why?" he asked. "Why did you think you had to lie?"

"I was going to tell you."

"Before or after the baby came?"

Leah shook her head. "You don't understand. If I had told you, you wouldn't have wanted me to come with you."

"You're damn right." He shoved his fingers through his hair. "I can't believe you risked our child. And for what?"

"No, no," she cried. "I would never—"

Hunter jerked up his hand, palm out. "Don't!" he shouted. "I don't want to hear any more of your lies!" With one last menacing glare, Hunter stormed past her. He wrenched open the door leading into the hallway, crossed the threshold and slammed it behind him.

The sound rang out like the blast of a shotgun, and Leah jumped.

He was gone. Grief and despair tore at her heart. She'd waited too late, and every fear that she had imagined had come to pass.

Chapter 17

Seething and cursing every step of the way, Hunter stomped toward the elevator. The rage inside him was like a cancer, eating him alive. He'd had to get out before he lost what little control he had left.

"Dammit!" he swore out as he hammered on the elevator button with his fist. He should have never trusted her, never let his guard down.

In the hotel suite, Leah stumbled over to the sofa. As she stared at the door, for a second a feeling of déjà vu came over her. She'd been given a second chance once, but she feared there would be no miraculous resurrection this time.

She closed her eyes and curled up near the armrest. She could run after him and try to explain. She could beg and plead, but until Hunter remembered it all, remembered their relationship and how much he had loved her, no amount of begging and pleading in the world would make a difference.

All he could see right now was that she had lied to him...
again.

If only she could rewind time back to that fateful night. If
only she had made Hunter stop at the drugstore on their way
from the airport...if he hadn't gone out that night, how different her life might.

A sudden, sharp rap on the door echoed throughout the
room. Leah's eyes snapped open and she jumped to her feet.
Hunter. He'd come back. A cry of joy escaped her lips as she
hurried toward the door.

"Room service," a muffled voice called out.

Leah froze and tears spilled down her cheeks.

The person on the other side of the door knocked again.
"Hello in there. Room service."

Leah blinked several times, then wiped her cheeks with the
back of her hand. Clearing her throat, she went to the door
and opened it. Too late she remembered that she should have
looked through the peephole first. If Hunter were here, he
would have given her a lecture...but Hunter wasn't here, and
the skinny balding man standing in the hallway was dressed
in a hotel uniform.

The smell of the food sent a wave of nausea through her,
and she swallowed several times. Motioning toward the small
table near the window, she said, "Just leave it on the table,
please."

The man tilted his head and gave her a curious look. "Are
you okay, ma'am?"

"I'm fine," she answered and stepped to the side of the
doorway.

The man stared at her a moment more. Then, with a slight
one-shouldered shrug, he entered the room. After he'd placed
the tray on the table, he handed her a ticket to sign. Leah
added a small tip to the total then scribbled her name and the
room number below the price.

After the man left and she'd closed the door, she returned to the sofa. Leaning her head against the armrest, she curled onto her side and closed her eyes. If only she could sleep, then maybe when she woke up, she'd find that it had all been just a nightmare.

But closing her eyes only made the ache around her heart worse, and she kept seeing the look on Hunter's face when he'd asked her if she was pregnant.

Leah moved her hand down and placed it protectively over her abdomen.

I can't believe you risked our child.

Hunter's words echoed through her head. How could he think such a thing, say such a horrible thing? She would never purposely risk her baby. Being shot at, being chased hadn't been a choice, certainly not *her* choice. Why couldn't he see that her only hope of protecting her baby had been to help him find out the truth?

Leah opened her eyes and stared at the opposite wall. She moved her hand in small circles as if soothing the baby inside her. "It's okay, baby," she whispered as tears filled her eyes. "Mommy will take care of you." Then she felt the small flutter within her belly, and her eyes filled with more tears.

Her gaze strayed to the food tray on the table. Whether she wanted to or not, whether she felt hungry or not, she should eat something.

Leah sat up, then pushed off of the sofa and went over to the small table. With a grimace, she uncovered the food and removed the salad, the carton of milk and a set of eating utensils. Replacing the cover over the remaining food, she settled in a chair at the table and forced herself to fork up a bite of the salad.

The salad might as well have been grass, but she chewed and swallowed every bite of it anyway. And while she ate she came to several conclusions about her predicament.

First and foremost, the part of her that believed in true, everlasting love still held out hope that Hunter would return, that he would either fully regain his memory, or that he would find it in his heart to forgive her in spite of the amnesia and fall in love with her again. Now that he knew she was pregnant with his child, surely that would make a difference. After all, the Hunter she knew and had fallen in love with valued human life, and though he might not return right away and might not ever remember that he'd loved her, she couldn't imagine that he would abandon his own flesh and blood.

But Leah was also a realist, and her practical side insisted that she had to prepare for the other possibility as well, the possibility that Hunter wouldn't come back.

She opened the carton of milk and took a long drink. While it was true that she and Hunter had uncovered the reason that his testimony was so important, it didn't make their situation any less dangerous or precarious. There were still men searching for them, men who wanted Hunter, and probably her, dead. With Hunter gone, there was only her to protect their baby now.

The first thing she needed to do was figure out how much money she had left. Hopefully it would be enough to pay the hotel bill and buy a bus ticket home. After all, the men who were after them were looking for a couple, not a lone woman. And even if they had distributed pictures of her at the bus stations, she could come up with a disguise of some kind. She could cut her hair, dye it, and get a cheap pair of glasses.

Satisfied that she was finally thinking with her head instead of her broken heart, she searched her brain for some way to protect herself once she got back home. Surely there was someone she could trust, someone who could get the truth out.

Then it came to her. A reporter. A newspaper reporter. If she told their story to a reporter and the story was printed, there was no way Carlos Lorio would dare harm her, the baby or Hunter.

But who? she wondered. Who could she trust?

Leah frowned. Hadn't she once had a patient who was a reporter? But what was his name? Leah's frown grew deeper. Blake somebody? Leah shook her head. Not Blake, but something similar. "Jake," she whispered. "Yes! Jake Logan had been the man's name."

Leah finished off the carton of milk. Once she got back to New Orleans she'd go straight to the newspaper and tell their story.

She pushed away from the table and wandered over to the window. It was midafternoon, and almost an hour had passed since Hunter had stormed out of the room.

How long? she wondered as she stared out into the clear blue sky. How long should she wait to see if he returned?

Leah alternately paced the floor, watched the clock and mindlessly flicked through the fifty or so cable-television stations as she waited two hours, then three.

As the third hour dragged by, Leah was channel surfing again, but thoughts of going to look for Hunter weighed heavily on her mind. Without transportation though, and being unfamiliar with the city, she finally decided that doing so would be impossible and foolhardy, like trying to find one particular grain of sand on a seashore.

Leah turned off the television and stood up to get herself a drink of water. Suddenly, without warning, the door burst open.

Two men entered the room, and Leah froze with terror. Each was pointing a gun at her.

"FBI, ma'am!" one of the men shouted and flashed a badge.

The other man went straight for the bedroom door, kicked it open then disappeared inside. After a moment, he reappeared at the door and shook his head. "No one there," he told his partner. He jerked his head in Leah's direction. "Where's Hunter Davis?" he demanded, glaring at her.

Leah felt faint with fear, and her mouth was so dry that she wasn't sure she could utter a sound. Then she felt a flutter inside, and she knew that now was not the time to show weakness. Her baby needed her to be strong, and for her baby's sake she had to somehow protect his father.

Leah swallowed hard and gathered her last shreds of courage. She lifted her chin defiantly and glared right back at the man. "He's not here." She spat out the words contemptuously. "We had a fight, and he left. I don't know where he went and I don't care," she lied. Then, for good measure, she added, "And if that bastard knows what's good for him, he won't be back."

For long, agonizing, tension-filled moments, both men stared at her as if doing so would reveal whether she was telling them the truth or whether she was lying.

Finally, the man who had searched the bedroom told the other one, "No choice. We'll take her with us. Then we'll have some bargaining power."

Bargaining power? Something in the tone of the man's voice set alarm bells clanging in Leah's head, and suddenly she wasn't so sure that they were who they claimed to be.

The other man nodded and waved his gun at her. "You'll have to come with us."

Leah narrowed her eyes and considered her options. Slim to none, she finally decided. Weren't they supposed to have a warrant or something? She could refuse and demand to see a warrant, but all they had to do was shoot her. She could scream the place down, but again, all they had to do to shut her up was shoot her. Or she could wait and bide her time on the off chance that she might get the opportunity to escape.

"Let's go," the man said, motioning with his gun. "And don't try anything funny if you want to live."

The warning bells clanged even louder. These men were either the shooters posing as FBI or they were the real thing, corrupt agents who were in cahoots with Lance Martin and Carlos Lorio. But how had they tracked them to the hotel? The question screamed through her mind, but Leah was afraid to ask and she doubted they would tell her anyway.

"I said, let's go," the man repeated.

She had to stall. If she stalled long enough, maybe Hunter would return. "May I get my purse?" she asked for lack of anything better to say.

Both men shook their heads no.

"But I need my purse," she insisted.

Then the man who had searched the bedroom grabbed her by the arm. "A purse is the last thing you need where you're going."

He shoved her forward, and Leah's insides shriveled. So much for stalling. Taking a deep breath and praying that her legs would support her, she let herself be propelled toward the door.

As they headed for the elevator, to Leah's acute disappointment, the hallway was empty; there was no one who could help her. Once they were inside the elevator, both men crowded closer, and Leah had to keep reminding herself that she could breathe, that she wasn't trapped in the small car, and that the doors would eventually open. Only thoughts of Hunter kept her phobia at bay. Where was he? Would she ever see him again? Would he ever have the chance to see his baby? Or would these men murder her and her precious baby in cold blood?

The elevator seemed to take forever to get to the first floor. When the bell finally dinged and the doors slid open, Leah had to bite her lip to keep from crying out with relief.

There were several people milling around the lobby. Leah was tempted to let loose and scream her head off, but the man on her left leaned down and whispered, "If you don't want to be responsible for getting innocent people killed, keep your mouth shut." For emphasis, he jabbed the gun harder into her left side. Leah winced with pain, and the scream died a silent death in the back of her throat.

Though several people stopped to gawk at them as they walked through the lobby, the man on her right kept saying, "FBI, official business. Stand back."

Leah broke into a cold sweat. No one was going to help her. If she got out of this mess, she only had herself to depend on.

As Leah and the men exited through the front door of the hotel, she squinted against the glare of the blinding sun, and the late-afternoon heat hit her like a blast from a furnace. With every step they took she could feel her opportunity to escape slipping through her fingers like running water, and she shivered.

In the parking lot, the men hustled her toward a white van. When they got to the van, the man on her left fished a ring of keys from his pocket and reached to unlock the sliding door.

Suddenly, out of the corner of her eye, Leah saw a dark blue sedan racing toward them. Both of the men with her looked up just as the car screeched to a stop behind the van. The car doors flew open, and two men with guns jumped out.

The man on her right grabbed Leah around the neck in a choke hold. When he jerked her in front of him, she stumbled and gagged. She clawed at his arm, but he tightened his hold and dragged her backward.

Her other captor scrambled to the front of the van for cover.

The men from the sedan took aim from behind the open car doors. The man on the driver's side shouted, "FBI! Drop your weapons. Let the woman go now!"

Leah's heart raced as she fought to breathe. They were almost to the front of the van when the man holding her fired his gun. The explosion was deafening, and Leah jumped. But her scream was cut off when the man tightened his hold around her neck.

Her other captor took aim and fired, but before he could fire a second time, two shots in rapid succession rang out from behind. The man holding her yelped in pain as the gun flew out of his hand. Her other captor grunted and fell to the ground beside them. The man holding her released his grip on her to grab his bleeding hand, and suddenly she was free. She'd only taken a step, when another shot rang out, and the man crumpled to the ground.

Leah gasped for breath. *Run! Run now!* a voice from within demanded.

Leah wanted to run, she tried to run, but her legs wouldn't do her bidding. Then everything began to swim in front of her eyes and turn dark. Just as she began to sink to the ground, strong arms grabbed her around the waist from behind.

"It's okay." The voice near her ear was low and husky with emotion. "You're safe now."

"Hunter?" His name was but a hoarse whisper on her lips. His arms tightened around her, and Leah closed her eyes. She was safe. Hunter had come back for her.

Around her she heard the rustling of running feet.

"Hunter Davis, NYPD!" Hunter shouted.

"We know who you are, Davis," one of the men said. Leah heard the skidding of metal against concrete as someone kicked the guns away from the injured men. "You're the reason we're here in the first place," the same man said. "That, and those two goons on the ground. By the way, that was some damn good shooting. I don't know many men who could have made that shot."

Leah's eyes sprang open, and she twisted within Hunter's arms to face him. "*You* shot those men?"

He nodded.

"Oh, Hunter—" Words failed her for a moment. That

Hunter had been able to fire a weapon could only mean one thing, could only mean that he'd finally come to terms with what had happened to him in New York.

Hunter hugged her close, and with her cheek pressed against his solid chest, she could hear the strong steady beat of his heart.

"Hush, sweetheart," he whispered in her hair. "None of that's important right now. All that's important is that you're okay." He took her by the shoulders and held her back from him. "You are okay?" His gaze lowered to her neck.

When Leah nodded, he slid his hands up and buried his fingers in her hair on either side of her head. His eyes darkened with regret. "I'm so sorry," he whispered. "This was my fault. I should never have left you."

"W-where were you?" she asked. "Where did you go? I—" Tears filled Leah's eyes. "I thought you were gone for good."

Hunter slowly shook his head as he slid his hands down and began massaging the back of her neck. "No, not for good. Never for good. And I didn't go far." He tilted his head toward the small diner near the hotel. "I was over there the whole time. I just needed to cool off." He reached up and smoothed away a lock of her hair. "Don't you know I'd never abandon you, not on purpose?"

Hunter's words were music to Leah's ears, and once again hope that he could forgive her sprang within her chest.

"Hey, Davis," a voice called out. "Better get her inside. You never know what other vermin might be lurking around."

"He's right." Hunter pulled away then bent down and swung her up into his arms.

"I can walk," she protested as he lifted her. But Hunter ignored her, and because being in Hunter's arms again, feeling the strength of them around her, was her heart's desire, she didn't protest a second time.

Once inside the hotel, Hunter lowered her onto a sofa then sat down beside her and slid his arm around her shoulders. Only then did she notice that the lobby was empty. "Guess everyone cleared out when the shooting started." But as she murmured the words, a sudden thought occurred to her. Frowning, she looked up at Hunter. "H—How did you know? How did you know which were the real agents?"

Hunter bowed his head for a moment, and Leah could hear the sound of distant sirens growing louder. He finally lifted his head again, his eyes dark and serious. "I knew because I recognized one of them from the night he helped Carlos Lorio murder Neil Turner in that alley by the drugstore."

Shock waves reverberated through Leah. "Oh, Hunter, does that mean what I think it means?"

Hunter nodded. "I remembered it. I remember it all."

"All?" she questioned. "Everything?"

Again Hunter nodded. Then a slow smile curled his lips. "The day we met it was pouring rain. I got soaking wet helping an old bag lady get her shopping cart across the street. And about your friend Christine Brady—she went with us to the justice of the peace when we got married. You wore a long-sleeved, white lace dress and a wedding veil. You said that the veil had belonged to your mother."

"You do remember," Leah whispered in awe, her heart soaring with joy. "When?" she asked eagerly. "When did your memory come back?"

Hunter shrugged. "All I know is that by the time I walked over to the restaurant and ordered coffee, everything started coming back. It's hard to explain, but it was like watching a movie in my head in fast-forward motion."

"I still can't believe that you were able to fire your gun though. Amazing."

"No, honey." He reached up and traced her lips with his forefinger. "Not amazing. What was amazing was that I was able to make that shot that took out that bastard's weapon without hitting you. But I'm fast finding out that true love can cure a lot of ills and cause miracles to happen. When I saw you being escorted out of the hotel and realized that they had a gun on you, I hightailed it around back and worked my way up from behind them. There was no way in hell that I was going to let them take away my wife and baby."

Out of nowhere, sudden doubts began crowding Leah's mind. She stared down at her hands clasped tightly in her lap. On the surface everything was perfect now, almost too perfect. But there was one source of contention that Hunter had yet to mention. Did she dare hope that he had forgiven her for doubting him, for keeping the secret of their baby from him?

Ask him, a small voice persisted. *Just come right out and ask him.*

Leah lifted her head and stared up into Hunter's blue eyes. "Hunter, there's just one more thing we need to talk about."

His expression grew tight with strain. Suddenly, his eyes shifted and narrowed, and he focused his gaze on something behind her. Then she heard the sound of approaching footsteps.

Leah turned her head and recognized the man coming toward them as one of the agents who had tried to rescue her.

The agent walked around to the front of the sofa and stopped in front of Hunter. "We need to talk," he said.

Hunter nodded, and when he slid his arm from around Leah's shoulders and moved away, her spirits sank and an inner torment began to gnaw at her. Maybe she was being paranoid, but she couldn't shake the thought that Hunter seemed relieved that the agent had appeared when he did.

The man sat in a chair near Hunter.

"Leah, meet Agent Steve Owens. Agent Owens was one of my keepers during my stay at the hospital."

Leah nodded and Steve Owens gave her a quick, uneasy smile. Then he leaned forward and rested his forearms on his knees. "First things first," he said. "I'm assuming that since you recognize me and, from what happened out there, that you got your memory back."

Hunter nodded.

"I thought so," the agent said. "So you recognized those two from the night that Neil Turner was killed?"

"Not both of them," Hunter replied. "Only one—the short stocky one."

"Damn." The agent dropped his gaze and stared at the floor for a moment. "I was afraid of that." He lifted his gaze again. "The one you recognized is Phil Shaw, one of ours. We've suspected for a long time now that we had a rogue agent, especially after Turner was murdered, but we didn't know who the Judas was. Now we know."

"And the other one?"

A feral grin pulled at Owens's lips. "Oh, he's a bonus. He's a high-ranking detective with the Orlando police."

"Well, I hate to be the one to tell you, but you've got another rogue agent."

"Damn," Owens whispered again. "I suspected as much."

"His name's Lance Martin."

The agent began nodding. "Makes sense. He and Shaw were partners for a while." He paused, then he said, "What about the other one, the other man who was with Shaw that night?"

"I might be wrong, but I'm betting that the other one was Carlos Lorio."

Owens's eyes widened. "How so?"

When Hunter glanced at Leah, the disapproving look he gave her made her cringe. And as he explained to Owens about how he and Leah had sneaked into her house for the money she had stashed away, Hunter's earlier accusation came back to haunt her. *I can't believe you risked our child.*

Leah swallowed the tightness in her throat and tried concentrating on what Hunter was saying. She hadn't thought it was a risk at the time, and there was no way she could have predicted what had happened. She stared at Hunter, but he was still talking to the agent.

"After I knocked the man unconscious," Hunter was saying, "I checked his wallet. According to his driver's license his name was Tony Lorio, and the man who did the shooting that night by the drugstore could have been Tony's twin, except that he was about twenty years older."

Owens suddenly let out a whoop and slapped his thigh. "Hot damn, we've got him!" the agent yelled. "We've finally got that SOB! Tony is Carlos's son, and you're right, add twenty years and you've got Carlos." He grinned. "It would be just like Carlos to want to take Turner out himself, make an example of him." He reached down and unclipped a radio from his belt, depressed a button and said, "Come in, Tommy."

A gruff voice answered back. "Yeah, Steve."

"Send someone after some mug shots of Lorio Senior, and I need two of our best to baby-sit Ms. Davis while we do some interviews with Hunter."

"Ten-four," the gruff voice answered.

Leah narrowed her eyes as something suddenly occurred to her. "I have a question," she said. "How did they know where we were?"

Owens grimaced and a tinge of scarlet darkened his cheeks. "My fault, I'm afraid. When we lost you in New Orleans, we figured you had to be headed this way. We just couldn't figure out how, not until we started checking around and discovered your friend had rented a car. We put out an APB on the rental car, but we also tapped your friend's phone."

"And followed her," Leah interjected.

Owens nodded. "Yeah, that, too. Anyway, we'd traced you to the other hotel from that phone call you made to her. But by the time we got there, y'all had cleared out. I knew, within reason, that you hadn't gone far. Just my bad luck that one of the Orlando PD spotted the car and called it in to that detective who was with Phil Shaw. By the time we got word, it was almost too late."

Owens suddenly directed his gaze toward the hotel entrance. "Here come my men now." He turned back to Leah. "They'll take you to your room."

"Uh-uh," Hunter grunted as he shook his head. "Where she goes I go. And I've got a few questions of my own before anyone goes anywhere."

Owens sighed and signaled to the approaching men. "Just stand guard for now," he told them. He turned to Hunter. "Okay, what now?"

"What now?" he repeated. "Well, for starters, how did you even know that I was the one who had witnessed Neil Turner's murder in the first place?"

The agent grinned. "That old man—the pharmacist—he gave us your description. He didn't see the men chasing you through the drugstore well enough to describe them, but when he called 911, he was staring out the front window and saw two men jump into a car. He figured they were the same two who were after you, and he was able to give us a pretty good description of the vehicle they were driving. One of the Orlando PD boys spotted the car, but before he could stop it, the chaser rammed your car and forced it into the path of that gasoline truck. Then, all hell broke loose when the gasoline truck exploded, and the chaser got away. You were just lucky that you hadn't fastened your seat belt, otherwise, you would have been fried, instead of being thrown clear."

"Then what?" Hunter asked.

"Then we got a look at you. Since you fit the description

that the pharmacist gave us—" he shrugged "—we figured
you were our witness. Once we found out that you were
NYPD, the boss pulled out all the stops to keep you on ice
until you'd recovered. The best we'd hoped for was that you
could ID the men who killed Turner, and that we could pressure them into giving up Carlos Lorio."

Leah lay in the king-size bed and stared up at the white
ceiling in the bedroom of the hotel suite. For security reasons,
she hadn't been allowed to return to the suite that she and
Hunter had stayed in. Except for being located on a different
floor and the color scheme being green instead of blue, the
new suite was almost exactly the same though.

In the next room, she could hear the low rumble of male
voices but she couldn't make out what was being said.

Leah still got the shivers when she thought about what
Steve Owens had told them and about all that Hunter had endured the night of the accident. Once the agent had answered
all of Hunter's questions though, Hunter had balked when
Owens had tried again to separate her from Hunter. Owens
had argued with Hunter, assuring him that Leah would be
safe, but in the end, Hunter had won.

The end result was that she and Hunter had been hustled
up to a suite together. While Hunter was being questioned in
the small living room, she'd been asked to wait in the bedroom.

Leah sighed, glanced at the clock on the bedside table and
shifted to her side. This was torture, she thought. An hour had
dragged by since they been taken to the suite, an hour in
which she'd had nothing better to do than to go over every
word Hunter had said to her after the shooting. An hour that
she'd spent second-guessing and agonizing over everything.

Leah glared at the closed door separating them. How much
longer? she wondered. How much longer before she could fi-

nally talk to Hunter alone? Until she talked to him, until she knew for sure how he really felt…?

Suddenly the doorknob rattled, and Leah pushed herself up in the bed as Hunter entered the room and closed the door behind him.

At the sight of Hunter, Leah's mouth felt dry and a cold knot formed in her stomach. She scooted back until she was leaning against the headboard. Nothing in Hunter's expression gave her a clue as to what he was thinking or feeling.

"Well?" she asked, her voice barely above a whisper. "Will we have to go into protective custody?"

Hunter walked over to the bed and sat down beside her, facing her. Instead of answering her question, he said, "You were right, down there. We do need to talk."

The knot in her stomach tightened.

"While I was in that restaurant this afternoon, I had a lot of time to do some thinking."

Leah held her breath as she waited for him to explain.

"I was wrong to blame you for the decisions you made. Given the circumstances, I realized that you had no choice. And once I regained my memory, once I remembered you and our love, I—I—" He shook his head. "I'm so sorry for all those things I said."

The knot in Leah's stomach loosened, and she reached up to caress Hunter's jaw. "It's okay," she whispered. "All that's important now is that we're together and that you know that I would never knowingly do anything to harm our baby."

"Oh, honey, I know you wouldn't." He reached out and folded her within his arms, and with a cry of joy and relief, she threw her arms around his neck.

Hunter held her for long moments and Leah savored being wrapped in his arms. Then he pulled away just enough to claim her mouth with his. The long, sensuous kiss was full of passion and promises, and left her senses reeling and aching for more. And when he ended it, his eyes glowed with a tenderness that brought tears to her eyes.

"Now, now, none of that," he whispered, kissing each of her eyes. "Besides, we don't have long before we have to leave."

Leah blinked several times and the glow of passion faded somewhat in the face of reality. "Will we have to go into protective custody?" she asked again.

Hunter nodded. "Yeah, for a while, but I made us a deal with the feds."

Leah frowned. "What kind of deal?"

Hunter grinned. "I made a call to my chief in New York, and we had a long talk. Bottom line, the chief is guaranteeing us around-the-clock protection until the trial. And he said to tell you that the NYPD takes care of its own. And that includes the wives and families, as well."

Hunter's words ebbed and flowed around her heart, and Leah, knowing that he'd truly forgiven her, felt the barrier of distrust between them shatter into a million pieces.

"I love you, Leah," he whispered against her lips.

The words she'd longed to hear flowed through her like warm honey, seeping into every crevice of her soul. "And I love you," she whispered back, and as she whispered the words, she felt a flutter deep in her stomach. Reaching out, she took Hunter's hand and placed it over her stomach. When the flutter happened again, Hunter's eyes widened with a look of surprise mixed with awe, and love darkened his eyes to navy.

* * * * *

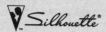

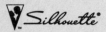

eHARLEQUIN.com

The Ultimate Destination for Women's Fiction

For **FREE online reading,** visit www.eHarlequin.com now and enjoy:

Online Reads
Read **Daily** and **Weekly** chapters from our Internet-exclusive stories by your favorite authors.

Interactive Novels
Cast your vote to help decide how these stories unfold...then stay tuned!

Quick Reads
For shorter romantic reads, try our collection of Poems, Toasts, & More!

Online Read Library
Miss one of our online reads?
Come here to catch up!

Reading Groups
Discuss, share and rave with other community members!

For great reading online, visit www.eHarlequin.com today!

INTONL04R

If you enjoyed what you just read,
then we've got an offer you can't resist!

Take 2 bestselling
love stories FREE!
Plus get a FREE surprise gift!

Clip this page and mail it to Silhouette Reader Service™

IN U.S.A.	IN CANADA
3010 Walden Ave.	P.O. Box 609
P.O. Box 1867	Fort Erie, Ontario
Buffalo, N.Y. 14240-1867	L2A 5X3

YES! Please send me 2 free Silhouette Intimate Moments® novels and my free surprise gift. After receiving them, if I don't wish to receive anymore, I can return the shipping statement marked cancel. If I don't cancel, I will receive 6 brand-new novels every month, before they're available in stores! In the U.S.A., bill me at the bargain price of $4.24 plus 25¢ shipping and handling per book and applicable sales tax, if any*. In Canada, bill me at the bargain price of $4.99 plus 25¢ shipping and handling per book and applicable taxes**. That's the complete price and a savings of at least 10% off the cover prices—what a great deal! I understand that accepting the 2 free books and gift places me under no obligation ever to buy any books. I can always return a shipment and cancel at any time. Even if I never buy another book from Silhouette, the 2 free books and gift are mine to keep forever.

245 SDN DZ9A
345 SDN DZ9C

Name	(PLEASE PRINT)
Address	Apt.#
City	State/Prov. Zip/Postal Code

Not valid to current Silhouette Intimate Moments® subscribers.

Want to try two free books from another series?
Call 1-800-873-8635 or visit www.morefreebooks.com.

* Terms and prices subject to change without notice. Sales tax applicable in N.Y.
** Canadian residents will be charged applicable provincial taxes and GST.
All orders subject to approval. Offer limited to one per household].
® are registered trademarks owned and used by the trademark owner and or its licensee.

INMOM04R   ©2004 Harlequin Enterprises Limited

SPOTLIGHT

**Every month we'll spotlight
original stories from Harlequin
and Silhouette Books' Shining Stars!**

Fantastic authors, including:
- Debra Webb
- Julie Elizabeth Leto
- Merline Lovelace
- Rhonda Nelson

**Plus, value-added Bonus Features
are coming soon to a book near you!**

- Author Interviews
- Bonus Reads
- The Writing Life
- Character Profiles

SIGNATURE SELECT SPOTLIGHT
On sale January 2005

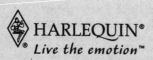

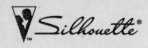

COMING NEXT MONTH

#1339 DANGEROUS DISGUISE—Marie Ferrarella
Cavanaugh Justice
Mixing business with pleasure wasn't in detective Jared Cavanaugh's vocabulary—until he saw Maren Minnesota walk into the restaurant where he'd been assigned to work undercover to catch the mob. But when their smoldering attraction for each other threatened his disguise, would he have to risk everything to protect the woman he loved?

#1340 UNDERCOVER MISTRESS—Kathleen Creighton
Starrs of the West
After a hit-and-run accident forced Celia Cross from Hollywood's spotlight, her only refuge was the beach. Then homeland security agent Roy Starr washed ashore, bleeding from an assassin's bullet. Little did she know her mystery man had gotten too close to an international arms dealer. With the killer determined to finish the job and Roy's feelings for his rescuer growing stronger, would this be their beginning—or their end?

#1341 CLOSE TO THE EDGE—Kylie Brant
Private investigator Lucky Boucher knew his attraction to fellow investigator Jacinda Wheeler was a mistake. He was a bayou boy; she was high society. But when a case they were working on turned deadly, keeping his mind off her and on their investigation proved to be an impossible task, because for the first time since he'd met her, their worlds were about to collide.

#1342 CODE NAME: FIANCÉE—Susan Vaughan
Antiterrorist security agent Vanessa Wade felt as false as the rock on her finger. Assigned to impersonate the glamorous fiancée of international businessman Nick Markos, she found herself struggling to remain detached from her "husband-to-be." He was the brother of a traitor—and the man whose kisses made her spin out of control. Could she dare to hope their fake engagement would become a real one?

#1343 RUNNING ON EMPTY—Michelle Celmer
Detective Mitch Thompson was willing to risk his life to uncover the mystery surrounding Jane Doe, the beautiful amnesiac he'd rescued from an unknown assailant. But the more time they spent together trying to unravel the secrets hidden in her memory, the more evident it became that they were falling in love…and that Jane's attacker was determined to stop at nothing to destroy their happiness—not even murder.

#1344 NECESSARY SECRETS—Barbara Phinney
Sylvie Mitchell was living a lie. Pregnant and alone, she'd retreated to her ranch to have the baby in hiding. Then her unborn child's uncle, Jon Cahill, appeared, demanding answers, and she had to lie to the one man she truly loved. She'd lived with the guilt of his brother's death and the government cover-up that had forced her into hiding. When the truth surfaced, would she lose the only man who could keep her—and her baby—safe?

SIMCNM1204